Bayou Justice

Ali Spooner

Affinity
eBook Press
NZ
2014

Bayou Justice
Copyright © 2008 by Ali Spooner

This book is Published by
Affinity eBook Press NZ LTD
Canterbury, New Zealand

ISBN: 978-1-927282-68-7

2nd Edition
Published: June 2014

Editor: Ruth Stanley
Cover Design: Irish Dragon Designs
E-mail: affinity@affinityebooks.com

Acknowledgements

I would like to thank Affinity Ebook Press, my publisher, and staff for the opportunity to publish this work. I would like to thank Terry Baker, whose wonderful reviews continue to inspire me to grow as a writer. Thank you also to Nancy K. for the beautiful cover art. To my readers, thank you for supporting me and providing feedback on my stories.

Dedication

Bayou Justice is dedicated to Cat M. Your belief in Sasha inspired me to continue this series. Thanks for the encouragement and support.

Also by Ali Spooner

Epitaph
Bailey's Run
Sugarland

Table of Contents

Chapter 1

Sasha crept out of her comfortable bed to pull the drapes in the master bedroom that were preventing the early morning sunlight from streaming in. Sasha had spent the previous night tossing and turning as she relived the past thirty years of her life without Milly. The memories of their life together haunted her sleep. They had survived so many tragedies together it felt ironic to her that the blood they needed to survive was the catalyst for Milly's death when she drank blood tainted with the AIDs virus. Sasha's dreams frequently ended with the memory of setting the ashes of Milly free in the soft breeze as she scattered them on the grounds of the home she loved. Sasha walked to the bathroom to splash cold water on her face to wash away her tears then wearily crawled back into her bed, hoping for a few more hours of slumber before she would have to rise in preparation for her arriving guests.

✝

For the past eighty-five years, Sasha Thibodaux had owned Sugarland Plantation, a working sugar cane farm that she leased out to local farmers. Besides this income, the history of Sugarland as a haunted plantation had added to her wealth. The bed-and-breakfast business had prospered and there was a long waiting list for reservations, many of which were returning patrons year after year. Sasha seldom traveled far from Sugarland, and when she did, she felt her heart longing for the comfort and seclusion of her home.

After Milly's death Sasha spent time learning more about the specters that lingered at Sugarland. Lizette was a seven-year-old child who had succumbed to the same flu pandemic in 1919 that had taken Sasha's mother. Visitors frequently reported sightings of Lizette skipping through the halls or playing the baby grand in the plantation's ample parlor. Several times as Sasha played the piano, she sensed Lizette's presence in the room and would at times catch a glimpse of the child dancing through the room to the music she was playing.

Luscious was a slave who had gone into the bayou to retrieve catfish from a trotline for the master's dinner. When he reached into the water, an alligator attacked him, severing his left arm from his body. Luscious was able to make his way back to the plantation, but died several days later from the loss of blood and infection. Over the years, and especially during the full moon, visitors spotted Luscious walking down the path toward the bayou, or roaming through the cane fields.

Finally, yet importantly, was Joshua. Joshua, a beautiful young slave, was hanged from the old oak out front when the landowner caught him in a compromising position with his daughter. Joshua was only sixteen when he died for his indiscretion. Visitors had seen Joshua, sitting under the oak where he died, weeping for his lost love. Of all the ghosts, Sasha felt closest to Joshua, as she understood the pain from the loss of a loved one.

Sasha felt at home with these specters, however, at times, she longed for companionship. The loss of Milly kept her secluded from the outside world. She doubted she could survive losing another lover if she would search for someone to share her life. Instead, Sasha preferred to dream of Milly and the love they had shared.

✝

Sasha detested the fact that she still had to feed on humans from time to time to continue her existence. The Network, a specialized laboratory in Atlanta, was working to create a liquid serum to replace the need for vampires to feed on humans to maintain their existence. However, the progress on perfecting the serum was painfully slow. Sasha and Milly had started with the serum years before, but it was not enough to prevent the need for feeding completely. Maybe if the serum had been further developed at the time, it would have prevented Milly from being infected. Instead, she suffered the horrible disease that took her from Sasha.

The Network's efforts were gallant, but the hunger still burned deep within Sasha. The synthetic blood the Network had developed could not satisfy the lust for human blood that made her nights unbearably restless. Sasha would battle the hunger until she could no longer tolerate the pain. She would then surrender and set out to hunt the bayou, to feast on a lone poacher, knowing the carnivorous denizens of the swamp were more than willing to dispose of the corpse to prevent detection.

✝

Sasha lay in bed contemplating a night of hunting when Marie came to the door, gently tapping. "Sasha, you awake?" she quietly asked her.

"Yes, Marie, what is it?"

Marie and her husband James, while not blessed with Sasha's immortality, received an excessively slow aging process and had served her well for many years. They were the second generation to reside at Sugarland and Sasha was thankful for their years of service. James's parents, James senior and Martha, had served Sasha for many long years and were finally enjoying the remainder of their lives in retirement in Shreveport.

Marie slowly entered the room and found Sasha lying on the bed.

"I wanted to let you know that James is going to drive me to town to purchase supplies before he leaves for the airport to pick up the guests. Is there anything I can get you before we leave?"

"No, thank you, Marie," Sasha said. "I am going to laze around a while this morning and then I will prepare for our guests as well."

"Very well then, Sasha, we will be back shortly." Marie left the room and closed the door behind her.

Sasha lay back on her bed and mentally reviewed the guest list. Four sorority sisters from Tulane were meeting at Sugarland for a long weekend reunion. The four women had not visited one another for several years and were excited about catching up with each other.

Lisa Thomas had been in regular contact with her as the organizer of the trip. A schoolteacher from Jackson, Lisa had arranged to sample some of the nightlife in nearby New Orleans while sharing the secluded resort with her college mates. She was successful in persuading Kara Stewart, a criminal attorney from Atlanta, to leave the rush of her busy practice behind. She enticed Susan Schultz, a successful realtor in Asheville, who was looking forward to the slower pace of the bayou, to join them in New Orleans. Cindy Search, the lone married woman of the four, welcomed the change from the doldrums associated with life as the wife of a prominent banker in Charleston.

Their host had made plans for the women to have a private ghost tour in New Orleans on Friday, after a day of shopping at The River Walk. Marie would be busy cooking her fabulous creations while James would provide transportation for the women during the weekend. Sasha would join her guests for drinks before the evening meal, but for the most part Marie and James would attend to their needs.

✝

Unable to sleep, Sasha decided to shower and dress for a ride around the property. As she dressed, she smiled at the misconception that modern vampires could not cast an appearance in a mirror. She gazed into the mirror, her deep lavender eyes framed by shoulder-length black hair, which, surprisingly, was lacking gray hairs for a person of one hundred and fifteen. Pleased with the reflection smiling back at her, she stepped out into a bright sunny day.

She walked to the stables and saddled up Thunder, her favorite mount. Sugarland encompassed over five hundred acres and she took pleasure in riding over the property. Sasha eased Thunder into a gentle trot, and rode past one of the sugar cane fields. Workers hacked at the stalks with sharp cane knives as they harvested the crop. Sasha waved to the foreman, who was angrily barking out orders to the migrant workers working the fields. She detested the way he treated the workers, but was unable to control how he addressed his workers.

The man cautiously raised his hand to wave back as the hairs on the back of his neck snapped to attention. A shiver passed through his body as her eyes fixed him with a cloaked stare. The foreman watched until she and Thunder were no longer in sight and again began shouting at the workers cutting the cane.

The harvesting of the cane had always been a painful time for Sasha. In the next few weeks, the harvest would be complete and Sasha would celebrate another anniversary of her lover's death. "I still love you so," she said, her voice filled with sadness.

✝

Sasha and Thunder cantered around the property. They were returning to the stable when she saw James arriving with the carload of guests. Leading Thunder to the stables to allow him to cool, she watched as James ushered the women into the house and then returned to unload their luggage. She removed Thunder's tack and brushed him down then walked up to the house as James removed the last of the bags from the trunk of the car. Taking one of the suitcases from James, she walked with him into the house.

"I think you are really going to enjoy this group of guests, Sasha," James said with a devilish grin.

"Oh really, James, why is that?" Sasha asked.

"You will see for yourself shortly," he said.

Sasha looked at him quizzically, wondering about the smirk that was playing around on his face, but followed him into the house, curious to get an answer to her question.

✝

She set the bag she was carrying on the floor in the foyer and stepped into the parlor where the women were seated sipping cool drinks while they waited to settle in their rooms. Removing her

5

sunglasses as she walked in and said, "Good afternoon and welcome to Sugarland. My name is Sasha and my staff, James, Marie and I, will do everything possible to meet your needs this weekend." Along with her welcoming words, she added a brilliant smile.

Sasha noted one of the women studying the painting of Milly hanging above the fireplace mantel. When the woman turned around, she felt her knees go weak and she understood why her guest was so interested in the portrait. The woman's likeness to Milly was uncanny, so much so that she could easily pass as a descendant of her former lover.

The women introduced themselves, which allowed Sasha a moment to regain her composure. When introduced, Sasha moved forward to shake hands with the woman, affixing her lavender eyes on her and heard the beating of Kara Stewart's heart jump noticeably. A slight blush graced Kara's face as Sasha held her hand for a moment longer than necessary. Sasha's eyes took in the beauty of the woman standing before her. Kara's sparkling blue eyes framed by her light brown hair, which fell to her shoulders, reminded her so much of Milly. Sasha's eyes drifted lower, marveling at the petite features of Kara's body. She could feel the blood racing through Kara's veins as she smiled.

"Marie will have fresh crawfish and cocktails prepared at five if you would like to settle into your rooms and freshen up from your travels. Dinner will be served at six and then you can make yourself at home and relax for the evening," she added.

"That sounds like a great plan." Lisa stood and joined the other women.

Sasha watched as Marie escorted the four women down the hall and took an opportunity to dip into Kara's thoughts.

I will definitely be visiting you later, Sasha projected into Kara's mind.

Kara turned to look back at Sasha, grinned broadly, and then rushed to catch her friends. Sasha enjoyed sending her mischievous thoughts into unsuspecting subjects, and watching as they responded to her suggestions. The young woman had stirred something deep in Sasha and for the first time in ages, Sasha felt her heart racing at the sight of another woman.

†

Sasha walked into her room and quickly stripped off her riding clothes and boots before starting the shower. She slipped under the tepid water and slowly caressed her body with fragrant soap, eliminating the evidence of her afternoon ride in the humid bayou. Her fingers softly brushed across her hardened nipples as she closed her eyes and imagined Kara's hands roaming her needy body. It had been much too long since Sasha had had the pleasure of a lover, and she looked forward to seducing the young, alluring lawyer.

Kara's physical features reminded Sasha so much of Milly that her heart sank with melancholy memories of the great love she had lost nearly thirty years ago. Sasha's heart still ached for the love that she thought would last for eternity.

Sasha remembered the conversation she and Milly had shared just before her death. *There will be a woman in your future, my love, that will return the love and passion you have to offer.* That left Sasha curious to know whether Kara could be the one Milly had seen in her future.

Sasha shook off the melancholy feeling and, after dressing, sprayed rich-smelling cologne along her neckline and across her wrists. She walked to the parlor, her body thrumming with excitement to see Kara again, and joined her guests for cocktails.

†

Once in the parlor Sasha sat comfortably in an oversized chair across from Kara where she could easily capture her gaze with quietly seductive glances. Marie poured a glass of red wine and handed it to Sasha before disappearing into the kitchen to finish preparing the crawfish.

Once everyone had settled, Sasha began to spin a tale about Sugarland's history. "Sugarland is approximately three hundred years old and, as you can imagine, it was a plantation served by slaves. The owner, however, was a gentle slave master and treated his servants with a gentility not normally seen in most southern plantations. It wasn't until after his death that the first violence occurred at Sugarland, when his son found his daughter in a rather intimate situation with a young slave named Joshua." Sasha smiled inwardly when she saw the intent looks on her guests' faces. "Her father was so enraged that he had the young man hanged and shipped his daughter off to finishing school," Sasha continued. "The landowner, just as many of his era, felt it was entirely proper for him to take pleasure from the many female slaves, but he would not tolerate this behavior from his daughter."

Sasha paused in her story when Marie returned to serve the crawfish cocktails.

"After the emancipation, the plantation was passed down from father to son for several generations until I purchased the property, and here we are today. Sugar cane is still the primary crop and the lease for the land allows me the opportunity to use the house as an exclusive resort. I am sure Lisa shared with you that Sugarland has a reputation for being haunted." Motioning toward Lisa, she said, "Keep your eyes and ears open during your stay." Sasha pointed upward. "The full moon occurs tomorrow night which will be a prime time for a possible haunting."

Lisa asked several questions regarding the three known ghosts of Sugarland. Sasha answered them professionally, glancing at Kara several times to gauge her response to the sordid history. Sasha smiled when she noted the pulse jumping along Kara's neck and the beating of her heart pounded loudly in Sasha's ears.

Marie entered the room, announced that dinner was ready, and led the four women into the dining room. Sasha excused herself and walked down to the stables to care for Thunder and the other horses housed there.

After feeding them, she stopped at Thunder's stall. His ears pricked forward, listening as she lovingly stroked his forehead. "We will go out again soon," she promised, slipping an extra-large block of hay in the bin before closing the door to his stall. She knew James would have devotedly tended to the horses, but she enjoyed the task of taking care of her powerful creatures.

†

Sasha sat on the porch in a well-worn rocking chair, watching the sun slip below the horizon while the night creatures came to life. Fireflies danced across the front yard to the music created by the crickets. Deep in the bayou, Sasha could hear the bellow of a bull alligator as he sought a mate. The slight creak of the door as it opened interrupted the concert of the night. Sasha intuitively knew that Kara was about to join her on the porch.

"Mind if I join you?"

"Of course not." Sasha motioned her toward a rocking chair.

Kara pulled a cigarette out of a pack in her pocket and lit it, offering one to Sasha.

"Thanks." Sasha took the offered gift and breathed deeply of the cool menthol.

"I had forgotten how peaceful it can be in the bayou." Kara slowly rocked back and forth. "Much different from Atlanta," she said as a quick smile crossed her face.

"I hope you will take full advantage of your time here to relax and take every pleasure Sugarland has to offer." Sasha locked eyes with Kara.

"I would very much like that." Kara's eyes widened with delight. "I noticed you riding a fabulous stallion as we drove up. Is there any chance of getting a horseback tour while I am here?"

"I am sure that can be arranged," Sasha responded. "I do believe Lisa has plans for a riverboat cruise for Saturday morning, but if you prefer you may remain behind and we will go for a ride." Sasha let out a soft chuckle.

"That would be delightful."

Sasha was about to make another comment but was interrupted when the door opened and Lisa poked her head out. "There you are. We thought you had disappeared on us."

"Just enjoying a smoke and the sounds of the night with our hostess," Kara replied.

"We thought we might play some cards in the parlor and do some catching up before heading off to bed. Will you join us?" Lisa asked.

"Thanks again for the smoke." Sasha watched as Kara stood to join her friends.

"You are welcome." Kara smiled before she disappeared into the house.

✝

Sasha finished the cigarette then walked into the kitchen to find Marie preparing for the next day's meals. She could hear the chatter and soft laughter of her guests as she watched Marie move gracefully around the kitchen.

"Can you believe how much Miss Stewart looks like Milly?" Marie asked.

"I was completely taken aback when she turned around while she stood by the portrait." Sasha sighed. "It was as if for a moment Milly had returned, young and full of life as ever," she said with just a hint of sadness in her voice.

"She appears to be a very sweet young woman too." Marie had a coy expression on her face.

Sasha gave a short laugh. "You are a marvel of a woman, Marie." Sasha softly touched the woman's shoulder before walking out of the kitchen and into the parlor.

✝

Sasha sat before the baby grand and let her fingers brush across the keys as her mind became lost in a cloud of Brahms and Beethoven. She was playing each delicate piece from memory. Playing music relaxed Sasha, and the concentration was taking her mind off the fire in her stomach, intensified by the appearance of the beautiful Kara.

After Milly's death, Sasha had played less and less. Playing the baby grand in the parlor brought back memories of their youth in Europe and their life together at Sugarland. Sasha frequently felt a connection with Milly when she played—her fingers stroking the keys lightly remembering the softness of Milly's skin.

She was deep in memory. Her eyes closed, watching Milly dance in front of her. She smiled as she watched her lover.

With her mind focused on the music and her memories, an hour passed quickly and Sasha opened her eyes to see Kara standing in the doorway watching her. Sasha fixed her eyes on Kara. "Join me."

"You play so beautifully." Kara sat in a chair across from Sasha.

Sasha found herself reluctant to break away from gazing into the woman's enchanting eyes. "Thank you." Sasha released Kara's eyes, permitting her to watch how sensually her fingertips brushed across the piano keys.

I could be stroking your breasts like this. Sasha planted the thought in Kara's mind.

She watched as Kara's nipples grew hard under the soft fabric of her blouse and a flush rose to her cheeks.

"Do you play?"

"Yes, but not nearly as well as you."

"Join me." Sasha again beckoned, pointing to the bench beside her. Kara slid beside her, their thighs touching.

Sasha placed her hand lightly on Kara's thigh as she began to play.

"It has been a long time and I am afraid I am a trifle rusty."

Sasha stroked Kara's thigh and leaned in close to Kara's ear. "Relax, you are doing just fine."

Kara softly sighed as she breathed in the rich cologne Sasha wore then closed her eyes to concentrate on the piece she was playing.

Sasha noted the heartbeat pulsing in Kara's neck and brazenly allowed her tongue to trail up the length of her jugular until her lips came to rest atop the pulse. Kara's body shivered and a soft moan escaped her lips.

Sasha softly kissed Kara's neck and listened quietly as Kara finished the piece she was playing.

Kara's fingers played the final note and she turned toward Sasha.

"Beautiful. You should play more often." Sasha looked into the deep blue of Kara's eyes.

"I know." Kara shrugged. "The music is very relaxing and gives me much pleasure."

"Maybe you will play again before you leave," Sasha suggested, "but for now I recommend you retire as Lisa has a big day planned for you tomorrow." Sasha stood and led Kara to her room. "I hope you have sweet dreams tonight." Sasha could feel Kara's eyes watching her as she walked down the hall toward the stairway and her room.

✝

Sasha started up her computer and busied herself updating the business accounts while she listened to the sounds of the guests sleeping in the house. Shortly after midnight, she walked outside, picking up another of the cigarettes from the pack Kara had left on the porch. She had forgotten how much she enjoyed smoking and marveled at the taste as she listened to the sounds of the bayou. Crickets chirped in song, and deep in the darkened forest animals called to their mates or sounded alarms at the presence of a predator in the area. Clouds passed quickly in front of an almost full moon. She sighed then returned inside the house in search of sleep.

As she passed each of the rooms, she could hear the soft heartbeats and slow breathing of their sleeping occupants. A strange sound caught her ear as she neared Cindy's room and she quickly recognized the sound as the rapid heartbeat of a baby.

Smiling, Sasha walked on and stood in front of Kara's room. She silently passed through the closed door and looked down onto the bed where Kara slept. A soft, full breast was uncovered and a bare thigh exposed as well, revealing that Kara slept naked on the cool sheets. Sasha watched as Kara's hand moved in her sleep to cover her breast. She slipped into Kara's dream.

Kara's dream was as vivid to Sasha as if it were reality. She observed her hands and mouth covering Kara's body, arousing the sleeping beauty with soft touches and nibbles. Kara's hands moved on her breasts with the exact motions Sasha was using in her dream and Sasha watched as she arched her back, begging for a firmer touch. She could hear the soft moans escaping Kara's lips and she resisted the temptation to give herself pleasure as she eavesdropped on Kara's dream.

Instead, she quietly turned away and retired to her room for dreams of her own.

Chapter 2

Friday began with a beautiful sunrise and Sasha was surprised to find Kara already on the porch drinking coffee when she stepped out into the morning.

"Good morning," Sasha said. "I trust you slept well last night?"

"Probably one of the best nights of sleep I have had in ages." Kara's face was aglow in the morning light, her beauty radiant, and she looked completely relaxed as she lounged on the front porch.

"I am so glad to hear that," Sasha said. "You look rested and more at ease than you were yesterday."

"I had forgotten how revitalizing the fresh air can be," Kara admitted. "I find it so refreshing and much different from the smog of Atlanta."

"Well, I hope you will visit again and often."

"Don't be surprised if I do," Kara boldly stated.

The front door opened and Cindy came out carrying a steaming cup of coffee. She sat down beside Sasha.

"Let me be the first to congratulate you," Sasha said to Cindy.

Cindy looked at Sasha quizzically and asked, "For what?"

"Well, if you don't know already, you are pregnant," Sasha said.

Cindy's coffee cup fell from her hand and shattered on the porch floor. "How on earth could you know that?" Cindy exclaimed.

"My dear, when you have lived in the bayou as long as I have you develop certain talents, and a strong intuition is one of mine," Sasha said to the two shocked women.

"Jarrod, my husband, and I have been trying for three years to get pregnant with no success," Cindy said.

"Well, if you see your doctor when you get home, I guarantee he will tell you the same news," Sasha replied.

Stunned, Cindy looked down at the shattered china cup.

"No worries," Sasha said, stopping Cindy's apology before she even uttered a word. "Let me get you a fresh cup and I will clean up that mess." Sasha left the two friends sitting in shock on the porch.

"I still don't understand how she could know that?" Cindy said to Kara.

"She appears to have many special gifts," Kara said, offering no further explanation.

✝

Breakfast and the rest of the morning passed uneventfully then James packed up the women for their trip to New Orleans. After a day of shopping, ghost and cemetery tours, James was to bring them home for the evening.

Sasha worked in the barn during most of the day, feeding the animals and preparing the tack for a horseback tour with Kara as she had requested. After sunset, she found herself watching the hours tick by slowly until she heard James coming up the drive. Loud laughter and off-key singing competed with the night sounds of the bayou. The women had obviously stopped off for a few of New Orleans's famous hurricanes before coming home.

"Welcome back," Sasha said, rising from her seat on the porch to open the door. Lisa was the tipsiest of the women and needed help to reach her room. While Susan and Kara got Lisa safely tucked away in bed, Cindy joined Sasha on the porch.

"I had James make a detour to a pharmacy for a home pregnancy test, and sure enough, you were right," Cindy said, still amazed at Sasha's earlier revelation. "I can't wait to get home to share the good news with my husband." She stood to enter the house. "Thank you," she said.

"No thanks are necessary, Cindy. I do believe you and your husband deserve all the credit," Sasha teased. "I didn't have anything to do with it," she added with a grin.

Chuckling at her quick wit, Cindy said, "Good night, Sasha," and disappeared into the house.

"Sweet dreams, Cindy," Sasha offered.

Though exhausted from the day's events Kara returned to the porch, drawn by Sasha's magnetism. Lighting a smoke, she handed it to Sasha, who could taste the faint sweetness of liquor on the filter from the touch of Kara's lips.

"Thanks," Sasha said as Kara lit another and sat close beside her.

Kara, still slightly buzzed, talked quietly with Sasha as they smoked. When they stood to go inside Kara stumbled and Sasha wrapped her arms around Kara to keep her from falling. They stood pressed together for a long moment. Kara's lips, only inches from Sasha's, seemed to beg for a kiss. Breathing in the richness of Sasha's cologne, a soft moan escaped Kara's lips as her mind wandered back to her dreams the night before. Smiling, Sasha released Kara, turned, and led Kara to her bedroom, bidding her pleasant dreams.

Two hours later, Sasha stood outside Kara's door and listened to the soft purring of her sleeping. She eased inside the room to find Kara naked and slipping into dreamland as her eyes moved from side to side under her pale eyelids. Sasha carefully pulled the silky covers back from Kara's body and lay beside her on the bed.

The light from the full moon bathed Kara's body in its softness. Sasha gazed down at the beautiful woman lying beside her and her body ached to touch her. She slowly reached out and allowed her fingers to caress the full breast, circling the nipple until it ripened with excitement. She moved closer to Kara, who briefly stirred as her nose caught the scent of Sasha's cologne, but she did not wake. Sasha's tongue gently caressed the hardened nipple. Soft moans emanated from within Kara as Sasha's fingers danced down her body. Instinctively, Kara spread her legs to welcome her touch and Sasha found a well of moisture awaiting her arrival. Her fingers dipped into the velvety dampness, making Sasha moan and sending vibrations onto the breast she was caressing with her tongue.

Sasha looked up into Kara's face to find that she was awake. Their eyes locked and Sasha put a finger to her lips, asking for silence. Kara's head dropped back on the pillow as her hands buried themselves in the softness of Sasha's hair. Sasha resumed suckling Kara's breast, her fingers moving inside Kara, causing her to catch her breath. Again holding Kara's gaze in hers, Sasha began nibbling the sensitive nipple while she pressed her fingers deeper inside Kara.

Kara's moans grew in volume and she raised her hips off the bed to rock with the motion of Sasha's urgent fingers driving deep inside her. The burning in Sasha's stomach grew to a blazing inferno as she listened to the coursing of blood through Kara's veins. Kara's body was on fire as well as she released the first orgasm into the palm of her lover's hand.

Kara's eyes begged for more as Sasha prayed they would, and she carefully moved her body between Kara's trembling thighs. She entered her again with her fingers as her mouth slowly encircled Kara's clit, swollen with the hot blood racing through her body.

Her exposed fangs grazed across the top of Kara's clit, opening a small puncture wound. Her lips surrounded the engorged clit and began sucking the hot nectar of life that her body so desperately craved. She drank in bliss as Kara's body reeled from the most intense sensation she had ever felt and she exploded with another forceful orgasm. Sasha was wary of drinking too much and used her soft, warm tongue to seal the small wound, while each new movement of her mouth resulted in violent convulsions as Kara's body danced with ecstasy. Kara pulled Sasha's face to her mouth, allowing her lover's tongue to snake inside her mouth and they kissed deeply as Sasha's fingers continued to produce waves of pleasure that overwhelmed Kara.

Kara was afraid to speak, fearful if she spoke, the dream she was enjoying so much would end prematurely. Instead, she allowed Sasha's tongue and fingers to bring her body to peak after peak of pleasure.

After several hours of slow lovemaking, Kara's eyes grew heavy and with a final kiss Sasha said, "Good night, my darling," and quietly left her side. Sasha walked softly to her room, climbing carefully into her bed where she slept peacefully for the remainder of the night.

†

The sun on her skin finally woke Sasha and she was surprised to find that it was ten in the morning. She showered and dressed in riding clothes then went downstairs to find Kara patiently waiting for her on the porch. Kara blushed as Sasha approached.

"Good morning, Kara," Sasha said.

"Good morning."

They chatted as they walked down to the stables and soon they were mounted and heading into the fields.

"Would you mind if I asked about the portrait hanging in the parlor?" Kara asked as the horses walked at a leisurely pace.

Sasha had been wondering when Kara would ask about portrait, the resemblance between Milly and Kara was so strong. "The woman in the portrait is Milly Vansant, my partner and lover since we met in London," Sasha said. She watched to see if Kara would blanch at the term "lover" but there was no outward change to her composure. Sasha did hear the racing of Kara's heart as she continued. "Milly was also the artist who painted that portrait for me prior to her death."

"I'm sorry if I brought up painful memories for you, but we share so many traits I find it unusual, so I had to ask."

"You do remind me very much of Milly," she answered and let the conversation stall for a few moments.

The women continued to chat casually for a while before falling silent and enjoying the sunshine and quiet companionship.

Kara broke the silence saying, "I had the most wonderful dream for the second night in a row."

"Really," Sasha said. "I hope it was very pleasurable for you," she added.

Kara's cheeks were blood red as she looked Sasha directly in the eyes and said, "I dreamed that you came to me last night and made love to me like no one has ever before."

Seeming almost relieved that she could make that statement, Kara took a deep breath as her eyes searched Sasha's face for a response.

"What if I told you that it wasn't a dream?" Sasha asked.

"I would have to say I was the luckiest woman in the world then," Kara said sincerely, making Sasha smile.

Sasha changed the direction they were traveling and urged the horses into a soft canter. Within minutes, they reached the small cottage tucked away in the bayou that Milly had used as her studio. Hidden from prying eyes, it now was a place of retreat for Sasha.

Sasha opened the door and led Kara into a dimly lit room. Removing her sunglasses, she moved to take Kara in her arms. Kara looked into her eyes, drinking in the sparkling lavender, and said, "You have the most beautiful eyes I have ever seen."

This time Kara initiated the kiss, beginning slowly then growing to a fevered pitch. Kara undressed Sasha as she backed her toward the small bed on the other side of the room. Pressing Sasha down onto the bed, Kara quickly removed her clothing and lay down on top of Sasha. Kissing her deeply her hips began undulating against Sasha, igniting a fire of a different kind. Kara's hand slipped between their bodies and she boldly entered Sasha, who allowed Kara to bring her body to peak after peak of pleasure before she rolled Kara over onto her back to repeat last night's performance.

Finally collapsing on top of Kara, they struggled to catch their breath before drifting off for a short nap. Just as Sasha began to fade from consciousness she heard a deep sigh of contentment echo around the room and felt Milly's spirit surround them, as they lay entwined on the bed.

When Kara awoke, she found Sasha lying in her arms, watching her as she slept; the lavender of her eyes deep with satisfaction.

"That was incredible all over again," Kara whispered to a smiling Sasha.

They slowly dressed and shared a deep, fiery kiss before leaving the cottage for the ride back.

When they arrived, the other guests had returned from the boat trip. None of them noticed the glow of pleasure gracing the face of their friend, but Marie was quick to notice when Sasha entered the kitchen.

"Been naughty, have you, Sasha?" she teased, delighted to see Sasha smiling again.

"Several times, Marie, several times," came her response. Marie answered her smug response with a pop of her towel across Sasha's backside. Sasha grinned and left Marie to toil in the kitchen as she headed upstairs for a shower.

✝

Sasha sat on the porch watching the sun slowly disappear, pondering the events of the past two days. Undoubtedly, she had left herself vulnerable to the charms of Kara, a luxury she couldn't afford to indulge in often. She wondered, had she dropped her defenses because Kara reminded her so much of Milly? Immersed in her thoughts, Sasha jumped when Kara sat beside her.

"May I expect a visit again tonight?" she asked.

"Would you like a visit tonight?" Sasha replied.

"I would love nothing more than to spend my last night here with you, Sasha," Kara answered honestly.

"I suggest you go inside and eat a nice meal then," Sasha said as she gazed into the sparkling blue eyes looking at her.

Kara smiled and joined her friends for another of Marie's Cajun feasts, eating heartily, but her mind drifted way beyond food. Her friends chatted excitedly about returning home after their short break, failing to notice that Kara wasn't as eager to leave. She was relieved when her friends chose to retire early to prepare for their homeward journey.

Chapter 3

Kara packed her bags and slipped beneath the sheets, awaiting Sasha's arrival. The full moon shone brightly in her window as it rose across the night sky, and she could hear the soft whispering of the wind as it moved among the ancient oaks surrounding the house. Her eyes began to feel heavy, and she closed them for what she thought was just a moment.

Sasha entered the room and again saw Kara's body bathed in the moonlight. She is so much like my Milly, and then so different, she thought as she climbed onto the bed. The feel of a naked body awakened Kara as it pressed close to her. She opened her eyes to find Sasha lying beside her. Wasting no time Kara took Sasha in her arms for a deep kiss, pulling her body over to cover hers. Kara locked her heels around Sasha's thighs and began to thrust her hips up to meet Sasha's as she ground into her. Their moans, muffled by deep kisses, grew to a fevered pitch. The rocking of the bed tapped against the bedroom wall as the lovers came together in violent spasms.

For hours, each woman took turns pleasing the other, eventually winding up in a sixty-nine position. With Kara on top Sasha slowly bled her clit, licking at the droplets of blood, teasing Kara into blinding arousal with her tongue and fingers, which were buried deep inside. When Sasha was convinced Kara could stand no more, she enclosed her clit with her hungry mouth and feasted on her lover's blood until Kara collapsed in exhaustion.

Sasha held Kara in her arms until the sun rose then quietly slipped from the bed to retire to her room to shower and dress. When she entered the kitchen, Marie was busy preparing a large breakfast that she hoped would hold their guests over until they reached their destinations. Sasha poured a cup of coffee and sat with an audible sigh to watch Marie cook.

"Did you have another sleepless night?" Marie asked.

"Something close to that," Sasha replied as the first of their guests followed the aroma of freshly brewed coffee and joined them in the kitchen.

"Good morning, ladies," Cindy said as she poured a cup of coffee and sat next to Sasha.

"Good morning. I hope you and your friends have had a pleasant stay," Sasha said.

"Oh, it was far more than we could have asked for," Cindy said. "Unfortunately we do have to get back to our lives, though."

Lisa, Susan, and finally Kara, who looked surprisingly well rested for the limited amount of sleep she had, joined them in the kitchen. In the midst of eating Marie's hearty breakfast Susan asked, "Did anyone else see the ghost last night?"

Her friends looked at her in disbelief as she went on to tell her tale. "About midnight I was awakened by a soft tapping on my wall and muffled moans coming from inside the house," she explained. "The moon was shining brightly and when I walked to the window I saw Joshua sitting under the oak, sobbing into his hands. A cloud crossed in front of the moon bringing darkness again, and when the cloud passed Joshua was gone." Susan paused to take a sip of coffee. "Then I crawled back into the bed and pulled the covers up to my chin and tried to go back to sleep, but the tapping and moans went on for hours."

Marie stole a knowing glance at Sasha and then at Kara, who remained surprisingly silent. Sasha caught Kara's eye, winked and smiled at the blushing young woman.

†

After breakfast, James brought the car around and began to load the guests' bags while they bid their good-byes to Marie and Sasha, thanking them for a wonderful trip. Kara was mysteriously absent from the group, and when Sasha went in search of her she found her waiting in her bedroom.

"I was hoping you would come looking for me so we could have a private good-bye," she said as Sasha entered. "I had the most amazing time with you and I hate to leave, but I must go for now. I hope the invitation to return still stands. I would love to come back to spend more time with you."

"You are welcome to return anytime, for however long you wish to stay," Sasha assured her. She leaned down and planted a soft kiss on Kara's lips. "Good-bye for now then, my love," she said softly as she led Kara out the door and walked her to the waiting car.

Sasha walked back to the porch and, with a heavy sigh, lit the last cigarette in the pack as she watched the car disappear down the drive. Donning her sunglasses, she slowly smoked the cigarette and then crushed the butt in the ashtray.

As the car disappeared in a cloud of dust, Sasha reached out to touch Kara's mind one last time. *I love you* was the thought projected and Sasha was surprised when from deep inside her mind, Kara answered, *I love you too.*

Chapter 4

The week following the departure of Kara and her friends turned into absolute torture for Sasha. She moped glumly around Sugarland each day, riding for hours through the fields and dense forest trying desperately to erase Kara from her haunted memories.

Meanwhile back in Atlanta, Kara also moved listlessly through her ordinarily bustling life. Her nights consisted of restless sleep filled with dreams of Sasha. She was haunted by the song *Bring me to Life*. She heard the song on the radio as she commuted to and from work, in the elevator of her office building and hints of the song danced in her head while she tossed in bed.

One evening, after Sasha had returned from one of her long rides, Marie finally confronted her. "Sasha, why don't you at least call her?"

"Call who?" Sasha asked coyly.

"Kara," Marie said.

"Is it that obvious?" Sasha asked.

"Yes it is, dear," Marie said with a smile.

"You would think by now that I would know better than to let someone get so close to me," Sasha said sadly.

"Sometimes your heart wins out over your head," Marie sweetly reminded her.

"I do miss her so," Sasha admitted, "but I really don't have anything to offer her."

"Sometimes you can be so silly, Sasha," Marie admonished. "All Kara wants from you is your love."

Sasha perked up as she let Marie's words sink in.

"But—"

"But, nothing," Marie interrupted. "That woman loves you dearly."

Sasha smiled again. "Do you think so?"

"I swear, for someone so brilliant, you can be intolerably naïve," Marie crowed. "Open your eyes and at least give her a chance to show you. You know James and I will be gone for the next two weeks while they burn the cane fields, so why don't you call her and invite her for a visit," Marie suggested.

"Oh Marie, the skies will be filled with nasty smoke and it won't be decent to be outside."

Laughing, Marie said, "I doubt the two of you would leave the bedroom, much less the house."

Sasha blushed furiously at Marie's speculation, knowing the woman's assessment was completely accurate.

"I will give it some thought," Sasha said as she moved past Marie to walk up the stairs.

"Good," Marie said. "I put Kara's telephone number on your desk just in case," she added.

Shaking her head, Sasha said, "Thanks, Marie," and continued up the stairs.

✝

Sasha picked up the note with Kara's phone number and looked at her watch. It was probably still too early to call, she thought, and decided instead to take a bath.

Sasha started the water to draw a bath. She located mulberry bath bubbles and lit a candle of the same fragrance sitting on the edge of the tub. Slipping out of her riding clothes, Sasha stepped into the sea of bubbles, sinking up to her neck as the water soothed her aching body. She rested her head against a bath pillow, closed her eyes, and allowed the tension in her body to disappear into the bubbles. The fragrance of the bubbles and candle reminded her of the sweet taste of Kara's kisses, especially the one before she left to return to Atlanta.

Sasha remembered the tears in her eyes as Kara said good-bye and her heart ached to hold Kara in her arms again. Her thoughts drifted back to the last night she and Kara made love, the tender moments and wild passion, which sent a wave of desire over Sasha as she soaked. She imagined the soft brush of Kara's lips against her skin as her hand disappeared beneath the bubbles to find her clit throbbing with need. Sasha whispered Kara's name as her fingers stroked her body to a shuddering orgasm.

†

Kara had just arrived at her studio and was pulling into her parking space when a rush of heat surged through her body and she heard Sasha's voice whisper her name. With a trembling hand Kara put the car in park and turned the key to shut down the racing engine. She leaned her head against the headrest and closed her eyes as images of Sasha filled her brain. Overwhelmed by the tremors Sasha was experiencing Kara could taste the sweet rush of Sasha's wetness as it filled her mouth.

Kara sat motionless behind the wheel until the current of pleasure passed, leaving her legs weak as she shuffled toward the elevator. She closed the door of her studio behind her and walked over to the love seat, collapsing into the safety of her sanctuary. Reaching for a remote, Kara dimmed the lights and turned on the sound system. Ironically, Evanescence was playing and Kara became lost in the haunting lyrics of *My Immortal*.

Kara listened carefully as the words echoed through the room. She thought the lyrics surreal as Kara realized how easily Sasha had entered her soul and how empty her life felt without Sasha in it. She closed her eyes and continued to hear the lyrics as if for the first time.

Kara wanted to be with Sasha forever and tears slipped quietly down her cheeks as the rest of the song played.

†

Sasha had finished her bath and was sitting out on the porch enjoying the evening when she felt tears flowing down her face. She reached up to capture a tear, touching it to her lips. She could taste the essence of Kara on her tongue and was relieved to discover the tears were those of Kara missing her. Unable to restrain herself further, Sasha went upstairs to her office and picked up the telephone. She was preparing to dial Kara's number when the telephone rang in her hand. Sasha smiled when she looked at the caller ID to see Kara's number.

"Hello, Kara."

Kara, taken aback by the luxurious tone in her rich voice, was certain Sasha's lavender eyes were alight with a smile.

"Hello, Sasha," she answered. "I will be honest and tell you I am missing you very much and needed to hear your voice," she blurted out.

Sasha smiled. "I was just getting ready to dial your number when the telephone rang."

"Were you really?"

"Yes, really, you have been on my mind a great deal since you left."

"I feel like you have been right here with me tonight, but I still needed to hear your voice," Kara said.

"I am so glad you called," Sasha said. "I was calling to invite you down for a visit."

"Wow, when did you have in mind?"

"Well, they burn the cane fields after the harvest which will start next week. Marie has horrible allergies to the smoke, so we usually shut down for two weeks while she and James take a vacation."

"So we would be all alone?"

"Yes, ma'am, we would."

"I have a case that should wrap up on Wednesday," Kara said. "Why don't you fly up this weekend and I can show you around the city. Then we can fly back after court on Wednesday."

"I haven't been to Atlanta in ages. Let me check with the airlines, and I will let you know tomorrow."

"So, that's a yes?" Kara asked excitedly.

"Most definitely a yes," Sasha said, a broad smile crossing her face. "I will call the airlines tonight and call you back tomorrow night with the details," she promised.

"I can't wait to see you."

"I look forward to it too," Sasha said, then bade Kara good night and returned the telephone to its cradle.

Kara was so excited she could not eat the salad she had prepared for dinner and decided instead to take a hot shower and call it an early evening. She climbed between the fresh sheets and slept soundly, dreaming of holding Sasha in her arms again.

†

After Sasha ended the call with Kara, she immediately called the airlines for arrangements to fly to Atlanta early Saturday morning. Only one more day and she would see Kara. Sasha grinned as she went downstairs to find Marie, who was bustling about the kitchen, cleaning and preparing for the next day's meals.

Marie noticed the smile on her face when Sasha walked into the kitchen. "Did you call her?"

Sasha quickly told her of their plans.

It was difficult for Marie to hide her excitement for Sasha. "James and I will be thrilled to drop you at the airport on our way up to Shreveport Saturday morning."

Sasha raced up the stairs to pull out a small bag and began the task of deciding what outfits to take to Atlanta. Two hours later, she climbed into bed for a restful night's sleep.

Chapter 5

She spent the following day setting up self-feeders for the animals, checking and rechecking her packed bag. She called Kara around seven to give her the details of the flight.

"I will arrive in Atlanta at noon on Saturday."

"Just a few more hours then," Kara said, unable to conceal her excitement.

They chatted for a few more minutes and then ended the call, both women excited about the weekend to come.

†

Saturday morning arrived and Sasha had her bag loaded in the car before James and Marie awoke. She could not hide her impatience as the couple brought out their bags, rushing to help James pack the car.

"You aren't excited about your trip, are you?" Marie teased.

"Me?" Sasha tossed back. "No, I just wanted to make sure you two make it to Shreveport before nightfall."

"Likely story," James teased as he closed the door behind Sasha and moved around to the driver's door.

†

Sasha checked in at the counter and arrived at the gate just moments before the call for boarding. She stowed her small bag in the overhead compartment and stretched out in a first-class seat while the remainder of the passengers boarded. She took the offering of a glass of sweet red wine from the flight attendant, and once they were in the air, reclined the seat for a nap on the short flight to Atlanta.

The bumpy landing woke Sasha. She retrieved her bag and stepped into the terminal, entering the mass of travelers rushing to find their next gate. It had been a few years since Sasha had been among a crowd and it took a moment to regain orientation to where she was and in what direction she should be heading.

She had forgotten how alive her special sense became around large crowds of people. She could sense happiness, anger, and vile evil as she made her way through the terminal. She also felt a familiar buzzing in her head, which grew stronger with each step. Sasha recognized the sensation of another Immortal being close and smiled warmly at the young man who passed within inches of her, returning her knowing smile. The sounds of so many heartbeats and the rushing of blood through veins became near deafening as Sasha struggled to control the sounds in her head.

She passed through the busiest of hubs and the crowds began to thin out. She followed the signs to the arriving passenger location and searched until she found Kara standing with her back to her, looking in the opposite direction.

Turn around, Sasha projected to Kara.

Kara immediately turned and smiled when she saw Sasha walking toward her.

Sasha returned the smile, knowing Kara's heart rate had nearly doubled as her blood was gushing through her veins at an incredible rate. She was pleased her physical presence had this effect on Kara. Sasha opened her arms and enveloped Kara in her warm embrace as she planted a soft kiss on Kara's lips.

"Hello, Kara."

"I am so glad you are here," Kara said as she hugged her tightly.

Kara ushered Sasha out to the short-term parking where she had left her car and tossed her bag into the backseat of the convertible. Turning again to face Sasha, she leaned in to her for a make-your-lungs-scream kiss, which left both women hungry for more. Kara opened the door for Sasha, and they rode into the early Atlanta afternoon. The wind whipped through their hair as Kara carefully wound the sports car through the busy metro traffic toward downtown.

Kara drove to a small park and parked the car under the shade of an old oak. She carefully raised the ragtop, securing it against the elements of nature and humankind, and then clicked the security system as they walked away. Sliding her hand into Sasha's, Kara led her across the park to where a horse-drawn carriage awaited passengers. The female driver welcomed them aboard and soon they were off for a historic tour of downtown. The driver, who introduced herself as Susan, was well versed in the history of her city and gave them a detailed tour of the city and special places of interest.

As they rode through the city, Kara cuddled into Sasha's body, stealing several kisses along the route.

Two hours later, Susan brought them back to their starting point, where she accepted a generous tip from Kara and bid them farewell. Kara and Sasha returned to the car and as the lights of the city began to come alive, they drove to Kara's home. Once there, she led Sasha through the parking garage into the elevator, pinning her against the back wall for a deep kiss as they rode up to her studio.

Kara opened her door into the wide-open studio, and the first thing Sasha noticed was the beautiful view of the city as seen from Kara's veranda. She walked over to the huge sliding doors and gazed out at the city below them as it glowed with manufactured lighting.

"This view is beautiful," Sasha said as Kara walked up beside her.

"It is the best part of living in Atlanta," she said, wrapping her arm around Sasha's waist.

Sasha turned in Kara's arms and took Kara's chin in her fingers, raising her lips up to meet hers they kissed, softly enjoying the closeness of their bodies.

Kara took Sasha's hand, led her into the large master bedroom, and pushed her back onto the bed. Straddling Sasha, she began to unbutton the deep red shirt, pulling it free from her body and dropping it over the edge of the bed. She leaned down, her lips brushing the soft skin of Sasha's neck as she moved toward her ear to softly whisper, "I need to taste you."

Sasha's smile gave Kara the impetus to move forward, her lips covering Sasha's body with fevered kisses. Sasha lay back, basking in the pleasure of Kara's mouth and touches on her body as her arousal soared. Kara's fingers manipulated the fasteners of Sasha's jeans and Sasha kicked her boots off and lifted her hips to allow Kara to push them down and off her body, leaving her naked body exposed to Kara's desires.

Kara's mouth covered Sasha's right breast, her fingers lightly raking down her abdomen, traveling to the core of the fire burning in her body. Her tongue flicked the erect nipple, trapping it between her teeth, nipping it lightly. Sasha's breathing became shallow as Kara suckled her breast and her fingers probed the steamy wetness, searching for and reaching the precise rhythm and touch that made Sasha cry out for more. Stroke after stroke, Sasha's body shuddered beneath her touch until she cried out that she was coming and filled Kara's hand with a rush of wetness.

Kara removed her fingers and slipped down between Sasha's trembling legs, driving her tongue deep into Sasha. One orgasm flowed into another.

Hungering for Kara, Sasha lifted her body and rolled Kara onto her back.

"Wait," she said. She left the bed long enough to hastily remove the clothing that prevented her from being skin to skin with Sasha. She returned to the bed covering Sasha's body with her own. Her clit rubbed against Sasha's wetness as their bodies entwined and their heartbeats raced together.

The sweet fragrance of Kara's blood as it streamed through her body drove Sasha mad with lust. She gently nipped Kara's lip, causing a drop of blood to form. Sasha licked the droplet with her tongue, the taste of it like a fine wine that left her hungering for more.

Sasha caressed Kara's body with kisses, driving her wild with passion until she begged Sasha to allow her release. Sasha continued her light kisses, unwilling to end Kara's torture just yet. Kara's moans turned into wails when Sasha's hot breath caressed her clit and her fingertips parted her soaked lips. The tip of her tongue finally reached the soft folds inside Kara. She attempted to grind her hips upward to meet Sasha's mouth, but one well-placed hand on Kara's stomach kept her pinned in place as Sasha's tongue traced her womanhood, licking ever so slightly over her clit. Kara convulsed with need, tormented by her desire.

Sasha slipped two long fingers deep inside Kara, withdrawing slowly and pressing deeper with each thrust. Placing her wrist to her mouth Sasha used her sharp fangs to open a small gash in her wrist, drawing a slow trickle of blood. Putting her wrist over Kara's mouth she wrapped her lips around Kara's clit, sucking it deep into her mouth. Sasha watched as Kara's tongue lashed out to catch the first droplet of blood, and then pulled her wrist down, covering it with her mouth. She drank from Sasha as her body exploded in violent spasms.

Sasha understood what Kara would experience next from her time with Milly. She felt Kara's mind go blank at the first taste of her blood and then erupt into chaos as images flashed inside her mind, briefly taking Kara into a world of madness. She heard her groans as Kara felt the enormous sensations of love and loss that Sasha had experienced over the past 115 years. Sasha moved up next to Kara, holding her body close as the images raged inside her mind, her body twisting with the torture Sasha had experienced. She hated that Kara had to experience this, but it was necessary for Kara to understand the choice she would be facing if she chose to be her life mate.

Sasha held her for hours until the torment subsided and Kara's mind and body faded into the blackness. She gently pulled the covers over Kara's exhausted body and listened for the soft purring of her sleep. Sasha watched over Kara closely, fully aware that if she chose to join her in eternity, there would be much more agony to come.

†

The next morning Kara awoke to the smell of Sasha cooking breakfast and crept silently from the bed to walk into the kitchen. Sasha felt Kara wake but allowed the smaller woman to walk up behind her and wrap her arms around her waist without spoiling her act of deception.

"Good morning, darling, how did you sleep?" Sasha asked.

"Very well, thank you, but every muscle in my body is sore this morning," she replied. "It must have been one fantastic workout you gave me last night."

"What, you don't remember climbing the walls last night?" Sasha asked with a wicked smile.

"I remember the tremendous orgasm you gave me and the sweetest of tastes in my mouth and then nothing. Did I pass out from the pleasure?" she asked.

"Something close to that," Sasha said. "Are you hungry?"

"I am starved," Kara replied as she stole a strip of bacon and moved to the refrigerator. "What kind of juice would you like?" she asked.

"Apple, if you have it," Sasha replied, carrying two plates to the small table.

Kara poured two glasses of juice and sat beside Sasha. "This tastes wonderful," she said as she feasted on the meal.

"Why don't we do a driving tour of the city today and then return here for some Chinese takeout and then maybe hit one of the local women's bars later tonight," Kara suggested.

"How early do you have court in the morning?" Sasha asked.

"Not until ten o clock," Kara replied with a smile.

They finished their meal and cleared the dishes together, sharing several warm, tender kisses as they labored.

✝

After a quick shower, Kara and Sasha drove through town visiting several historic sites before deciding to head back home for a short nap then ordering Chinese for an early dinner.

She snuggled in close to Sasha as they slept. In her dreams, Kara relived the many times they had made love and the way Sasha took control of her body, bringing her the most powerful orgasms she'd ever had. In her slumber, Kara's body reacted to her dreams, wetness soaking the silky panties she wore.

The scent of Kara's arousal lingered in Sasha's nostrils, stirring her from her sleep. With ease, Sasha slipped into Kara's mind to discover she was dreaming of their lovemaking and a smile crossed her lips. Sasha glanced over to the clock to see that it was fast approaching five, plenty of time for a quick snack, she thought.

Kara had rolled onto her back in her sleep and Sasha watched the rhythmic rise and fall of her chest as she dreamed. A smile played across her face as Sasha again entered her mind. Sasha whispered softly *Pull up your top,* and Kara slowly responded to her suggestion. *Touch your nipple*s, Sasha instructed and Kara's hands began to circle her nipples. They sprang to life under her caresses.

Sasha slid her hand between Kara's thighs, her fingertips brushing across the damp fabric, tracing the outline of her feminine lips as Kara moaned softly. Kara began rolling her hips and Sasha took advantage of her movement to slide the soaked panties off her aroused body. *Wouldn't it feel good to touch yourself?* Sasha suggested. Sasha watched as Kara's right hand moved to her mound. She smiled as Kara began stroking her wetness and her clit began to swell. Kara's left hand rolled her nipples between her fingers as her fingernails grazed across the top of her blood-engorged clit. Sasha watched as Kara's skin flushed with desire and her breathing became more rapid.

Propped on her elbow Sasha leaned into Kara's body. Her tongue traced the outer edges of Kara's left ear and then she whispered, "Enter yourself, baby." Kara's fingers parted her lips and two fingers disappeared into her wetness, burrowing deep before emerging and plunging back inside her. "Oh yes, that's it, make it feel good," Sasha whispered her instructions as Kara picked up speed with her strokes. Sasha watched the tremors take control of Kara's body as her fingers continued to pleasure her body. "Come now," she commanded and Kara's body exploded, her eyes flying open as she cried out with pleasure.

Kara looked deep into Sasha's lavender eyes and found herself hypnotized by her stare. Her body continued to shake with arousal as Sasha instructed Kara to roll over and rise to her knees. Moving behind Kara, Sasha spread Kara's knees wide then lay on her back and slid underneath Kara's body. Kara's full breasts swayed underneath her body and Sasha easily suckled her as her fingers played in Kara's wetness. Sucking Kara's breast deep into her mouth Sasha formed a cone shape with the fingers of her right hand and entered Kara. Kara groaned loudly, her muscles spreading wide to accept the penetration of Sasha's hand. Sasha's thumb stroked furiously across Kara's clit as her fingers worked deep inside her. Kara shook uncontrollably as Sasha's knuckles rubbed against the outer edges of Kara's lips with each downstroke. Kara released a flood of wetness as her body erupted in a second powerful orgasm.

Sasha was not yet satisfied. As Kara's body recovered, Sasha slipped her own shirt and panties off and lay on her back. She guided Kara's body to straddle her face and lowered Kara's head between her spread thighs. Kara covered Sasha's wetness with her mouth, stroking deep with her tongue as Sasha parted her lips and began slowly licking from her lips to her clit, teasing Kara to the brink of madness.

Sasha lifted her hips, pressing Kara's hand deeper into her wetness, and entered Kara with her tongue. Sasha grasped Kara's hips and rolled her over onto her back as her hips ground her wetness into Kara's face. Sasha allowed her body to release further, coating Kara's face with her juices just as Kara shook violently in a final exhausting climax.

Sasha turned Kara around in her arms and pulled her body close. "Sleep now," she whispered softly, and Kara closed her eyes and allowed her body to tumble into sleep. Sasha lay awake for several minutes, struggling with the hunger her sexual arousal had awakened. It would be difficult to feed without arousing suspicion, but Sasha would find a way to satisfy her need. Finally succumbing to the warmth of Kara's body, Sasha closed her eyes and dreamed.

✝

Kara awoke two hours later, refreshed and excited about taking Sasha for a night on the town. With soft lips, she kissed Sasha awake and led her beautiful lover into the shower. They caressed one another underneath the tepid flow, arousal continuing to build between them. Kara finally reached down to turn off the water and then patted Sasha dry with a thick towel before wrapping her in a warm robe. Kara quickly dried and donned a robe of her own before leaving the bedroom to order their dinner.

"Delivery will take a half hour," Kara said as she reentered the bedroom.

"That will give us time to figure out what we will wear tonight then," Sasha said as she looked up at Kara from the edge of the bed.

Kara and Sasha walked into the large closet to choose outfits for their evening on the town. With Sasha's approval, Kara selected black jeans and a lightweight blood-red sweater with black leather boots. Sasha also chose black jeans and boots but selected a tight-fitting black spandex pullover, which would leave nothing to the imagination. The doorbell rang as they laid their outfits across the bed, and Kara went to the door to retrieve their dinner.

Kara spread the feast across the small table out on the veranda, and they dined together, looking down into the city now ablaze with lights. "What a beautiful night," Sasha said as she picked up the noodles with her chopsticks and made her offering to Kara.

"It is very nice for a change," Kara said. "The humidity has been horrible lately and it is a welcome relief to feel the first signs of fall in the cool night air."

She watched the pulse jump in Kara's neck as she talked and the burning in her stomach intensified. She cursed herself now for not venturing into the bayou to feed before leaving, but her eagerness to see Kara had outweighed all other appetites.

They ate their fill of the sumptuous meal and Sasha helped Kara store the leftovers in the refrigerator for a late-night snack when they returned. They then decided to dress and prepare for their night on the town.

Kara dressed quickly and watched with anticipation as Sasha dressed in all black, the tight jeans and snug-fitting shirt enclosing her body like a second skin. She would definitely be turning heads at the club tonight, Kara thought, as Sasha bent down to slip into her boots.

"You look very sexy, darling," she said when Sasha glanced up for her approval.

"You, my dear, look good enough to eat," Sasha said as she stood and kissed Kara softly on the lips.

"I guess we will be the envy of the club tonight then," Kara teased as she led Sasha to the door, and they headed down to the garage.

Her hair blew in the wind as Kara wound the car through the city, and her heart raced every time she could look over to catch a glimpse of Sasha. Sasha's hand rested on Kara's thigh and her touch intoxicated her as she drove, a dampness growing between her thighs. Though her fingers remained static, Kara's imagination knew exactly the profound effect Sasha's touch had on her body.

When they arrived at the club, Sasha took Kara's hand, and led her through the doorway, stopping briefly to pay the cover charge before entering the tightly packed club, full of raging hormones. As they searched for an open table, Sasha could feel her senses vibrating, making her aware that she was not the sole Immortal on the prowl tonight. Her eyes searched the darkness to locate the source of vibration and she found herself locking eyes with a ravishing blond-haired woman with deep green eyes.

Greetings my sister, Sasha projected.

Welcome my sister, the blond-haired woman responded. Would you care to sit with us?

That would be lovely if we aren't intruding, Sasha replied.

I would be honored the woman spoke into Sasha's mind.

"Follow me, sweetie, we have been requested to join a private table," Sasha whispered to Kara.

She had no idea what Sasha was talking about, but trusted her completely. She would follow Sasha blindly wherever she chose to lead.

Sasha walked over to the table and held out her hand in welcome. "Sasha and Kara would be pleased to join your table," she said as she introduced them to their host.

"I am Katrina, the owner of this establishment, and this is my lover, Elise," the blond-haired woman said as she motioned to the dark-haired beauty sitting to her right.

"Very nice to meet you," Kara said, still slightly bewildered as she took the seat Sasha offered.

"What may I offer you to drink?" Katrina inquired.

"How about two gin and tonics," Kara suggested.

"Elise, would you get the ladies their drinks, my sweet?" Katrina requested.

"Certainly, love," Elise said and she slipped away from the table.

"What brings you two ladies out tonight?" Katrina asked.

"I'm visiting from the bayou and Kara promised me a sample of the nightlife here in Atlanta."

"I have heard about your club, but have never visited before," Kara said. "This place looks fantastic!" she added with excitement as her eyes surveyed the club.

"Why, thank you," Katrina said. "We take pride in catering to a variety of tastes here at the G Spot," she added with a grin.

Elise returned to the table with the drinks and asked if Kara would like to dance. Kara looked at Sasha, who smiled and motioned for her to go. Kara disappeared with Elise into the mass of bodies on the packed dance floor.

"So, my sister, what brings you into the city?" Katrina asked.

"I desire to take Kara as my mate and wanted to spend time with her before she made the difficult choice," Sasha said.

"Does it look promising that she will choose our way of life?" Katrina asked.

"I think so, but I want her to take as much time as needed to decide. Forever can be so much longer than a mortal can comprehend," Sasha replied.

"Understood, my friend," Katrina said. "I hope she will choose wisely and become your companion."

"Thank you, Katrina," Sasha said with sincerity. "She has become very important to me in such a short time. I would hate to imagine a life without her in it."

"Elise has been with me almost a year and I have loved every minute of being with her," Katrina said with pride.

"She is a beautiful woman," Sasha said as they watched the women dancing together.

"I sense your hunger," Katrina said. "Have you fed since you have been here?"

"No, not at all," Sasha admitted.

"Well, I am sure there will be opportunities for you to snack here tonight if you choose. I have a private office in the back, and I am sure Elise can keep Kara entertained on the dance floor if you would like to indulge," she offered. "In case you haven't noticed, there is a young blonde sitting at the bar who has been drooling since you came in. I am certain she would love to disappear with you for a few minutes," Katrina suggested.

Sasha's eyes scanned the bar until she located the woman Katrina spoke of and smiled at her. *Come to me*, Sasha planted in her mind. The young woman crept down from her barstool and made her way toward their table.

Katrina pointed out a door as the young woman approached them.

"I will let Kara know you will return in a few minutes if she beats you back to the table," Katrina promised.

"Thanks," Sasha said as she joined the young woman and led her into the small office. Locking the door behind them, Sasha pinned the woman against the door, kissing her deeply, their hands exploring each other's body. The scent of her arousal droned in Sasha's brain as the woman raised her leather skirt and placed Sasha's hand directly on her mound.

Her moans vibrated in Sasha's mouth as she entered her with three fingers, plunging deep inside her on the first stroke. The woman broke the kiss long enough to urge Sasha to fuck her harder before she sucked Sasha's tongue deep into her mouth. Sasha's blood lust grew each time her fingers rammed into the woman; she could hear the woman's blood rushing through her veins.

Sasha kissed her way to the woman's neck, slowly licking tiny circles as her fangs appeared, the licking replaced by sharp nibbles. The woman's jugular grew large beneath her tender skin as the coursing of her blood roared in Sasha's brain. Sasha could feel the woman's muscles begin to contract tightly around her fingers and her moans grew louder to signal her impending climax. Sasha sank her fangs into the soft skin of the woman's neck and she cried out as her orgasm began. Sasha drank freely from the woman, her fingers pounding into her, extending the woman's pleasure. Sasha's mind reeled with ecstasy as she drank the life-sustaining blood that her body craved so deeply.

The intoxicating rush from her feeding coursed through her body just as the woman's orgasm started to end. Withdrawing her fangs, Sasha licked the small wounds until they disappeared from the woman's neck, leaving smooth, flushed skin intact. Carefully removing her fingers Sasha led the exhausted woman to the small couch near the back of the office. She stretched the woman out and kissed her lightly as her eyelids fluttered and then closed. "Sleep now," Sasha said as she entered the small bathroom and washed her hands. With a final look at the young beauty, Sasha slipped quietly out the door and back to their table just as Elise and Kara were returning from the dance floor.

"Whew, your woman sure can dance," Kara said as Elise led her back to the table.

"You weren't doing too badly yourself," Katrina replied with a smile.

Kara took the drink Sasha offered and drank a large swallow of the cool liquid. "Thanks baby," she said, setting the drink back on the table. "This club is one fantastic place you have here," Kara said as she tried to catch her breath.

"Business has been good for us," Katrina said as she scanned the busy dance floor.

"I can see why. I have never seen so many gorgeous women in one place in all my life," she declared.

Elise laughed at Kara's comment. "It is kind of like being a kid in a candy shop, isn't it?"

"You can say that again," Kara said with a grin as she fanned herself.

"See anything you like?" Sasha asked.

"Yes, and she is sitting right next to me," Kara responded to her question.

"Very good answer," Katrina said from across the table with a wink to Sasha.

"How long will you be in town?" Elise asked Sasha.

"Just until Wednesday," Sasha replied. "When Kara finishes at work, we plan to fly back to New Orleans."

"Ah, New Orleans, such a beautiful place," Katrina sighed.

"You and Elise will have to come for a visit," Kara said. "Sasha owns a wonderful place in the bayou and there is plenty room for the both of you."

"You will be welcome at any time, should you choose to visit," Sasha assured them, passing one of her business cards to Katrina.

A slow song started to play and Sasha asked Kara, "Would you care to dance?"

"I would love to, darling," she responded as she accepted her offered hand, allowing Sasha to lead her to the dance floor.

"Lovely couple," Elise said to Katrina.

"Yes, they are," Katrina, replied. "I hope Sasha finds what she is searching for in Kara," she said, as much to herself as to Elise.

Out on the dance floor Kara pressed tightly into Sasha's chest. "Are you having a good time?" Sasha asked.

"Absolutely," Kara responded. "This place is amazing."

"Katrina definitely has herself a gold mine here," Sasha admitted as she nuzzled into Kara's neck. "By the way, you smell absolutely delicious," Sasha said as she breathed deeply of Kara's scent.

"Why, thank you, ma'am," Kara answered. "It is called *eau de* dance floor," she said with a chuckle.

Sasha's tongue trailed up the length of her neck, causing Kara to shiver. Sasha whispered, "Tastes good too." Her hands pulled Kara's hips deeper into hers.

The erotic allure of Kara's body intoxicated Sasha. As their bodies moved together on the dance floor, Sasha's lips found Kara's and they kissed deeply, oblivious to anyone else.

Kara's erect nipples pressed against Sasha's chest as her fingers traced the fine line down Sasha's jaw. Her eyes moved up to meet Sasha's, and the passion she found waiting there nearly caused her knees to buckle.

Sasha could hear the pounding of Kara's heart and the rush of her blood as it pulsed through her veins seductively. "How disappointed would you be if we cut out early and headed home?" Sasha asked.

"I would be disappointed if you had not asked," Kara answered.

"Why don't we pay homage to our hosts and make a beeline for home then?" Sasha suggested as the song ended.

"Lead the way, lover."

Sasha took Kara's hand and led her back through the crowd to their table. "I hope you two don't mind, but we have decided to call it an early night. We have greatly enjoyed your hospitality and hope you will visit us in the bayou soon," she said to Katrina and Elise.

"We don't mind," Katrina said. "Maybe one day before you leave, you and I can get together while Kara is at work," she suggested as she wrote down a number for Sasha. "Give me a call, if you can."

"You have a deal, my friend," Sasha said as she leaned in to hug Katrina. "I will call you tomorrow morning."

After their good-byes, Kara led Sasha from the club at a frantic pace, all but running toward her car. She wanted nothing more than to be back at her apartment, passionately entwined in Sasha's arms.

Chapter 6

The ride home passed quickly as Sasha's hand caressed the wetness between Kara's fevered thighs. When they were in the elevator, Kara pinned Sasha against the back of the elevator with a crushing kiss while her hands disappeared underneath her shirt. "I want you so very much," she groaned into Sasha's ear as the elevator came to rest.

Inside the apartment, clothes vanished as they made their way to the bedroom. Hands worked furiously removing bras and panties until they stood together bare skin to bare skin, the heat building between them in volcanic proportions. Sasha lowered Kara onto the bed and covered her body with feverish kisses, the movement of her hands stoking the fire burning between her legs. She felt her excitement trickle down her thighs as Sasha's hands expertly teased her throbbing nipples.

Sasha moved further down the bed between Kara's thighs and forced them wide as her mouth attacked the small rivers of arousal now flowing freely from her body. Her tongue traced the flow of the sweet nectar to its origin, slowly circling Kara's lips with the tip of her tongue as she inhaled the scent of her desire. Kara's body squirmed and she spread her legs wider, begging Sasha for more. Sasha's tongue probed deeply inside her wetness. Kara's hands tore at the sheets as Sasha's tongue teased her to the edge of climax before withdrawing, leaving her panting, and begging for release. After what seemed an eternity to Kara, Sasha covered her engorged clit with her mouth and entered her forcefully with two fingers. Kara cried out in pleasure. Obsessed with the sound of her wails as they echoed throughout the room, Sasha thrust her fingers in and out of Kara's body uncontrollably as her mouth wildly sucked her clit.

Restraining her desire to ravage Kara, Sasha reached up with her free hand and painfully twisted Kara's nipples until her body ignited with an orgasm so intense she fainted from the extreme pleasure. Sasha watched anxiously until Kara's breathing deepened, indicating her body had succumbed to sleep. She carefully pulled the covers over her exhausted lover before she slipped out of bed.

Donning a robe, Sasha walked out onto the balcony and into the cool night. The light breeze bathed her heated body as she gazed out across the city. Her brow wrinkled with concern as she thought how close to losing control she had been this evening with Kara and worried that she was pushing her too far too fast. Pulling the thick robe around her body, Sasha leaned against the cool railing and watched the rising of a brilliant moon as she contemplated her future with Kara.

When she finally grew tired of thinking, Sasha walked back into the bedroom and placed the robe on the end of the bed before she crept between the sheets and snuggled into Kara's warmth. Burying her face in Kara's neck Sasha breathed deeply of her essence and fell into a dream-filled sleep.

✝

Kara stretched and woke Sasha early the next morning. "Good morning, darling." "Morning," Sasha said, before she kissed Kara's soft lips. "What time is it?"

"Almost six," Kara replied.

"Good, have we time to snuggle awhile then?" Sasha asked.

Kara encircled Sasha with her arms, pulling her on top of her body to answer Sasha's question. "I think we have plenty of time for that," she added as her hands slid down Sasha's back to cover her ass.

Kara pulled Sasha's hips between her heated thighs and Sasha began to grind slowly into her body. Kara's moans broke the silence in the room as Sasha began to lick slowly up her neck to her ear.

"Feels good, doesn't it?" Sasha breathed into her ear.

"Oh yes, baby, it feels wonderful," Kara groaned as their clits made contact, sending shock waves through her body.

Sasha felt her body throb with need as she picked up speed with her hips, thrusting into Kara. Kara's nails dug into Sasha as they ran up and down her hips, which drove Sasha into a frenzy of movement. She slipped a hand between them and entered Kara with two fingers, driving them deep into her body, each long stroke causing her to shake violently with need. Sasha covered Kara's mouth with a bruising kiss, kissing her deep and hard as her body writhed underneath her.

She broke their kiss and Sasha blazed a trail of heated kisses down Kara's body as her fingers continued to thrust deeply. "I want to taste you," Kara groaned as Sasha kissed down her belly.

Sasha turned her body on the bed to straddle Kara's face, lowering her wetness onto Kara's waiting tongue. She covered Kara's clit with her mouth, running her tongue around it in tight little circles as it throbbed against her lips. Sasha shivered as Kara's tongue licked strongly inside her.

The muscles deep inside Kara pulsed around Sasha's fingers as she caressed her G-spot. Flicking her tongue over Kara's clit, she felt Kara begin to climax. Feeling, tasting, and hearing her lover come sent Sasha tumbling over the edge and she flooded Kara's face with her sweet wetness. They lay spent and panting for breath for a few minutes before Kara reluctantly left the bed to shower and dress before heading into the office. Kara hated to leave Sasha alone on the bed, but duty called. She leaned down to kiss a napping Sasha on the forehead and slipped quietly from the apartment.

Sasha woke an hour later, showered before dressing, and then retrieved a vial of the Network's serum, which she downed in one long drink. She had fed well the night before, but she was curious about the taste of the serum. The taste was not nearly as pleasurable as human blood, but it would serve to fight off the urge to feed, at least for a short time.

She picked up the telephone and called Katrina, setting a time to meet her at the club the following day, then spent some time looking through photograph albums and perusing the large collection of books in Kara's home office. Her fingers traced the outline of Kara's body in a picture that showed Kara in hiking shorts on a tree-covered mountaintop. "I do love you," Sasha whispered to the picture before setting it down on the shelf and going to the kitchen.

Sasha reviewed the contents of Kara's pantry and freezer and found items necessary to cook a surprise meal for Kara. She toiled in the kitchen for hours, marinating chicken breasts and cooking pasta for a light, satisfying meal.

Kara managed to finish her day sooner than she thought possible and walked into the apartment to find Sasha preparing the chicken for baking.

"That looks like it will be fantastic," Kara said as she wrapped her arms around Sasha.

"You are home earlier than I thought," Sasha said, turning to face Kara.

"I just could not stay away from you any longer," Kara replied as she leaned in to trace Sasha's lips with the tip of her tongue.

Sasha opened her lips to invite Kara's teasing tongue inside and they shared a long, sensual kiss. Their hands caressed each other's body, reigniting their passion. Sasha broke the kiss, taking Kara's hand and leading her into the bedroom. Sitting Kara on the edge of the bed Sasha began to undress her lover. Kara sat speechless watching Sasha remove the business suit from her body. Sasha's fingers then manipulated each button until Kara's blouse fell open to reveal her soft, smooth flesh.

Kara whimpered softly as Sasha licked and nibbled her way up from her collarbone to her ear. Her hands trembled as she reached up to take Sasha's face in her hands and saw the desire burning deep within her eyes. Sasha removed Kara's blouse and bra then pressed her back against the bed and slowly slid the skirt off her hips, leaving her in her panties. Kara moaned softly as Sasha leaned forward to lick the dampness that had soaked through the soft fabric.

Sasha knelt before her and gently removed the panties, sliding them down Kara's long, slender legs as her tongue trailed their passage down her body. Loud moans filled the room as Sasha's tongue traced its way back up Kara's leg and her warm breath covered her swollen clit.

Sasha traced the outlines of Kara's lips with her fingers, coating them with her wetness as Kara squirmed beneath her touch. Kara covered her own breasts with her hands, squeezing them and rolling her nipples between her fingers as Sasha gently entered her body. She pressed two fingers deep into the wetness, moving them in and out of Kara's body as the tip of her tongue flicked across her blood-engorged clit.

Kara's hips bucked wildly as Sasha's fingers took her deeply, stroking faster and harder with each new thrust. Her mouth enclosed Kara's throbbing clit, sucking it roughly. Kara wailed she was coming and her body thrashed on the bed. Sasha continued stroking and sucking Kara until a second and third orgasm ripped through her body, leaving her soaked and trembling with exhaustion. Sasha helped Kara move further onto the bed and whispered, "Rest until dinner is ready."

Back in the kitchen, Sasha smiled to herself as she placed the chicken and pasta in the oven and poured herself a glass of wine. When dinner was ready, Sasha woke Kara and led her to the table where they dined on the fabulous meal. After dinner, Kara sipped her wine as Sasha cleaned up the kitchen and then led her lover into a shower, before tucking her gently under the covers. Sasha kissed Kara softly on the lips and headed out to the veranda to enjoy the night chill. She sat for an hour and watched the rising of the moon as it illuminated the vast city below her. Feeling the most peace she had felt since Milly's death, Sasha left the veranda and crawled into bed to encircle the woman she loved with her arms, and joined Kara in her dreams.

✝

The next morning they showered together and made plans for a late lunch downtown after Sasha met with Katrina. Kara left her cell phone with Sasha, who promised to call by the middle of the afternoon.

✝

When Sasha arrived at the club, Katrina met her at the front door. "Good morning, sister," she said, hugging Sasha.

"Good morning, my friend," Sasha returned her greeting and her hug. "How are you today?"

"I am doing great and I am so excited to be able to show you something wonderful today," Katrina said as she led Sasha inside. "May I offer you something to eat or drink?"

"No, thanks I'm good," she answered.

Sasha followed Katrina through the quiet bar to a door into a dim hallway, which led to a small staircase. Sasha's curiosity grew as they descended the stairs in tandem. At the base of the stairs, a large metal door opened revealing an underground laboratory.

"Welcome to the Atlanta Network Lab," Katrina said as she led Sasha into a room that bustled with workers.

"This place is amazing," Sasha said as she watched the workers mixing a variety of solutions for testing.

"We are very close to creating the serum that will allow us to abandon our need to feed on the human population," Katrina said. "Our scientists, as you know, have developed many formulas, but their latest discovery holds good promise to be the one they have been searching for." Katrina moved to a large refrigerator and pulled out a vial of a deep red serum. "Would you care to try the new formula?" Katrina asked as she handed the vial to Sasha.

Sasha had long prayed for a breakthrough that would allow Immortals to co-exist harmlessly with humans. Her heart raced with the possibility that she may be holding the answer to that enigma in her hands as she took the offered vial. Sasha opened the vial and sipped the thick liquid to sample the taste, then returned the vial to her lips to down the remainder of its contents.

She handed the empty vial back to Katrina and could feel a warm sensation start in her stomach and work its way through her veins, a sensation close to what she felt when she fed off human blood. The look of surprise on her face made Katrina smile as she placed the empty vial on the counter.

"That is amazing," Sasha finally managed to say. "What is the longevity of the serum?"

"We have had very positive results in the study which show that a vial the size you just consumed would hold back the urge to feed for at least six days on most test subjects, some longer," Katrina said.

"Much longer than the current formula that barely holds back the desire for three days at best," Sasha said.

"We have been testing for only three months so far, but ninety-five percent of the test participants have reported that when used regularly, their desire for human blood was completely quenched," Katrina said. "Curiously, the five percent who still need human blood are all male and have fed on human blood for fifty years or longer."

This comment sparked Sasha's curiosity. Katrina, sensing her interest, said, "I have been feeding for almost two hundred and fifty years, and I can comfortably make eight days on the formula before a next dose is needed."

"Those are amazing results, Katrina, and this could have a dramatic impact on our lives moving forward."

"I thought you might be interested in this new development, not only for yourself, but also for Kara, if she chooses to become your mate," Katrina said. "Could you imagine being transformed and never suffering with the need to feed on a human being?"

"That is such an incredible prospect," Sasha said as she thought of Kara.

"I will have several cases shipped to you, if you wish to participate in this test."

"I would like that very much," she answered, her mind whirling with this new development. One reason she was reluctant to transform Kara, was that she was not sure how Kara would react to having to take a human life to sustain her existence. If the formula were as successful as test results promised, there would never be a need for Kara to harm another living soul.

Katrina could clearly see the excitement on Sasha's face as the realization of what she was hearing struck home. Sasha listened intently as Katrina finished the tour of the lab and the process they had developed in creating the formula. She could barely contain her eagerness to share this news with Kara and to determine how this may affect their future together. Sasha's heart pounded with the realization that Kara may soon choose to be her mate for eternity.

After the tour was complete, Katrina again stopped at the refrigerator and picked up a small case, which held two vials of the precious liquid, and handed it to Sasha. "Just in case Kara chooses to join you before you make it home," Katrina said as she grinned at Sasha.

Sasha took the case and with a firm hug said her good-byes to Katrina. "I hope you and Elise will join us soon in the bayou," Sasha said as they walked back to the front of the club.

"We will see you before the end of the year, I promise," Katrina said as she held the door for Sasha.

Sasha stepped back into the bright sunshine, donned her glasses, and started to walk downtown. She took Kara's cell phone out of her pocket and dialed the direct line into her office.

"Hello, this is Kara Stewart."

"Hey, sexy," she said when Kara answered.

"I was hoping you would call soon. I'm almost finished for the day and thought we could pick up some sandwiches and have a picnic somewhere."

"That sounds beautiful," Sasha said as she continued to stroll along the sidewalk.

"Where are you, my baby?" Kara asked. Sasha told her she was walking down Peachtree and would wait for her to arrive at the next intersection.

"I will be there in ten minutes," Kara said and ended the call.

Sasha continued to walk until she reached the next intersection and then sat on a bus bench to wait on Kara. Sasha wanted to share this new development with Kara, but decided she would wait until they returned to her apartment. She wanted them to enjoy the afternoon together under the beautiful autumn sky.

Kara arrived as promised and together they found a sandwich shop where they bought items for a picnic lunch. They drove to a nearby park and located a picnic table close to a small pond. They shared their picnic as they watched children in the playground and couples walking through the park.

Kara sensed Sasha had something very important to say, but did not push the subject, choosing instead to let Sasha broach the subject when she felt the time was right. They finished their meal and headed back to the apartment just as the sun was beginning to set.

✝

Sasha took the case Katrina had given her, placed it in the refrigerator, and then joined Kara on the couch.

"Okay, so tell me about your visit with Katrina," Kara said as Sasha sat next to her.

"I know you have sensed there is something very different about me, Kara."

"Yes, but I can't quite place my finger on it, Sasha," Kara said.

Sasha took a deep breath, hoping Kara was prepared for the information she was about to give her. Better now, she thought, to go forward with complete honesty. "I am what your society would call an Immortal, or in more recent terms a vampire," Sasha said. "I have lived for over a hundred years and I will continue to live for hundreds more if I am careful to remain concealed."

Kara looked at her. "It doesn't matter to me who or what you are, Sasha. I love you, and that is all that matters."

Sasha smiled at Kara.

"I love you too, very deeply, and your acceptance means the world to me. In the basement of Katrina's club is a secret lab called the Network," Sasha said. "The Network is an important team of scientists and Immortals who are searching for a serum formula that would allow my kind to be forever free of the need to seek human blood for sustenance."

"Is that what you just placed in the refrigerator?"

"Yes, it is. Katrina shared with me a breakthrough on the formula that has demonstrated positive results in replacing the need of human blood."

Kara moved closer to Sasha as she continued explaining the details of her morning spent with Katrina and the possibilities it held for the future.

"I do not want to appear to be pushing the issue, but you should know that I want you to give thought to becoming my mate

51

and spending eternity with me," Sasha said. "Now with this new formula, you can join me and not be dependent on the need for human blood."

Sasha watched Kara's face carefully as the meaning of her words slowly sank in.

"There are still many things we need to discuss before you decide, but I am very encouraged about the future for us as well as others of my kind," Sasha said animatedly.

Sasha's eyes glowed with excitement and Kara looked deep into her eyes.

"I have already made my decision, Sasha. No matter the cost, I want to be with you forever."

"Forever can mean hundreds or even possibly a thousand years. There is no need for a decision now," Sasha said, even though her heart raced at the mere possibility.

Kara lifted her hand and placed a finger across Sasha's lips to silence her. "I had already decided that I was going to ask you to take me as your mate when we got back to the bayou."

"Though the formula will take away the physical discomfort associated with the need for blood, the process of becoming immortal remains incredibly painful," Sasha warned.

"It does not matter as long as you love me and want to spend eternity with me," Kara said.

Sasha leaned forward and kissed Kara softly. That kiss led to many more then Kara took her hand and they walked into the bedroom, stripping off their clothes as they entered the room. They made love for several hours, until finally exhausted, they pulled the covers over their bodies and snuggled the night away.

Chapter 7

Kara was up early the next morning to finish packing her bag for their afternoon flight. Sasha watched her from the bed as she placed the last of her items in her suitcase and zipped it up. "I should be home by noon to pick you up, and we can grab a bite to eat at the airport before our flight," Kara said.

They showered together and Kara dressed for court while Sasha made them breakfast. Sasha noticed a glow about Kara as she moved about the apartment, collecting her briefcase before stopping to kiss Sasha deeply and then disappearing out the door.

Sasha packed her bags and took both hers and Kara's bag to the front door to await Kara's return. She was out on the veranda when she saw Kara's car turn into the parking garage. Walking through the apartment to greet her at the door, she waited until Kara closed the door behind her before taking her in her arms and kissing her deeply, astounding her. "Welcome home, lover."

"Another kiss like that one and we will definitely be missing our flight," Kara said with a grin.

"What can I say, I missed you," Sasha said, returning Kara's grin.

The doorbell rang then, surprising them. "Our taxi awaits us," Kara said as she kissed Sasha one last time before they left the apartment.

Check in went smoothly at the airport, and within the hour, they had eaten, and were seated in first class. Kara snuggled into Sasha as the flight took off and they napped together until the touchdown of the wheels in New Orleans jarred them awake.

Sasha had ordered a car service to drive them to Sugarland and her heart raced with each passing mile. She longed to be home and was even more excited to have Kara accompany her. At last, the house came into view. Sasha paid the driver and tipped him well for his services. They entered the house and set their bags by the door.

"I want to go check the animals."

"May I come with you?"

"Of course you can," she said, taking Kara's hand as they walked toward the stables.

Thunder had been grazing in the pasture, but once he saw his owner he raced to greet her inside the stable. The large horse nuzzled her neck while she patted his strong shoulder.

"I do believe he missed you," Kara said as she witnessed the exchange.

"I missed you too, my friend," Sasha said, stroking Thunder's neck.

Sasha and Kara filled the bins with fresh food and water for all the animals before returning to the house. Sasha carried their bags up to the bedroom as Kara made them a small salad and poured them each a glass of wine.

They ate their light meal before heading upstairs to the master bedroom. Sasha drew a hot bath for them as Kara stripped out of her clothes. They soaked in the fragrant bubbles, Sasha's arms wrapped around Kara until she turned to face her lover.

"Tonight, Sasha," Kara said as she looked deep into her lavender eyes. "Tonight, I want you to make me yours forever."

Sasha looked into Kara's pleading eyes and knew she sincerely wanted to be with her. She replied, "Tonight."

Kara reached down and pulled the drain plug on the tub, and they quickly rinsed the bubbles from their bodies in the shower. When finished, Sasha led Kara to her large bed and laid her down. Sasha had no means to prevent the pain Kara was about to experience and prayed that the transformation would happen quickly for her lover to lessen the pain.

"There will be an intense pain as I drink the life from your body, and then it will seem like an eternity of darkness where you don't feel at all, until my blood brings you back to life." She looked into her lover's eyes. "I wish there was some way I could take the pain from you, but it's part of the process. When you return, you may not be able to speak for a period, but I will never leave your side. I will be able to read your thoughts and provide whatever comfort I can for you."

"I know you will."

Sasha lay down beside Kara and looked deeply into Kara's shining eyes and one last time asked, "Are you certain?"

"I have never been more confident of anything in my life, Sasha."

Sasha kissed her lips softly and whispered, "I love you."

Those would be the last words heard by Kara as a human being as Sasha's fangs sank deep into her jugular to begin the transformation. She drank freely from Kara, Kara's heart raced at first, and then slowed as Sasha drained the fluid of life from her body. Sasha listened as Kara's pulse slowed and then stopped completely and tears ran freely down Sasha's face.

"You are so beautiful, my love," Sasha said as she kissed Kara's lips.

Sasha opened her wrist with her fangs and placed the flow of blood above Kara's open mouth. She watched as the blood trickled past Kara's lips and listened for the return of a heartbeat. It felt like an eternity before Sasha heard the first faint sign of a pulse as her blood mixed with Kara's, nourishing Kara back to life.

Kara's lips began to smack together as she tasted the blood offering from Sasha. Her eyes opened and grew wide as she grabbed for Sasha's wrist and drank greedily. Sasha knew Kara could not hear her words, but she still tried to comfort her as much as possible as the agony began to grow inside her. Kara stopped drinking as the first wave of convulsions ripped through her body, leaving her soaked with sweat and writhing in pain as the physical changes began.

Sasha lay beside her, embracing her lover whenever the convulsions subsided, holding her close, comforting her until the next seizure struck. Sasha knew the pain Kara was experiencing and was relieved when the duration and frequency of seizures slowed and then halted completely.

Thirty-six hours later, Kara's eyes fluttered open and she attempted to focus her eyes. "Just relax and let your eyes adjust," Sasha said as she kissed Kara's forehead. Kara covered her ears as if protecting them from a loud noise.

"That is the beating of our hearts you are hearing, extremely amplified at this point until you learn how to control the volume in your head." Sasha took Kara's hand and placed it over her beating heart. "You will find that your senses—sight, sound, hearing, and taste—have become more acutely sensitive. In time you will learn to control and adjust each of them."

Kara could not speak, but she could project a thought inside Sasha's mind. *I love you, Sasha.*

"I love you too, baby," Sasha said as she rocked Kara in her arms.

Sasha encouraged Kara to try to rest and held her until the sun started to rise the next morning. When Kara awoke, her speech had returned and her first words spoken as an Immortal were, "I am yours completely now, Sasha."

Sasha could no longer hold back her tears as she remembered when Milly had transformed her, and tears ran freely down her face. Kara propped up on an elbow and gently wiped the tears from Sasha's face, then leaned in to kiss her deeply.

Sasha pulled Kara back down beside her, enclosing her within her arms as she listened to the beating of her heart.

"Listen carefully," she said.

Kara concentrated until she heard two heartbeats. Slowly they began to synchronize until the two beats joined as one pulse, indistinguishable and never again to separate.

"Now we are one, together forever." She then whispered to Kara, "Sleep, and when we awake again, our lives will have changed forever."

Kara allowed her exhaustion to take her. With Sasha's arms wrapped around her she slept, Sasha following her into dreams that would last for eternity.

✝

Sasha and Kara spent the remainder of her visit adjusting to her new senses. Kara learned quickly to control her heightened senses and showed great discipline in her lessons. The night before Kara was due to fly back to Atlanta, she and Sasha sat in bed talking.

"I plan to go into work on Monday and put in my resignation."

"Are you certain that is what you want to do?"

"I want nothing more than to be here with you."

"I am not going anywhere if you need time to make decisions."

"I made my decisions when I asked to join you, Sasha, and I intend to be with you for eternity, as promised."

Sasha smiled, very pleased with Kara's decision.

"Should I put my home on the market or do you think we would continue to use it?"

"Why don't you keep it, at least for now," Sasha suggested.

"Very well, Sasha," Kara said as she kissed her softly. "I cannot wait to live with you here."

"It will be very soon," Sasha promised. "Will you need me to help with your preparations to move?"

"No, I think I can make all those arrangements. You could fly up and drive back with me, though. I can't stand to part with my little convertible," she said with a sheepish grin.

"No problem there," she said as she pulled Kara back into her arms and they made love until the sun came up the following morning.

Before Sasha drove Kara to the airport the next morning, she took her into the kitchen and gave her a dose of the formula. "I don't know how long this formula will hold off your hunger, so it is important that you contact Katrina for a supply when you return."

Kara drank the thick liquid in the vial and felt the warm rush flow through her body. "I will call Katrina when I get home and ask her to have the formula delivered as soon as possible," Kara promised.

"Your body will determine its need for more formula, but it is very important that you do not wait too long between doses. When the hunger burns deep in your body, it is time for another dose," she instructed. "Promise me you will never wait too long and follow your instincts to search for human blood. I could not bear losing you to disease or, worse yet, to have your hunting discovered, jeopardizing not only your safety, but the safety of all Immortals."

"I promise to dose appropriately and not take unnecessary risks."

"Thank you, my love."

"I would never dream of jeopardizing our life together," Kara said as she hugged Sasha tightly.

"I know you wouldn't do so intentionally, but there will always be those that hunt us, so you must remain vigilant at all times."

"I will be careful."

They drove to the airport and Sasha told Kara she would fly up in two weeks to spend her final weeks in Atlanta with her. "Let me know when you get home today," Sasha said as she hugged and kissed Kara good-bye.

"I love you, Sasha."

"I love you too, and I will see you again soon. Then it will be us forever."

Chapter 8

Bo Logan stalked his prey in the back alley of a New Orleans nightclub. Tommy Gore was a local drug dealer who had the audacity of snubbing the powerful Bellfontaine brothers. He had received a shipment of methamphetamines and had not paid them for the drugs. Tommy was a frequent user of the drug himself and sold the drug for high profit to tourists on Bourbon Street. When the Bellfontaines learned of Tommy's lack of respect, they issued an order for Logan to track Tommy down and make an example of him.

It hadn't taken Logan long to locate Tommy at one of his frequent haunts. He sat at the bar and ordered a beer as he observed Tommy in action. Tweaking, Tommy bounced around the bar and made several obvious transactions with the club's patrons. Logan had dealt with tweakers before, knew it could be dangerous to confront them while they were riding their high. He quickly decided to wait until Tommy started to come down before he acted on his orders.

An hour later, Logan saw Tommy head toward the back door of the club. The door led into the alley and he guessed Tommy was going outside to take another hit of the drug. Logan followed him across the bar and out into the alley, placing brass knuckles on each hand as he walked.

Tommy was so delirious from the drug, he had no clue Logan had followed him into the alley. He cried out in surprise when he turned around to find Logan right behind him. "You shouldn't make trouble for the Bellfontaine's," Logan said as his first blow landed across Tommy's jaw. He felt the bone snap under the blow as Tommy fell back into a dark corner of the alley.

Tommy raised his hands in front of his face and even though his jaw was broken, he managed to slur, "Hey, man, I was going to make good on my payment tonight."

"Tonight is too late," he said as his next blow shattered Tommy's nose and the blood gushed down the front of his face.

"I swear, man, I have the money right here," Tommy said as he reached behind his body and grabbed a gun out of the waistband of his jeans.

Logan caught the glint of the nickel-plated gun in the dim light and pounded Tommy's face with both hands before Tommy could raise the gun to fire a shot.

"You stupid tweaker," Logan said in a rage as he beat Tommy into unconsciousness, blood and bone fragments pouring out of his shattered face. Tommy fell backward, striking his head against the brick wall, snapping his neck instantly and his body slid down the wall.

The back door flung open as a pair of the club's bouncers arrived to take a smoke break and saw Logan standing over Tommy's ruined body. Logan put up a valiant fight, but the two large men overpowered him while another bystander called 911. The police arrived and arrested Logan for Tommy's murder. Logan realized he had made a horrendous error, and he knew his life was forfeit from that point forward. The police had witnesses and all the evidence they would need to put him away for life, or worse sentence him to death.

Tears rolled down his cheeks as he entered the back of the police cruiser. He knew his life was over, but he feared for the future of his wife and infant son. He had been a loyal employee of the Bellfontaines for several years, but once he was rotting away at Angola Prison, they would not give a second thought to him or his young family.

Detectives Doug Johnson and Kyle Brody lucked out when they caught the Logan case, knowing it would be an open and closed case. An officer on the vice squad confirmed their murder victim was a local drug dealer and word on the street was that he had duped the Bellfontaines out of a payment.

The detectives were quick to put the puzzle together. Logan, an enforcer for the Bellfontaines, had received an order to eliminate the dealer to set an example for the other small-time dealers on the street.

"Put in a call to the DA's office," Kyle told the unit secretary. "I do believe they will want to be in on this case from the beginning." Kyle looked at Doug and smiled. "We play this one right and we will make first grade," he said to his partner who smiled and began planning ways to spend the large raise that would come with such a promotion.

"First things first, lover boy," Kyle said as he ushered Doug into the shift commander's office to bring him up to speed on their case and the potential to connect the Bellfontaines to the crime. If they could succeed in this endeavor, they would be local heroes for bringing the drug kingpins down. Their success would send the local drug crime rates spiraling downward, when the flow of drugs would slowly stop.

The district attorney received the page as he was enjoying a dinner at a political fundraiser for a candidate for the upcoming mayoral race. The smile on his face widened as the chief of police filled him in on the details of the arrest. He arrived at the precinct to personally witness the interrogation of Bo Logan. The DA knew a case of this import would bolster his run for judgeship in the coming months, and he knew he had just the assistant to prosecute this case.

Kyle and Doug started the videotape rolling as the chief of police and the district attorney watched from behind the mirrored glass. They read the Miranda rights to Logan again as a precaution to prevent a sharp defense attorney from getting him off on such a simple matter.

Kyle sat across the table from Logan as Doug paced the room behind Logan, his footsteps ringing in the silent room.

"Let's run through this quickly," Kyle said as he looked Logan dead in the eyes. "The security staff from the bar apprehended you at the scene of the crime with two bloody hands, standing over the body of Tommy Gore, a local tweaker and drug pusher." Kyle sat back in his chair with a wide grin. "Our job has never been this easy," he said to Logan. "In a very short time you can bet you will be rotting away in Angola while you await fulfillment of a death sentence. Once a jury gets a look at the demolished face of your victim, I would suffice it to say you will be riding Old Sparky on your trip to hell," he said.

Logan sat mutely across the table as he weighed his limited options. He knew he was a dead man no matter what plan of action he took. Even the best public defenders couldn't get him out of the murder charge. Logan would die in the electric chair or he would be "taken care of" by an associate of the Bellfontaines once inside the walls of Angola, to minimize their liability in the murder case or any other crimes he had committed for them.

"Now would be the time to help your case, Logan," Kyle said. "We know you were acting on the orders of the Bellfontaines and if you testify against them we can offer protection for you and your family." Kyle rocked forward in his chair. "We understand you have a wife and an infant son." He placed his hands on the table in front of him. "Do you really think the Bellfontaines will take care of them after you are out of the picture?" he asked.

Kyle saw Logan flinch at this last statement. He sat back in his chair and allowed Logan to dwell on the thoughts of his wife and son.

Kyle and Doug left the room and joined the chief and DA in the small room outside the interrogation room. "Great job so far," the chief said as they entered.

"He knows he is a dead man. I think he will crack soon," Kyle said. "What can we offer him in exchange?"

"If he agrees to cooperate fully, we will recommend a minimum sentence in a low-security prison out west, and his wife and son will be placed in the witness protection program," the DA said.

"We will make the play then," Kyle said as they left the room.

When Kyle and Doug entered the room again, Kyle tossed a legal pad and pen down on the table in front of Logan. "It's now or never," he said.

"Can you guarantee my family will receive protection?" Logan asked.

"We will take them into custody tonight and by tomorrow they will be on their way to a brand-new life, out of harm's way," Doug said.

Logan looked at Kyle for confirmation and Kyle shook his head in agreement with his partner's statement.

"Can I see my family tonight before they are taken away?" Logan asked.

"If you agree to cooperate with us fully, then we will send someone for your family while you give us your statement," Kyle promised.

"I am a dead man either way, so what do I have to do?" Logan asked.

"You can begin by outlining your association with the Bellfontaines, up to and including tonight's activities," Kyle said. "We will videotape your confession and then ask you to write your account into a statement as well."

"And you will bring my family in so I can visit with them one last time?" Logan asked.

Kyle nodded to Doug who left the interrogation room. "Doug will have officers pick up your wife and child while you make your statement," Kyle said.

Logan sighed and slumped in his chair. He knew his life was over. Maybe he could do one thing right and care for his family before the Bellfontaines could take any action toward them.

Doug stepped back into the room and said, "A unit is on its way to pick up your wife and child."

Logan took a deep breath and began to tell the detectives the story of how he met the Bellfontaines and the services he had provided for them for the past four years. The DA and chief of police crowed with excitement when they realized they had their first real shot at prosecuting the Bellfontaines and sending them away for a long time. All they had to do now was keep Logan alive for the time it took for a trial to be set and to get his testimony in front of a judge and jury. Once the Bellfontaines were arrested that would be a difficult task. There would be a contract on him once they realized Logan would testify against them.

The DA left to obtain warrants for the arrests of the Bellfontaines and the chief began working with the shift commander to set up a tight ring of men to serve as a protection detail for Logan.

Logan would now be on the run, from one safe house to another to prevent detection or a leak from within the department. The Bellfontaines would spend top dollar to make sure the DA's main witness disappeared. Many crooked cops on the force could retire handsomely with the money paid for information.

After his videotaped confession and written statements were complete, Logan's family entered the interrogation room. Arrangements were made for Logan's and his family's safety for the night while they visited. They would be placed in a safe spot for the night and when the morning came, his wife and child would be ushered away to begin a new life. Logan and his protectors would then be on the move, keeping him safe until he could testify at the trial of the Bellfontaines.

The DA returned to the precinct with arrest warrants in hand. He smiled as he shared his agreement with the chief for the Bellfontaines' arrest the following morning. By then, all the current prisoners in the lockup would be finished with their arraignments and either released or placed in long-term holding, which would prevent the Bellfontaines from learning too quickly of Logan's arrest.

Logan and his family spent the night in a posh suite at one of New Orleans finest hotels. He and his wife spent their final night together in marital bliss and deep into the morning fell asleep with their son protectively shrouded between them. The next morning, Logan kissed his wife and son good-bye, knowing he would never survive to see them again. He raised his hand to wave as they disappeared in a black SUV. He was ushered into the backseat of an unmarked police cruiser with blacked out windows.

The game began to keep Logan alive. It would be a major challenge to keep him safe until the trial concluded. There would be no rules of engagement left unbroken as the Bellfontaines sought to end Logan's life and preserve their freedom.

Chapter 9

After her transformation to an Immortal, Kara transferred her law practice from Atlanta to New Orleans. When she decided to switch from a criminal defense attorney to a prosecutor, the city of New Orleans offered her the position of assistant district attorney.

The first year she practiced in New Orleans passed in a relatively bland manner. She rarely felt challenged by mediocre cases selected for her to prosecute, while the district attorney's office evaluated her skill in the courtroom. She developed each of her cases with the expertise and detail that she had been renowned for as a defender in Atlanta, and it did not take long for Kara to climb the ladder within the DA's office.

Kara vigorously pursued more high-profile cases to establish her reputation. Her hard work paid dividends when assigned lead counsel on a conspiracy to commit murder trial involving an evil pair of brothers, the Bellfontaines. Curtis and Ray Bellfontaine had grown up as local thugs, strong-arming their way into the local drug market first with marijuana then quickly penetrating the cocaine and heroin trade. As their business grew, their connections also expanded into the South American drug cartels that had spread into the United States as recreational drug use exploded in the early nineties.

With several corrupt officers on their payroll, the Bellfontaines controlled the major drug traffic in New Orleans, and the Crescent City quickly became a portal for major drug trafficking. Arrests had been frequent, but charges never stuck, and the brothers ran rampant in the city and ruled the streets with brutal efficiency. Finally, one of their enforcers, Bo Logan made a mistake. Arrested for murder while shaking down a local dealer, he was encouraged to cut a deal with the prosecutor's office by turning State's evidence against the Bellfontaines.

The DA called Kara into his office early one morning and handed her a videotape. "This is your first big case, Ms. Stewart," the DA said rather formally as he passed her the tape. "In just a few moments, the Bellfontaine brothers will be taken into custody and charged with conspiracy to commit the murder of Tommy Gore, a local drug dealer that duped them on payment of a drug shipment." He smiled brightly as he sat down behind his desk and offered Kara a seat. "Bo Logan, one of the Bellfontaine's enforcers, was ordered to make an example out of Tommy. He took his level of force too far and Tommy died from a brutal beating at the hands of Logan."

"Am I to assume then that we have Logan in protective custody in agreement to turn State's evidence?" Kara asked as she quickly assembled the pieces of the puzzle handed to her.

The DA smiled at her clever deduction and knew he had made an accurate assessment of her skills and ability to handle this high-profile case. "Yes, Logan is in protective custody and will be moved frequently to insure his safety until we can get him on the witness stand."

"The videotape you hold in your hands is the taped confession of Logan. A copy of his written statement will be available when you arrive at the precinct. The evidence against the Bellfontaines has never been this good, so we finally have a decent chance of getting them off the street," he said with a broad grin.

Kara was excited to have her first high-profile case. At the same time, she questioned why the DA didn't take the case for his own so he could garner all the credit for putting such vile criminals away for a long time. It only took Kara a few more seconds to deduce the DA did not want to jeopardize his safety by trying this case, and, in his position, he would still receive much of the credit if one of his minions prosecuted the pair.

Kara stood to leave his office. "I will review this tape quickly and then head down to the precinct to watch our boys being processed. I doubt there will be much coming out of their interrogations, but I will be close by until their arraignment is scheduled."

"I assume you will request a high bond be placed on each of them," the DA said.

"Five million dollars each, but we will be lucky if we get a million," she answered.

"Well, that is a good place to begin. I hope the Bellfontaines will feel a little pinch in their bank accounts to have to pay for their freedom," he said. "Also, push for a quick trial date," he instructed as Kara opened the door.

"I will do my best," Kara said as she closed the door behind her.

Kara rushed back to her office. She and her assistant, Ted, quickly reviewed the tape as she brought him current on their assignment before they drove to the precinct house.

†

At eight a.m. sharp, SWAT teams simultaneously entered the homes of Ray and Curtis Bellfontaine and took the brothers into custody for conspiracy to commit the murder of Tommy Gore. Neither brother bothered to resist arrest; they were confident they would be out of jail by midmorning. Curtis instructed his wife to call his attorney while Detective Brody escorted him from his posh home.

As expected, the Bellfontaines' legal counsel was waiting for them by the time they were booked and fingerprinted. Placing them in separate interrogation rooms, Kyle and Doug squared off against the famed drug lords. Their attorneys had already warned the brothers about answering any questions, which was unnecessary, as both remained mute. The arrogant smiles on their faces made it evident they were confident there would be no way to link them to any crimes. Kyle enjoyed watching the smug look disappear when he told Curtis they had plenty of evidence and a witness who would be testifying against them, linking them to Tommy Gore's murder and a laundry list of other violent crimes.

The arrogance returned to Curtis's face as he boldly said, "Even if these charges stick, there will be no witnesses, and with no witness you have no case."

"That's enough, Curtis," his attorney said, fully aware his client had just made a threat to the life of anyone who would testify against him and his brother.

Kara had been watching closely behind the mirrored glass as Curtis made his threat. She smiled when he gave her additional ammunition to request a speedy trial during the arraignment. The prosecution's only hope hung on its ability to keep Logan alive and deliver him to the witness stand. Each day would be a challenge to keep him alive and out of the hands of the Bellfontaines, who would be desperate to end his life.

Two hours later the Bellfontaines made their "perp walk," and were ushered into the courtroom for their arraignment. Each received bond for two million dollars, and the judge, who was anxious to set the trial in motion, set a trial date for two weeks in the future.

The Bellfontaines smirked at Kara and gave their attorney the order to make their bond and then take them home. Officers took the brothers back to the precinct where they lounged confidently in separate holding cells. Their attorney took less than an hour and they were once again free men, albeit four hundred thousand dollars lighter in their bank account.

Kara was pleased with the date but knew she would be working long hours to ensure she was ready to prosecute. Normally, this would be a very tight timeframe to work such a case, but given the volatility of the Bellfontaines, she was eager to get underway.

Kara was sitting at the desk of Kyle Brody where they watched the brothers released from custody.

"Arrogant bastards," Kyle said loud enough for Kara to hear. "They walk out of here without a care in the world."

"Well, hopefully, we can bring them down a notch or two and send them away for a long while," Kara said as she read Logan's written statement.

"You have to know that these guys will do anything, and I mean anything, to stay out of prison," Kyle said. "They wouldn't hesitate to assassinate a pretty little ADA either, so watch your back." Kyle leaned forward across his desk toward Kara. "If you feel unsafe at any time or you get any threats, you must let us know immediately," he told Kara.

"Understood," Kara said, confident she could protect herself with her immortal powers.

"We can arrange escorts to and from the courthouse for you in a heartbeat," Kyle said, "and protection at home if you need it."

"I don't think that will be necessary," Kara said. "If I am no longer in the picture, another ADA will step in to finish the case. Logan is the one we need to concentrate on keeping alive for a few more weeks."

"We have some of the best men on the force working the protection detail," Kyle said.

"You can bet the Bellfontaines will be offering top money to buy information on Logan's whereabouts and even the best of cops have been known to cave in to six-figure amounts," Kara said.

"We will do our best to deliver Logan for testimony," Kyle promised.

"Fair enough, I will use your evidence to build the strongest case possible against the Bellfontaines," she said.

When they left the precinct, Kara and Ted locked themselves away to begin the process of cataloging the evidence and making duplicates to release to the defense team as part of the discovery process. Kara would drag her feet as long as possible releasing this information, knowing that once the Bellfontaines knew exactly what the evidence was they were facing, the clock would begin counting down the time remaining in Logan's life.

Late that evening Ted locked the evidence in the vault, and he agreed to meet Kara at seven the next morning to resume work cataloging the evidence. Ted walked Kara to her car, and she drove home quickly, excited to tell Sasha about her big case.

She walked into the house to find Sasha in the kitchen with Marie, preparing the evening meal together. "Something sure smells good," she said as she entered the kitchen.

"Marie's spicy Creole," Sasha said as she turned and welcomed a tight hug from Kara.

"Guess what?" she said as she placed a soft kiss on Sasha's lips.

"What?" Sasha said.

"I have my first high-profile case assignment," Kara said, the excitement in her voice evident in the quivers.

"Congratulations! Let me pour us a drink and we can sit at the table and you can tell us all about it," she said as she poured two glasses of a dry white wine and joined Kara at the table.

"There was a murder in the Quarter last night," Kara began. "The police were very lucky and have a rock-solid case against the perpetrator."

"That sounds like it will make the case a walk in the park for you," Sasha said.

"But, that's not the entire story," she said.

"What more is there?" Sasha asked.

"The killer was working under the orders of a couple of drug lords, and he has agreed to turn State's evidence against the Bellfontaine brothers," Kara said.

Marie let out a gasp and dropped the large spoon to the floor when she heard the name Bellfontaine.

"Kara, you must be careful! Those two are ruthless and will stop at nothing to remove anyone they feel is in their way," she said.

Sasha eyed her closely. "They do have a vile reputation, my love. Are you sure you really want this case?" she asked, knowing Kara was not going to back down from the assignment.

"More the reason to do my best to take them from the streets," Kara said as she sipped her wine. "I am not the one in jeopardy here. The State's witness is the person the Bellfontaines will be gunning for. They will want to erase the one key witness the State has against them."

"I hope they have some good people working the protection detail," Sasha said. "The Bellfontaines would have no problem funding the retirement of several good cops to get the information they need to rid themselves of your witness."

"The detectives working the case assure me they have the best possible men working the detail," Kara said.

"I am surprised the FBI hasn't taken over the case," Sasha said. "The federal government has tried for years to get the brothers off the street, and your case sounds like the first strong case against them in years."

"I am sure the feds are dying to get their hands on the case, but the conspiracy to commit murder indictment is a local charge.

It would weaken their case, to try to extend it to a federal charge," Kara said.

"I will rest easier once this case is over and done," Sasha said.

"I know you will, Sasha, and I will do everything within my power to make the case proceed as fast as possible." Kara reached over, covered Sasha's hand, and said, "If our luck holds, the case should be over within a month."

"Keeping your witness alive for a month will take a small miracle," Sasha said. "The Bellfontaines will have a healthy bounty on his life and every hit man in the United States will be looking for him."

After eating Marie's spicy Creole, Sasha and Kara sat on the front porch to enjoy a peaceful late summer evening. As they rocked, Sasha heard a soft breeze as it sighed and whispered through the moss-covered cypress surrounding Sugarland. The sultry summer heat had been unusually mild the past week and Sasha prayed that the case Kara was working on did not explode into a tempest of deaths, furthering the reputation of New Orleans as a hotbed of crime and corruption.

Sasha knew Kara would not place herself in jeopardy and had confidence that she would remain vigilant to prevent harm coming to herself or any of her co-workers.

They retired early that evening and Sasha fell asleep with her body entwined with Kara's, holding her protectively as her excited, young attorney dreamed of the case of her lifetime.

Chapter 10

The night creatures of Sugarland had come alive with their songs as Sasha paced the front porch while she waited for Kara to return from New Orleans. Sasha walked the front porch each evening until she heard the powerful engine of Kara's sports car returning down the driveway. Tonight, Sasha felt a knot in her stomach growing more powerful as the minutes ticked slowly by.

Kara would usually call when she was running late. Sasha began to worry when night fell and there was no call. She had been trying for hours to locate Kara through her mind projection, but there was no answer, only a deep blackness as Sasha searched for her lover. Something drastic had to have occurred to prevent Kara from receiving her projections. Sasha could not help but remember the time she had lost contact with Milly, when she feared she was dead in Ireland, and a tremor of unease surged through her body. Unable to wait any longer, she walked to the garage, slipped behind the wheel of her truck, and drove through the darkness into the shadowy lights of New Orleans.

Sasha continued to mind search to no avail for Kara as she drove, and when the river came into view Sasha had broken out in a cold sweat as her fear continued to flourish. Sasha hoped Kara was at the office working on the case and had allowed time to slip away, but somehow she sensed this was not the case.

Her heart raced when she arrived at the district attorney's office and found Kara's sports car parked and in good condition. Sasha ran up the stairs and checked in at the guard's desk to see if Kara was still in her office.

"Good evening, Ms. Thibodaux," the pleasant, young guard said. He was familiar with seeing Sasha when she visited Kara.

"Good evening, Roger," Sasha said. "Is Ms. Stewart still in her office?"

"No, ma'am. Ms. Stewart signed out about two hours ago." The young man checked the register to confirm his statement. "Yes, she left the building at five fifteen," he said with a puzzled look.

"Is there something wrong?" he asked.

"She hasn't made it home yet and her car is still in the parking lot. Did she leave with anyone that you can remember, Roger?" Sasha asked.

"No, Ms. Stewart was alone," he said. "She set her briefcase down on the counter as she signed out and then left the building." Roger swallowed hard under the glare of Sasha's eyes. "Is there anyone I should call?"

"No, not yet, let me check her car and I will be right back."

She rushed outside to the parking lot and over to Kara's car. Anxiety knotted in her stomach as she looked inside the car. This was not Kara's usual behavior. Kara would have called if delayed in coming home, or if she had made plans to meet someone after work. There was no sign of Kara, but her briefcase was sitting on the passenger's seat, so Kara had made it at least as far as her car. Her hands shook as she opened the unlocked door and found the keys in the ignition. She sat in the driver's seat and reached over to open the latch, the case files and her notes for the trial rested in the main section of her briefcase. A large clasp envelope caught her attention from one of the accordion storage areas. She withdrew the envelope and opened it.

There were several smaller envelopes inside, each with a handwritten scrawl on the outside addressed as confidential to Kara with the district attorney's office address. When she opened the first letter, Sasha's heart dropped to her stomach. Kara had received a death threat and not mentioned anything to her about it. In total, Kara had received six letters, all with various threats if she did not drop the case against the Bellfontaines. Sasha placed the letters back inside the envelope and took the briefcase and its contents back inside the building.

Sasha laid the briefcase on the counter and a wide-eyed Roger looked at it glumly. "I think it is time to call in the authorities, Roger." All the evidence pointed to the fact that Kara had been involved in foul play.

Roger picked up the phone, dialed 911, explained the situation to the authorities, and then dialed the district attorney to apprise him of the situation as well. As Sasha waited for the authorities, she drilled Roger for information on the Bellfontaines.

"What do you know of the Bellfontaine brothers, Roger?" she asked.

"They are some seriously dangerous men to deal with, Ms. Thibodaux," he said. "They are the major drug runners here in the city and rumor has it they have expanded their territory to major cities in the south with the assistance of the South American drug cartel."

Sasha leaned in close to him and asked, "Where can they be found?"

Roger did not miss the look burning in Sasha's eyes, and swallowed hard before he formed his answer.

"They own several large mansions in the Garden District for starters, Ms. Thibodaux," he said. "Do you think they have something to do with Ms. Stewart's disappearance?"

"Given the case she is prosecuting right now, I would bet my last dollar they are involved in some way," she said, holding back a growl.

"I surely hope not. Those men have a reputation for being ruthless," he said.

Anger flared in her eyes as she listened to Roger, and she could barely contain her rage when two New Orleans detectives arrived and began interrogating her and Roger. She remained long enough to give them her statement and then left her cell number with them. The district attorney had also arrived and promised they would do whatever was necessary to ensure Kara returned safely.

She walked back out into the humid night and was still unable to reach Kara. Had Kara perished, Sasha felt that she would know immediately, but her inability to reach her lover left her confused, and her distress growing. She returned to her truck and drove as a woman possessed back to Sugarland. She stopped in to explain to James and Marie what had happened and then she headed upstairs to their bedroom.

She turned on her computer and searched the Internet for all the information she could find on the brothers Bellfontaine. She remembered Roger's warning and soon determined his assessment had been accurate. The Bellfontaines had been instrumental in a variety of crimes in the city, their reputations as drug traffickers and slumlords well documented in the local papers. She turned off her computer and went to speak to James and Marie.

"I need one of you to spend the night in the house and listen for the telephone," Sasha said. "I do not anticipate a ransom call, but I want someone to be there just in case."

"Where are you going, Sasha?" James asked.

"I am going out in search of Kara," she said. "I will go insane if I just sit back and wait for the authorities to act. I will be back sometime tomorrow, but you can reach me on the cell if you hear anything," Sasha said to James.

Their daughter, Little Milly, woke from the sound of the conversation and the five-year- old walked into the living room still wiping the sleep from her eyes. "Hi, Aunt Sasha," she said so sweetly. "Where is Aunt Kara?"

"Hello, Milly. Aunt Kara will be away for a while for work," Sasha said to keep the child from being alarmed.

Milly walked over to Sasha who bent down to pick up the small blond child. Milly wrapped her arms around Sasha's neck and kissed her cheek. "Are you okay?" the small girl asked, surprising Sasha.

"Yes, Milly, I am fine," she said, returning the child's kiss. Go back to bed, now little one," Sasha said as she placed the child on the floor and watched as she walked back toward her room.

Milly stopped and turned around and said, "I love you, Aunt Sasha," and then disappeared down the hallway.

Tears came to her eyes as she watched the small child, named after her first lover, Milly Vansant. Each passing day Milly took on more and more of her namesake's personality and she had Milly's love of art. Sasha made sure she was receiving the finest education money could buy and encouraged Milly's painting and drawing talents. She sometimes caught Milly studying her closely, her large blue eyes and dimpled cheeks grinning at her, and Sasha felt she was looking at her old love as a child.

James had disappeared into the kitchen while Milly was in the room. He returned and walked Sasha out the door, handing her a small cloth-wrapped bundle. She opened the cloth to find a shiny nine-millimeter pistol, fully loaded, and wrapped to conceal. "If you feel you must go, at least give me the comfort of knowing you carry this. I know you probably don't need it for protection, but I feel better knowing you have it just in case," James said. With a hug, they parted ways and he walked toward the main house.

Sasha took the gun, laid it on the seat next to her in the truck, and brought the engine roaring to life. She had looked up the addresses of the Bellfontaines and planned to pay each of them a visit tonight. Her heart longed for Kara as she concentrated on the road ahead, cloaked in a thick cloud of fog in the early morning hours. Sasha had faith she would be able to find Kara and bring her home safely. Her anger turned to rage as she drove and thought about what she would do to the person or persons who dared harm her beloved Kara. Their lives would not end pleasantly she vowed as she drove across the river for the second time that night.

She located the first of the two homes, this one belonging to Ray, the younger brother and found it completely empty as her mind searched each room closely for signs of life. She then drove on to the home of Curtis, the older of the brothers and found that he and his family were at there. Sasha slipped quietly into the home, passed the drowsy guards positioned inside the front door, and searched through the home for any evidence of a plot against Kara. Finding none, Sasha crept silently up the stairs, past the room of two children, and entered the master bedroom.

Lying in the bed next to his beautiful wife was Curtis Bellfontaine, clothed in deep blue silk pajamas. It would be so easy for Sasha to slit his vile throat and watch him drown in his own blood, but she thought she might need information from him later, so for tonight, she would spare his life. Sasha did invade his dreams long enough to plant a suggestion of a brutal death for him at the hands of a tall dark-haired woman. Sasha grinned wickedly as she saw the sweat break out across his body as he tossed and turned. When she sliced a gaping wound in his neck in his dreams, Curtis's bladder released and he soaked the bed with urine. Sasha slipped through the darkness of the room and out the door as he woke.

Curtis felt the presence of someone foreign in the house and chalked it up to the horrible nightmare he'd had regarding his death. Just as Sasha hoped, Curtis's thoughts drifted to Kara and Sasha could vaguely see a vision of Kara, bound and gagged and concealed in an area Sasha could not determine. She was relieved Kara was alive and well, but still disturbed by the fact she could not discover her whereabouts.

Sasha spent the remainder of the evening driving around New Orleans, trying to locate Kara but with no success. Sasha growled with frustration when her efforts to project to Kara remained unanswered.

Chapter 11

Ten days after their arrests, Kara could no longer stall and had released the discovery evidence on the case. Curtis and Ray Bellfontaine met with their attorney to review the evidence against them. When they reviewed the videotaped confession of Bo Logan, their attorney told them they had no chance of escaping jail time. Their best course of action would be to try to plead out their case to a lesser offense and attempt to avoid jail time at all. Their attorney wasn't confident of the latter, but he threw the information in on a lark.

After they left the attorney's office Curtis looked to Ray. "We have no choice now," he said. "Have the attorney abducted as a diversion. With luck, the cops will panic and begin moving that rat Logan to prevent detection," he said. Curtis looked at Ray with a determined gleam in his eyes. "Have everyone notified there is a million dollar price tag for anyone who brings me Logan's head."

Curtis stepped into a waiting black limo to head back to his home while Ray opened his cell phone and began making calls. Within minutes, the plan to abduct the young assistant district attorney was set into motion and the bounty on Logan's head spread like wildfire through a forest of dry timber.

†

By four, Kara was exhausted and ready to head for home. She and her assistant, Ted, had spent the afternoon with Bo Logan, their star witness in the case, rehearsing for the beginning of his testimony, scheduled for the following morning. Kara had drilled him with questions until he answered them with the same ease as taking a breath, and her confidence grew. Kara knew she had developed a strong case against the Bellfontaines, and with the damning testimony from Logan, she should be able to send them away for many years.

The security detail assigned to Logan was ushered into the room and four men escorted Logan out the back entrance to return to the safe house. Kara had worried at first that the Bellfontaines would be able to infiltrate the security detail with some of their dirty police officers and take out her witness. The chief of police assured her that he had deployed the best officers on the force to protect Logan, and no one outside the detail knew the location of the safe house. After tomorrow's testimony, she could relax, as Logan's story would be part of the official court record.

Ted packed up and left the office, leaving Kara behind to review the script for tomorrow's testimony and to plan for countering the cross-examination that was sure to come from the clever defense attorney she was facing. When she felt comfortable with her game plan, Kara packed her briefcase with the case files and notes. Her fingers brushed against the envelope containing the threatening letters and she shivered as she remembered the contents of the letters. She had intentionally kept the letters a secret from her boss, Sasha, and from the authorities; a decision she would later regret. Kara felt that with her heightened senses she would be able to detect a threat against her and would take action in her defense if necessary.

Kara snapped the catch on her briefcase and headed out of the office. She stopped at the guard's desk to sign out, and after a brief conversation with Roger, left the building. Kara walked down the steps quickly and unlocked her car from a distance using her remote device. She opened her door, placed her briefcase on the passenger's seat, and put the key in the ignition. Anxious to get home to Sasha, she let her guard down briefly and that was enough time for her attackers to strike.

When she leaned over to close the driver's door, Kara saw a flash of movement and felt a cloth pressed across her face. The sickening sweet smell of ether rushed into her nostrils and Kara's world turned black.

Kara's attackers quietly lifted her into the back of a cargo van and disappeared into the early evening, completely undetected. Returning slowly to consciousness Kara's mind was flooded with confusion and she was unable to move. Her hands were cuffed behind her back, her feet bound with tape and there was a blindfold covering her eyes and ears. She could hear her attackers—their voices muted by the effect of the ether on her senses. She felt the sting of a needle as it pushed into her arm, and then nothing but blackness.

When the drug began to wear off, Kara found herself restrained by metal cuffs on a small cot. Her body ached, a side effect of the drugs. One of her captors heard her stirring and she felt a blood pressure cuff inflate. Someone was closely monitoring her vital signs. If they intended to kill her, Kara felt they would not be taking the precautions to prevent over sedation. She had no idea how long she had been out, but the scents in the air made her think she was captive deep in the bayou.

"Put her back out," Kara heard a gruff male voice instruct and she felt the sting of the needle as she was administered another dose of the unknown drug. Kara attempted to project a thought to Sasha but was unable to formulate a coherent message. She drifted in and out of consciousness and had no idea how much time had passed when she awoke again.

This time she could hear her captors talking across the room. Kara determined there were at least two males and one female in the room.

"I am sure by now they have discovered the attorney has been taken captive," one of the men said.

"That should delay the trial and allow the boss to track down Logan and have him eliminated," another male voice said.

Kara knew the two men were correct. When they found her missing, the judge would delay the trial and, she hoped, the authorities would take extra precautions to keep Logan safe. Logan would move to a new location, and Kara prayed the security detail would keep him safe until the DA's office decided to proceed with the trial with substitute counsel. Ted was more than prepared enough to step into her shoes and finish the trial.

"I think she is waking again," Kara heard a female voice say. "She probably needs a bathroom break and some food. It has been almost sixteen hours and I can't dose her again until she has some food in her system."

"All right, but she will remain cuffed so you will have to assist her in tending to her needs," the man with the gruff voice said.

Kara heard a cell phone ring and heard one of the men answer the call. "We will be right outside," the other man said to the woman as he followed the first man out the door.

Kara felt the tension relax on her hands and though still cuffed, she could move her arms from above her head. The movement allowed her circulation to return. She was surprised to feel the restraints on her legs loosened and then removed. "I know you probably need a bathroom break by now," the woman's voice said as she helped Kara sit up on the bed. "Take it slow at first. You have been heavily sedated for a while and may still feel groggy when you try to stand."

"How long have I been out?" Kara asked.

"Close to sixteen hours," the woman said.

Kara did the math, figuring it was near nine in the morning. The trial was scheduled to start at eight and would have been delayed temporarily by now so that the DA's office could regroup and continue with the prosecution.

With the woman's assistance, Kara stood and followed her into a small bathroom. She left Kara to attend to her needs in private and when the woman heard her flush, she opened the door and guided Kara to a small table.

"You will be safe as long as you don't try anything foolish," the woman whispered to Kara. "They are using your disappearance as a diversion while assassins hunt down your witness. As far as I can tell, you will be released once he is taken out of the picture and no harm will come to you as long as you relax and don't learn any of our identities."

"You appear to be an educated woman in the medical field," Kara said. "So why are you involved in this?"

"Some of the Bellfontaines' henchmen have my husband and will hold him until your safe release," the woman answered. "They are taking precautions to ensure you are safely sedated and protected to prevent the possibility of further charges." The woman sighed audibly. "So as long as I keep you safely sedated for a few days and prevent you gaining additional information that may lead to your harm, then my husband will be returned."

Kara heard the woman open a small cooler. "I am sorry to have to treat you like this. I hope you understand I have no other options," the woman said.

"I can understand being in your shoes. The Bellfontaines wouldn't hesitate to harm any innocent bystander to insure their freedom," she said.

"I hope you like bologna and cheese," the woman said. "Our options are fairly limited."

"Bologna would taste like steak right now," Kara said, trying to put the woman at ease. She felt for the woman's plight and would assuredly do whatever necessary to make sure Sasha were safe if she were in a similar situation.

The woman placed a sandwich on a paper plate in front of Kara and opened a bottle of water for her. Kara used her cuffed hands to pick up half the sandwich and took a large bite, letting out a soft moan as she savored the taste.

"I wish I could tell you more, but that is all the information I have," the woman whispered as she heard the men returning from outside.

"Thank you," Kara said quietly before they returned.

When Kara finished her meal, the woman returned Kara to the cot and replaced the restraints around her arms and legs.

"Give her another shot," the gruff voice said.

The woman prepared another injection and Kara felt the prick of the needle as it pierced her skin and the warm sensation as the drug penetrated her system. She reached out with her mind and tried to locate Sasha.

Sasha can you hear me? Kara waited patiently for a reply from Sasha. She could feel Sasha's presence in her mind, but she could not hear any response as she drifted into drug-induced sleep. The next time she awoke, she would try again to contact Sasha to let her lover know she was safe.

✝

Sasha was sitting in the parlor reading the morning paper when she felt a faint tingling in her mind. Kara was trying to project to her but for some reason, her thought was blocked, and when Sasha tried to return her projections, she reached only the blackness that surrounded Kara.

The newspaper's front page was filled with headlines of Kara's abduction, and the affect it would have on the Bellfontaine case. The more she read, the more irate she became and disgusted with the media coverage. Sasha picked up the telephone and dialed the DA's office. She asked to speak to Ted, knowing he would share whatever information with her that he could.

When he answered his extension, Sasha said, "Ted, this is Sasha, have you heard any new information?"

"Very little, Sasha," Ted said. "Now that they have kidnapped a state employee, the Feds are threatening to take over the case, which plays right into the Bellfontaine's plan," he said in disgust. "As far as I know, Logan is still alive and being moved almost hourly to prevent detection and only the chief of detectives know where he is scheduled to be housed."

"Do they have any information on where Kara is being held or by whom?" she asked.

"They haven't received any ransom calls or anything like that to my knowledge," Ted said. "I am not sure they would share that information with me if they had though."

"Thanks, Ted," she said. "Please give me a call if you hear anything."

"I sure will," Ted said then hung up the telephone.

Sasha had not heard the front door open while she was on the telephone, but when she had replaced the receiver, she turned to find Milly sitting beside her on the love seat. The child was looking up at her with her deep blue eyes, searching Sasha for signs of emotion.

Sasha smiled at Milly and took her in her arms for a hug. "Good morning, Sasha," Milly said.

"Good morning, Milly," Sasha returned.

"You look sad," she said, her intuition far beyond her young years.

"I am fine," Sasha said not sure, if Milly was convinced. "What are you doing today?"

"Mother sent me over to tell you that we are going to town and to ask if you need anything," Milly said as she snuggled into Sasha.

The young child looked up to find Sasha gazing at the portrait of Milly hanging on the wall. "Hera was such a beautiful horse," Milly stated.

"I am sorry, Milly, what did you say?" Sasha asked.

"I said, Hera was a beautiful horse," Milly repeated as she pointed to the portrait.

"Yes, she was and she was Milly's favorite horse, even though she had others after Hera," Sasha said.

"Do you want anything from town?" Milly repeated her question.

"No, I think I have everything I need," Sasha said. "Stop by when you get back from town, though," Sasha said to the young child who worshipped her.

Milly kissed Sasha on the cheek. "I sure will," Milly said and then bounced down from Sasha's lap and out the front door.

Sasha's eyes drifted back to the portrait of Milly. Often when she found herself stressed, she looked at the portrait to give her peace of mind and to help relax her. Milly had been her first and greatest love, and though Sasha loved Kara dearly, Milly would always hold a special place in her heart. As she gazed once again at Milly on the handsome horse, a realization struck Sasha like a bolt of lightning.

Milly had used Hera's name and to her knowledge, Sasha had never spoken the name of the horse in front of young Milly, or her parents for that matter. There should have been no way for her to know the name of the horse, leaving her confused by Milly's knowledge. The child seemed to know information that she found remarkable for someone of her tender age, and her maturity never ceased to amaze Sasha.

Chapter 12

Bo Logan slumped in his chair as he watched the morning news that reported Kara's abduction. He knew the ending of his life had begun in earnest. The officers assigned to his protection detail had been busy on their cell phones since the news of Kara's abduction had hit the air. They would be ending their twelve-hour shift within the hour and handing Logan over to a new set of protectors. The tension in the room hung like a thick curtain as the men watched the final minutes of their shift approach. They handed Logan a hooded sweatshirt to wear and placed the hood over his head in an effort to prevent detection. Then they would drive to the pre-arranged meeting spot where they would turn over Logan and the bulletproof vehicle to the oncoming shift. Up until now, they had been safe staying in one location for several days, but now that the Bellfontaines had posted a bounty on Logan's life, he would move much more frequently. The chief of detectives would be the only person who knew where Logan would be at all times.

Logan hunched underneath the hood and walked quickly between his guardians as they ushered him into the black SUV. The driver and his partner took their positions, and began monitoring traffic, remaining alert for signs of another vehicle following their path. They pulled away from the curb and began a circuitous route through the city to deter anyone from tracking their route.

When they arrived at the back entrance at one of the local hospitals and saw their replacements step from a similar black vehicle, Logan's current protectors put the SUV in park and quickly departed the vehicle as the new shift climbed inside. The total exchange took less than thirty seconds and Logan was again securely on his way to the next safe house.

As luck would have it, a drug dealer dropping his sister off at the hospital to begin her shift noticed the exchange of men between the two relatively unremarkable vehicles. He wrote down the tag number and description of the two vehicles used to transport Logan. He smiled, knowing the Bellfontaines would reward him handsomely for this information. His efforts to track the vehicle failed as he came to a stop in the snarl of traffic in the downtown district and lost sight of the vehicle.

In the next half hour, the Bellfontaines had the information on the vehicles used to transport Logan and the word spread quickly on the streets to be on the lookout for both vehicles. Every local thug and Bellfontaine employee joined the hunt for the vehicles, eager to collect on the reward money placed on Logan's life.

Events were spinning wildly out of control as the smell of blood money attracted every shark on the streets of New Orleans. The police had already taken into custody two henchmen who had come to remove Logan's wife and child to use as leverage against the witness.

The chief of detectives smiled to himself when he learned of the arrest of the two hit men knowing that they had beat the Bellfontaines on one account at least by removing Logan's family and relocating them out West, hopefully beyond the reach of them. Everyone involved in the case understood that Logan's life was forfeit the moment he got himself arrested. His fast thinking, though, had allowed him to arrange for his family's safety.

The shift of cops that were going off duty failed to notice a nondescript Crown Victoria that had tailed them back to the precinct. The Crown Vic circled the block as they pulled into the police garage and headed into the precinct before retiring for the day. They would reassemble at the station at nine thirty that evening and await rendezvous instructions from the chief of detectives.

The dark, sullen man behind the wheel of the Crown Victoria, known only as Wilson, pulled gently next to the curb. Fortune had smiled on him when the black SUV pulled out in front of him, making it so effortless for him to begin his hunt. It would be simple for him to sneak inside the police garage and pack a load of explosives under the SUV the off-duty cops had left behind. But the Bellfontaines wanted undeniable proof that Logan was dead. An explosion would always leave a small amount of doubt that his mission was successful. Instead, he would wait and watch to see if the same men that had left the vehicle returned to retrieve it and then he would carefully follow them to their destination. If his luck held, he would be able to track them directly to the next rendezvous point and follow Logan to the next safe house.

Earlier in his life, Wilson had been one of New York's best police detectives, but his love of the finer things in life led him down a path of corruption and he found himself far beyond the point of no return. He had frequently performed various jobs for the Bellfontaines and many other crime families, which enabled him to live a life in South Beach with all the amenities a man of his tastes, could enjoy. Having knowledge of how the police department operated gave him an edge in many cases, this being one of those occasions. He knew the protection detail would be working twelve-hour shifts, which would allow him to return to his hotel on the River Walk for several hours of sleep before he returned to the station to pick up Logan's trail. Checking the time on his watch, he felt certain he would have at least until eight that evening to rest and continue making his plans.

He returned to the hotel and ordered a nice steak dinner from room service before taking a shower and slipping between the fresh, clean sheets of the king-sized bed. He was not concerned about the success of his plan, but was worried that one of the lesser skilled local yokels would hit a lucky streak and bumble his way into the secreted location of the next rendezvous, placing the protection detail on a higher level of alert. Wilson was worried. He knew that scenario was always a potential, especially when news spread that a handsome bounty was involved. Every wannabe thug with a weapon would hit the streets chasing the lure of big money.

He set his bedside alarm just as a precaution. In his line of work, sleep came less frequently and he would be lucky to sleep for four hours before his internal clock awoke him. He pulled the sheets up over his body and reached under his pillow to touch the cool metal of a nine millimeter, Feeling completely secure he closed his eyes to welcome much-needed sleep.

As Logan's nemesis drifted off to sleep, Kara began to wake from her drugged slumber. She remained quiet and still and as her mind began to clear, she attempted to focus on Sasha. She had no clue if it was day or nighttime, but she knew that Sasha would remain vigilant in her search for her. She focused on a visual of Sasha in her mind and had to fight off a smile that threatened to cross her face.

Sasha my love, are you there?

Oh my God, yes, Kara, how are you? Sasha responded.

I am safe, and will be okay.

Do you have any idea where you are?

I think I am far away from New Orleans. I can hear the breakers as they crash on the shore and smell sea spray in the air, but the sound is not close. I think I'm in some sort of equipment storage area. I can smell oil and diesel fumes, but they are not overwhelming, so this place may have been vacant for some time.

What have you learned of your abductors? Sasha asked.

They are two men and one woman, Kara answered. The woman is a nurse or someone in the medical field that they are forcing as an accomplice, using her husband as ransom for her skills. She is keeping me drugged to keep me quiet and to prevent me from learning too much information. She told me that they are using my abduction as a diversionary tactic to allow the Bellfontaines' hired guns to locate and dispense of Logan. The plan is to release me after he is dead.

Drugged, no wonder we have not been able to communicate, Sasha said.

The woman caring for me administers the injections to keep me sedated, but there has not been any act of violence against me, Kara stated. The two men I know only by their gruff voices, and I have had no contact with them since my arrival here. Other than being restrained to a cot except for mealtimes and restroom breaks, I am doing well. If the Bellfontaines are successful, I should be home very soon.

The newspapers claim that the FBI has picked up the case and is handling your abduction, Sasha said. From the sounds of it, though, you will be out of harm's way before they can assemble their troops. Do you want me to see if I can locate you or take any other course of action?

I really do think I am safe here, Sasha, so there is no need to take any unnecessary risks. I am more concerned for Logan's safety at this point than my own. Without his testimony, the Bellfontaines will be free to continue their activities and future prosecution will become even more difficult.

Would you rather I track down Logan and give him whatever protection I can?

I know that is a lot to ask of you and it may delay my return, but yes, Sasha, I would love to hear that Logan makes it to the witness stand tomorrow. Once he testifies, the Bellfontaines would have no need to continue to hold me captive.

Very well, I'll do my best to track Logan down and see if I can keep him alive.

I think they realize that I am awake. I'll try to contact you again later, my love, Kara said and then disappeared from Sasha's mind.

As Kara lay on the cot, she silently cursed herself for not following the detectives' orders and notifying them when she had gotten the first of the threatening letters. Maybe if she had, she would not be in the predicament she thought, but there was little use in following that train of thought any further. She acted foolishly and now would suffer the consequences of her arrogance.

Sasha showered and dressed in black jeans and a long-sleeved black pullover shirt, in hopes that the dark clothing would help conceal her in the deep shadows of the night. She had no clue where Logan was and her only hope was to try to find out as much information on the streets as possible. Just after nightfall, she climbed behind the wheel of her truck and headed into New Orleans.

Her first route was to drive past the homes of the Bellfontaine brothers to see if they were at home and to determine if she could get any information from their thoughts without directly having to confront them. As she rode past Ray's large home, she once again found the house dark and empty. Ray had apparently never married and spent a great deal of his nights out on the town, enjoying the pleasures his wealth could afford. She continued down the avenue and parked outside Curtis's home. Unlike Ray's, Curtis's home buzzed with activity. Sasha could detect the two security guards inside stationed near the front door, and she was certain they would patrol the grounds throughout the night. Sasha also located two children in their bedrooms as they finished their schoolwork and prepared for bed. Curtis's wife was watching television in the large den in the front of the house and Curtis himself was in the back of the house in his home office.

Sasha turned off the dome light and slipped quietly from her truck and through the front yard. She used the concealment of darkness to carefully climb over a small balcony and stood outside a pair of sliding glass doors leading into the home office. Sasha could see Curtis sitting behind an immense mahogany desk drinking a cocktail. She was preparing to enter his mind when his cell phone rang. Ray was calling to give Curtis an update, telling him they had information on the two vehicles used to transport Logan. In addition, Wilson had made it into town and would take care of their problem tonight.

Sasha had no idea who Wilson was but she quickly deduced that he would be a hired gunman employed by the Bellfontaines to kill Logan. Sasha listened further, but gleaned no additional information she thought would be of help to locate Logan. As quietly as she arrived, Sasha slipped through the dark and climbed back inside her truck. She knew that the Bellfontaines had the vehicle information and by now, it would be common knowledge on the mean streets of New Orleans. Every minor crook would be on the lookout for the vehicles to claim the bounty for themselves or to improve their status with the Bellfontaines by passing on valuable information to help their cause.

Sasha drove toward the east side of town. She drove past her and Milly's first home, her parents' home and passed her father's shipping business that had changed hands several times but remained a thriving business. The streetlights became fewer as she entered the lower Ninth Ward and the less prosperous side of New

Orleans. It was here that the minor drug dealers prowled the streets to take advantage of the less fortunate residents of the Crescent City. Sasha parked her truck deep in the shadows of an alley and prayed it would still be there when she returned. She took a left turn at the end of the alley and walked down a sidewalk, her mind searching the thoughts of those she encountered for news of the Bellfontaines or of Logan himself.

Having little luck on the streets, Sasha entered a small bar and ordered a beer, trying to blend in with the rough crowd, but having little success. She had barely sat at the bar and begun drinking her beer when a young man sat down next to her and asked if he could buy her a drink.

"No thanks, I am good," Sasha said, trying her best to be polite to the man who, from the smell of his breath, had already exceeded his limit. She was more interested in the two men shooting pool across the room and tried to concentrate on them.

"Woody said he saw one of them SUVs the Bellfontaines was looking for out by the battlefield," one of them said to the other.

"Woody stays so stoned I don't think he could recognize his own mama most of the time," the other said with a laugh.

"Maybe so, but don't you think it would be worth a million bucks to at least check it out?"

"Well, hell yeah, we ain't got nothing better to do tonight anyhow," the second man replied. "You packing heat?"

"Always," the other man said with a smile.

"Let's go hunting then," the second man said as he slapped his friend on the back. They finished their beers and walked from the bar followed closely by Sasha.

She was only a few blocks away from her truck and knew where they were headed so as they walked toward a beat-up Ford truck she walked quickly back to the alley to reclaim her truck from the dark shadows. She breathed a sigh of relief when she found her truck just as she had left it and drove calmly out to the Chalmette Battlefield, the site of a Civil War battle. Sasha had been to the battlefield many times in her life and now remembered a small house behind the museum. It was secluded from most traffic passing by, and a dense woods that could easily hide a vehicle surrounded it. Not a bad place at all for a safe house, she thought as she drove across one of many sets of railroad tracks onto a smaller side road.

Had she known what type of vehicle to be looking for, Sasha may have noticed the sleek black SUV that she passed at the old train depot. Her concentration, however, focused on the action she would need to take once she reached the battlefield. She looked down at the clock on the truck's console and saw that it was eight forty-five.

Chapter 13

Wilson crushed out a butt of a Marlboro Red and then pulled a light black jacket over his heavy shoulders. It was eight thirty and time for him to take up his watching position near the precinct house. He had called the front desk and the valet attendant had his Crown Victoria waiting for him at the front entrance to the hotel. He tipped the driver and then placed a slim, long package on the passenger seat next to him. It wasn't the most romantic of weapons, he thought as he drove, but the razor-honed cane blade would be sufficient to do the job he had planned for the night. Earlier he had placed a silencer on the barrel of the nine millimeter and now had it tucked securely in the back waistband of his jeans.

He parked next to the curb a few blocks away and killed the engine as he began his wait. He smiled to himself as he watched each of the three cops assigned to the protection detail pull into the garage in their personal vehicles and walk quickly into the precinct.

✝

In the small house behind the battlefield museum, a cell phone rang promptly at eight thirty. The officer that answered it took down an address and after ending the call told his companions, "Time to move."

One of the officers quietly slipped from the house, surveyed the surrounding distance between the safe house and the SUV, and then quickly ran to unlock it and drive it next to the house. Logan had become used to being rapidly ushered from house to vehicle. He allowed the remaining two men to surround him and thrust him quickly into the backseat.

Logan had had a growing knot in the pit of his stomach all evening long. His testimony at the trial was barely twelve hours away and for a short time, he felt like he was going to make it to the witness stand after all. Then as night fell, so did his hopes of remaining alive until the next morning. He did not say anything to the cops who were working diligently to keep him alive, but he knew they felt the same feeling of impending doom. They would only feel relief once they had passed Logan off to the next shift, their job complete for the evening. If all went as planned, that would occur within the half hour.

The black SUV barreled down the side road leading from the battlefield and was nearly sideswiped by an old beat-up Ford racing in the opposite direction, followed closely by a dark truck. They circled around the Ninth Ward, giving it a wide berth, leery of prying eyes and headed north to Interstate 10, before heading west toward downtown New Orleans.

✝

Wilson watched as the black SUV pulled out from the police garage and headed west. He followed them through the busy streets and mimicked each of their turns until they flashed their lights and were given entry to a locked gate at the Superdome. Wilson pulled his car under the elevated interstate underpass and using the silenced nine millimeter took out the remaining streetlight, leaving him concealed in total darkness. He watched as a second black SUV pulled into the lot. The exchange took a total of thirty seconds and then the vehicle carrying Logan made a U-turn and headed for the exit gate. Turning right, they pulled out onto the one-way avenue followed closely by the off-duty cops. At the next intersection, the off-duty vehicle took a left as they headed to the precinct and Logan's vehicle went right and headed out toward the zoo. Ironically, they passed by the homes of the Bellfontaines on their route and Logan felt a shiver run down his spine as if icy fingers traced his backbone.

✝

At the battlefield, Sasha parked behind one corner of the museum and hugged the shadows of the building as she stalked toward the small hidden house. The two men from the bar had pulled their truck into a small copse of woods two hundred yards away from the house and were sneaking up the driveway when Sasha caught up with them. Sasha snapped the neck of the larger man then dragged the smaller of the two into the woods. The man pissed his jeans when Sasha pressed him against a large oak and fixed him with her rage-filled eyes. These bumbling idiots could put Kara in jeopardy and she would not allow that to happen. Sasha's large hand circled the terrified man's throat and with ease, she slipped inside his mind. The information she had learned at the bar was all she could gain from him. The men had come to look around on a lark that Logan and his protectors were hiding in the small house. Useless for any additional information, Sasha snapped his neck and allowed his body to slump to the ground.

She quickly approached the dark house and searched with her mind to find it empty. Her acute olfactory senses could still smell the fumes of gasoline and she knew a vehicle had left the premises a short time ago. She approached to find the door locked. A quick elbow to a small glass pane gave Sasha access to the doorknob and she quietly slipped inside the house. She could smell the sweat of fear masked by unknown hours of cigarette smoke. Sasha looked around the rooms for signs that Logan, and his protectors had recently been there. Her eyes fell on the tangled sheets of a small daybed. Someone had recently occupied the bed. Sasha doubted that sleep had come to the man who had lain there. Again, she could smell the fear as it enveloped the bed linens and Sasha knew that Logan had lain here not long ago. In the living room, a newspaper was open to the coverage given to the Bellefontaine trial as one of the cops had undoubtedly been reading before they left the house. A can of soda sat on the coffee table and the condensation still dripped from the chilled can.

Sasha was late in arriving to track Logan and his guards. Now she would have to drive around the city in hopes that she could again pick up the trail. She closed the door behind her and slowly jogged back to her truck. When she passed by the larger of the two men lying beside the road, Sasha sarcastically thought, you should have trusted Woody's comment earlier. As she drove, back toward the city Sasha could feel Kara reaching her mind out to hers.

Hello, darling, how are you?

I am missing you, but I am fine, Kara said. I just had a sandwich and restroom break while my mind was clearing. Have you any luck in finding Logan?

I just missed him by minutes when they left their last safe house, Sasha reported. I followed two local thugs who were attempting to cash in on the bounty, but they also were too late. Now I'm going back into the city to see if I can find their trail so wish me luck.

Good luck, Kara replied. Finding them will be like finding a needle in the proverbial haystack, but I know you will try your best.

Yes, my love, I will, Sasha said as she felt Kara slipping away. *I love you.*

I love you too, Kara said and then her mind went blank.

Sasha's mind boiled with rage over Kara's mistreatment. If the state could not find a way to make them pay for their crimes, Sasha would certainly take matters into her own hands. They had crossed a boundary when they abducted Kara and would receive punishment for their treatment of her lover. Their actions were now personal and Sasha had an eternity to exact her revenge.

Sasha tried to clear her mind of the rage to allow her to focus on finding Logan. The hours were ticking by rapidly, and Sasha knew there would be an attempt on his life tonight. Whether it was successful would be depend on her ability to locate them and the officer's skill at keeping their witness alive.

She drove down endless streets without detecting any sign of Logan. She knew her time was running out. She passed many vehicles with passengers looking intently out of the windows and Sasha knew she was not the only one looking for signs of Logan.

✝

Wilson sat in the rented Crown Victoria smoking a Marlboro that he kept hooded by his hand to prevent the bright orange glow of the cigarette from alerting anyone to his presence. It was almost three in the morning and he had not seen anyone pass by for the last two hours. He would strike soon. The inside of the small apartment only had one light burning and he hoped that he would catch the officers off guard as he stormed through the door. He smiled to himself as he saw a storm approaching from the west. The rumbling of thunder would do well to mask his crashing through the door and Wilson knew he was only moments away from being a million dollars richer.

As the first raindrops pelted the glass window of the apartment, two of the three cops were dozing lightly on the couch while the third remained alert to any movement outside the apartment. Wilson watched a curtain waver as the cop peered out the window in search of possible assassins.

In the bedroom, Logan had broken out in a cold sweat. He knew death was coming for him. He listened to the soft purrs of the cops asleep on the couch and felt even less confident that they would be prepared to protect him when the time came. Logan thought he might as well gamble on his own skills for survival as his eyes came to rest on the small window. He looked out into the darkness and when the next bolt of lightning flashed, he could see that the window led out onto a small private deck and then a small copse of woods. With the approaching storm, Logan knew his protectors would be worried about losing power and a breach of the apartment. Logan decided that is when he would make his break.

He timed the bursts of lightning and the cracks of thunder to gauge the nearness of the storm. When the flash of light and the rumble of thunder came almost simultaneously, Logan acted. He had already pulled on the dark, hooded sweatshirt and unlocked the window. The next bolt of lightning made the light in the living room dim and then flicker and the thunderous boom that followed masked the sound of Logan opening the worn window and pushing out the screen. Without another thought, he jumped into the dark, wet night.

Wilson moved quickly from the car and ran across the street to the apartment. His minutes were ticking away. As a precaution, he moved to the back of the apartment to scope out a secondary means of escape. Wilson stepped around the corner of the apartment as a flash of lightning landed close enough to make the ground tremble. When his eyes adjusted from the bright light, Wilson looked directly into the terrified eyes of Bo Logan.

Wilson brought his right hand up, and pistol-whipped Logan across the face and then lifted the smaller man over his shoulder. He ran across the street and popped the trunk with the remote, tossing Logan deep inside the voluminous trunk before sliding behind the wheel of the Crown Victoria.

Wilson chuckled as he reached down to turn the key to start the engine. "This is fucking unbelievable," he said aloud. Wilson had suffered a brief pang of guilt regarding potentially killing a fellow officer, but he would not have hesitated in killing them to get to Logan. Fortune had indeed smiled broadly on him. Wilson pulled the Crown Victoria away from the apartment with his prey safely tucked away in the trunk without having to fire a single shot.

Wilson drove south and in minutes had crossed the river as the rain lashed against his windshield. He had made it safely out of the city before the protection team realized that Logan had flown the coop. The city roiled in uproar as every available policeman searched for Logan, presuming he would be on foot and desperate for a safe hiding spot. Little did they know that death had already found Logan and he was headed into the bayou with him.

They traveled south in the pouring rain for nearly half an hour before Wilson found a small clearing and pulled the car off the road onto soft gravel. He dared not drive any further and risk becoming stuck as the ground continued to weaken with the soaking rain. He looked over at the package resting on the seat and decided to leave it there for the moment. Logan's luck had turned bad enough already, and Wilson would not torment him by showing him what was to become of his body. Instead, he left the car and popped the lid to find a terrified Logan huddling in the far corner of the trunk.

"You really should not have crossed the Bellfontaines," he said to Logan as he motioned him out of the trunk. Wilson held the nine millimeter firmly in his right hand as he pointed to a spot on the ground. Logan boldly knelt there in his final act of submission in his short-lived life. He felt the cold butt of the silencer press against the back of his head and when he heard the sharp click of the trigger, he knew nothing more of this world. The shot ripped through his brain, killing him instantly, then exited through the crown of Logan's head. Wilson watched as Logan's body fell forward in slow motion and the blood began to run from his wound mixing with the muddy storm water as it flowed downhill.

Wilson returned to the car and opened the package holding the cane knife. He preferred a quick, silent kill, but the terms of this contract included the head of the cursed one. After swallowing hard to hold back his gorge, Wilson landed a single blow across Logan's neck, separating his damaged head from his body in a clean cut. Logan's blood flowed like tiny rivers from his neck and with grave caution, Wilson picked up the severed head and wrapped it in several thick plastic bags and placed it in the spare tire well in the trunk. With a final look back at Logan's body, his blood covering a large patch of ground, Wilson said, "Poor bastard," and then drove silently back the way he came.

Wilson pulled the car over while still several miles from the river and returned the cane blade to its original wrapping and then took a side road parallel to the river. When he found a secluded spot, he pulled the car off the road again and heaved the package as far into the fast- moving water as he could. He watched as the package slipped from view as it drifted under the waters of the Big Muddy. Wilson then pulled out a cell phone and dialed the number given to him earlier by Ray Bellfontaine. After reporting his success and agreeing to meet at a previously designated spot, Wilson closed the cell phone and it joined the cane blade at the bottom of the river.

He was eager to make the exchange and head out of town. Driving around with a decapitated head in his trunk gave him the willies and the sooner he was on the road back to South Beach the better.

Ray called Curtis with the jubilant news and stopped by his brother's home moments later to pick up a briefcase holding the million dollars promised to Wilson. "Money well spent," Curtis said to Ray as he handed over the briefcase. "You know what to do afterward correct?" Curtis asked.

"Yes, I do," and with that confirmation Ray left the Garden District to meet Wilson.

The exchange went well and Wilson was on his way to Interstate 10 heading east toward home as the first rays of the rising sun crested the horizon. Eager to leave the state, Wilson stopped at the Mississippi Welcome Station to change out of his still-wet clothes. He later stopped in Mobile, Alabama to change rental cars, unwilling to drive the vehicle that had memories of Logan's head in the trunk. He glanced over at the briefcase and smiled, turning on the radio to an oldies station that would help the miles disappear more quickly.

✝

After exchanging the briefcase for the soggy plastic bag, Ray Bellfontaine drove the few blocks to Jackson Square. They had agreed that Logan's head would sit atop one of the iron spiked fence posts to serve notice to all who would dare to cross the brothers in the future. Ray drove away with the head of Bo Logan smiling a macabre smile as his blood continued to trickle slowly forming a puddle in the drizzling rain.

An hour later, a city worker on her way to work placed a 911 call. She reported the decapitated head hanging on the fence at Jackson Square. The police knew immediately that the Bellfontaines had defeated them yet again.

✝

Sasha had driven around the city all night, but could not pick up Logan's trail. She was making a final round of the Quarter when she heard a siren scream past her. When she drove in front of Jackson Square, she saw the crime scene staff removing Logan's head from the iron fence spike.

She deflated with defeat. Within hours, the trial would begin and charges against them dismissed when the state could not present the star witness. Sasha drove home and with the last ounce of her energy tried to contact Kara, but reached only blackness.

Sasha entered the house and slipped from her rain-soaked clothing and between crisp clean sheets in total exhaustion.

Deep in the heart of the bayou, Kara's mind was still reeling from her latest injection, but she was coherent enough to realize that somewhere across the room a cell phone was ringing.

"Got it," was the only response she heard from the man who answered on this end.

Kara drifted back to sleep. When she awoke hours later, she found her arms and legs freed and her blindfold removed. She squinted as she looked around the room, seeing daylight for the first time in days. The room was empty of other occupants, a cell phone sitting on the table where she had taken her meals.

Still suffering from the effects of the drug, Kara did the only thing she could think of, she dialed Sasha's cell number, and left a message, letting her know she was all right and would be home very soon. She then dialed 911 and kept the line open while the police traced the direction of the call and dispatched an ambulance. It took nearly an hour to pinpoint her location. When Kara and the 911 operator heard the wail of the siren together, Kara knew she was going home.

Chapter 14

Kara stumbled outside into the bright sunlight as she heard the blare of the sirens moving closer. She had no idea how many days had passed since her abduction, and she was suffering from a severe case of disorientation. Kara's body crumpled when she saw the ambulance approach, followed closely by an unmarked police cruiser.

The emergency medical staff helped Kara onto a stretcher and gave her a close examination before they would allow Detective Brody to approach.

"How are you feeling?" he asked as he took her hand.

"A bit worn, but safe and ready to go home," Kara answered. "I suppose my release means the Bellfontaines got to Logan before he could testify."

Brody sighed deeply. "Unfortunately, Logan slipped away from the protection detail only hours before he was scheduled on the witness stand," Brody said. "It is still unsure how it happened or why he suddenly felt the need to leave protective custody, but his body was found early this morning."

Kara had tears in her eyes as Brody made his last statement. She knew her carelessness played a part in his death and that there would be repercussions from the media and political arenas when the Bellfontaines would escape incarceration yet again. She could kiss her aspirations at the DA's office good-bye, as she was certain to play the role of scapegoat in this case. She knew there was a great risk of this occurring when she took on the case, and she would be strong when it was time to face the consequences of her failure.

Brody sensed her distress and did what he could to comfort Kara. "Logan's death was inevitable from the start, we all knew that. I am just glad you are alive and well," he said.

The emergency medical staff started an IV in her left arm. "Other than a case of exhaustion and dehydration, Ms. Stewart is in good health." The young woman gave Kara a winning smile. "We will take you to the hospital just as a precaution and to be more closely examined, but you should be headed home later today."

"Where am I?" she asked Brody.

"You are just outside a town called Grand Isle, and this building you were being held in appears to be a storage building for offshore oil drilling equipment," Brody said. "It doesn't appear to have been used recently by anyone other than you and your captors. We will go over the place with a fine-tooth comb, but honestly, the place was carefully clean. Is there anything you can tell me about the people that abducted you?" he asked.

"I was blindfolded and restrained except when I was given a sandwich or a restroom break, so I didn't see any faces, but I know there were two men." Kara did not know why she did not tell him about the woman, but she did not feel compelled to do so. "They kept me sedated and had very little interaction with me, but I could hear two separate voices in the room."

He nodded as Kara disappeared into the back of the ambulance.

†

Sasha received a call from Brody telling her that Kara was on her way to the hospital in New Orleans for a thorough evaluation. As soon as she hung up the telephone, she raced to her truck. She stopped in to tell James and Marie the news and then drove directly to the hospital. Though she would be there hours before Kara was ready for release, Sasha wanted to be there the moment she arrived.

I am so glad you are all right. I will be waiting for you at the hospital, she said to Kara.

I am so sorry to have put you through all this, Kara said.

Hush now, Sasha said. I love you and right now, nothing else matters but that you are alive and well.

I love you too Sasha. I can't wait to be in your arms again.

Soon, very soon, Sasha promised. Rest now and I'll be waiting for your arrival, my love.

The tires on Sasha's truck squealed as she turned the corner to enter the parking lot at the hospital. She whipped the truck into a parking spot and jogged across the street to enter the emergency room. She went directly to the admitting desk and told the nurse working the triage station that she was waiting for Kara to arrive via ambulance. The nurse smiled warmly at her and told Sasha to make herself comfortable in the waiting room, promising to let her know when Kara arrived.

Sasha paced the floor for a few minutes and then sat down in an uncomfortable chair. She looked up at the television that played constantly in emergency room waiting area. The television sound was low. Sasha scrambled around the room until she located the remote. She turned up the volume and watched as the news camera captured the Bellfontaines walking down the front steps of the courthouse. Both brothers were smiling widely for the cameras and a reporter asked, "How does it feel to walk out of the courtroom today free men?" she brazenly asked.

Curtis looked directly at the camera and said, "We were never guilty of the crime we were charged with, so we never had any worries."

"The whole city thinks you were involved with the abduction of the prosecutor, Ms. Stewart," the reporter stated.

"Well, we hear she has been released by her captors and is on her way back to New Orleans," Ray said. "Had she not been involved with this atrocious allegation, she would have not been in harm's way," he said with an evil grin and turned away from the cameras.

You will pay for your actions one way or another Sasha silently promised the smug pair, who had once again avoided prosecution for their crimes. The reporter continued with the story, relating how Bo Logan's head was found earlier this morning hanging in Jackson Square, and that without his testimony the State had no case against the Bellfontaines and all the charges had been dismissed. Sasha ground her teeth to hold in the seething rage she felt watching the two men disappear into a stretch limo amidst all the cameras and publicity.

There was no way Ray Bellfontaine could have known Kara had been released and was on her way back to New Orleans, unless he or his brother were the ones to give the order to release her. His statement to the reporter was just his arrogant way of telling the authorities that there would be no way to connect them to Kara's abduction and they walked away free men once more from a crime they orchestrated.

Sickened, Sasha turned the volume back down and resumed her pacing. She watched as a small crowd of reporters and camera operators started to form in front of the emergency room. The information regarding Kara's return to the city had already leaked to the press and they were anxious to get photographs and an interview from her. The same nurse who had talked with Sasha earlier came out to the waiting room and ushered Sasha into a private examination room to prevent the press from hounding her as she waited for Kara.

"She will be here very soon," the nurse said then closed the door behind her as she left.

Sasha watched the clock on the wall, time ticked by painfully slow. After she had been in the room for twenty minutes, Sasha heard voices talking excitedly and the rear doors of the emergency room crash open. The door to the private exam room opened and Kara rolled into the room on a stretcher. Her face and clothing were dirty and disheveled from her experience, but the smile on Kara's face sent Sasha's heart plummeting to her stomach and her knees felt weak. She leaned down, kissed Kara's cheek, and was brushed away by a doctor who came rushing in to examine Kara.

"Get a phlebotomist down her stat to draw some blood so we can determine what they were using to sedate her," he barked. The nurse who had accompanied him into the room rushed back out the door.

"How are you feeling, Ms. Stewart?" he asked.

"Very relieved to be on my way home," she answered.

"Not so fast," the doctor said. "We need to determine what drugs they were giving you to make any necessary plans for your treatment. Hopefully they used a drug that is not addicting, and will not cause any withdrawal symptoms for you. Are you hurting anywhere?" he asked.

"No, I am just little sore from being restrained, but I have no pain anywhere," Kara said.

How will my blood look when they examine it? Kara projected to Sasha.

Relax your blood will look just fine under inspection. They will just be performing a blood toxicology test to determine what drugs are in your system. It has been over a week since your last dose of formula, so that will not show up at all, Sasha said.

On cue, the phlebotomist came through the door, placed a tourniquet around Kara's left arm, and located a vein in the crook of her elbow. She quickly withdrew three vials of Kara's blood and rushed them back to the laboratory. The doctor told the nurse to start another bag of sucrose and then left the room.

The nurse left and then returned to the room carrying a bag of sucrose and replaced the empty bag on the IV pole.

Detective Brody knocked on the door and then stepped into the room. "I don't know how, but the press has gotten wind of your arrival," he said. "We are keeping them at bay for now, but Sasha will have to sneak out to get her vehicle and park it near the morgue if we are going to be able to sneak you out once you are released." Brody grinned wildly. "Better yet, why don't we have one of the staff bring it around for us."

"The news is already broadcasting Kara's release as reported by Ray Bellfontaine on the steps of the courthouse a little while ago," Sasha growled.

"That smug bastard," Brody said with disgust. "So it was broadcast all over the news then I am sure."

Sasha handed him her keys and told him where she had parked her truck. "Once the doctor says Kara can be released, I will send someone for your truck, Sasha. When you are safely loaded, I will walk out front and create a diversion while you drive quietly away," he said with a grin. "As a precaution, I have asked the chief to order an unmarked unit to monitor your driveway, just to prevent any of these rodents from sneaking in if they can find out your home address."

"Thank you," Kara said and Brody slipped quietly from the room.

When they were alone in the room, Sasha bent down and kissed Kara softly on the lips. "I am so relieved to know you are really all right," she said. "You really had me worried, you know."

"I am so sorry, Sasha. If I could do it all over again, I would not have been so arrogant. Maybe things would have turned out differently."

"I doubt anything would have changed, my love. Logan was destined to die, and nothing you could have done would have prevented that," Sasha said. "I think it is amazing that he was the only one to lose his life; the men assigned to protect him could have died, as well."

"I guess I will always wonder what he was thinking when he escaped from the protection team," Kara said.

"We will never know for sure, but maybe he felt like his chances were better if he was on his own those last few hours," Sasha said. "He could probably feel death coming for him and decided to run instead of sit there and wait for it to come to collect him."

A soft knock came to the door and the doctor walked back into the room. "I have your drug test results and everything looks good." He placed the report in her chart and sat down next to her on a stool. "You were being dosed with a combination of valium and Ativan," he said. "Your captors were smart enough to give you the smallest possible doses and you should have no unusual side effects." He looked directly into Kara's eyes and said, "But, if you have any pain or unusual motor sensations, come back here immediately to get checked out."

"I will," Kara said as Sasha noted the doctor's warning. She would drag Kara back if necessary to ensure her future health.

"As soon as a nurse can come in here and remove the IV you can go home," he said. "Take it easy for a few days and let your body catch up on its rest," he said before he left the room.

A nurse returned to the room to remove the IV and to bandage Kara's arm. Detective Brody stepped inside the room and ushered Kara and Sasha through the hallway and down to the morgue. When he saw them safely through the door, he headed back through the emergency room. His departure through the door would cause the media hounds to flock to him and he would keep them distracted as Sasha drove quietly from the hospital.

As he stepped through the doors, the first of the reporters rushed to him. "Detective Brody, what is Ms. Stewart's condition?"

Video cameras were rolling and flashes burned in the dimming light. "Ms. Stewart has been examined and is being treated for exhaustion and dehydration," Detective Brody answered honestly. "She will be admitted to the hospital for several days for further observation and treatment," he said as he watched Sasha's truck pull away from the hospital. He hoped this ruse would allow Kara a few days to recuperate before the media swarmed her. Detective Brody pushed his way through the mass of media and walked to his car. The last few weeks had been exhausting for him as well. He looked forward to a good night's sleep as he drove the short distance to his home.

†

Sasha wasted no time in leaving the city. Kara sat next to her and Sasha's right arm draped over her shoulder, holding her close. She would think twice about letting Kara beyond arm's reach again, at least until the heat of the case had passed.

James, Marie, and Milly were waiting for them in the parlor as they entered the house. "Welcome home," they said in unison when the two women walked in.

"I missed you, Aunt Kara," Milly said as she ran up to her and gave her a tight hug.

"I missed you too, Milly, but I am home again," she said with tears in her eyes.

"I have a pot of chicken and dumplings and fresh biscuits on the stove when you two are ready to eat," Marie said.

"Thank you so much, Marie," Sasha said. "I will get Kara in a nice soaking bath and then come back down to serve up a hearty meal for her."

"We will see you both tomorrow then, but do not hesitate to call if you need anything," James said.

"I promise," Sasha said as she walked them to the door and for the first time ever, she turned the key in the lock. Sasha felt comfortable with the fact that there was an unmarked patrol vehicle stationed at the head of the driveway, and that they would pick up on an intruder's presence, but there was no need to underestimate the persistence of a reporter on the trail of a story.

She then led Kara up the stairs and started a warm bath as Kara removed her soiled clothing. Sasha sat on the edge of the claw-foot tub and watched as Kara quickly removed the blouse and pants from her body. The last few weeks had not been pleasant for Kara or kind to her body. Sasha saw the outline of ribs that had previously been invisible to the naked eye and she knew Kara had lost weight. She would enjoy putting some meat back on her small frame and Marie would be in her glory as she toiled in the kitchen cooking for Kara.

She helped Kara into the steaming water and watched as she laid her head back against the tub. Kara was pale, the dark circles under her eyes revealing her exhaustion.

Sasha sat beside the tub, watched as the water relaxed, and soothed her lover's aching body. Kara began to bathe and after a soft kiss, Sasha went downstairs to prepare their dinner.

Sasha returned to the bedroom carrying a large tray filled with platters of food and a large pitcher of sweet tea just as Kara was slipping on a thick robe. She placed the tray on a small table and then sat Kara in a chair and took a seat next to her. Kara looked more relaxed after the bath and her eyes grew wide as the aroma of the meal bombarded her senses. She knew Kara was past due for a dose of serum and she handed her a vial, which Kara gratefully downed.

Kara ate a healthy portion of the food and drank several glasses of the tea. When she pushed her plate away, she looked at Sasha with complete adoration. Sasha left Kara propped up in the bed as she took the dishes to the kitchen.

When she returned to the bedroom, Kara whispered, "Hold me."

Sasha removed her clothing and climbed naked between the sheets. She took Kara in her arms and held her close as the first rumble of thunder echoed in the distance. Sasha's hand stroked through Kara's hair as she held her lover close, their hearts beating together as they listened to the approaching storm. The pelting of the rain on the windows and the warmth of Sasha's body comforted Kara and she silently drifted off to sleep. Sasha held her for several hours as the storm outside matched the one raging inside her lover's body. She entered her mind and felt Kara's distress as she dreamed of Logan and his final demise.

When Kara turned onto her side, ready for deep sleep, Sasha curled around her body and draped a protective arm across her waist. Content that the emotional storm had passed for now, Sasha closed her eyes and joined Kara in much more pleasant dreams.

Chapter 15

The next morning Sasha awoke to deep blue eyes staring at her, and she returned the smile on Kara's face. Her arm still draped across Kara's waist, but she was now lying on her back watching Sasha.

"How did you sleep?" Sasha asked.

"So well I cannot remember falling asleep," Kara said. "I remember the rain striking the windows and that was all."

"Are you hungry?" Sasha asked concerned with Kara's weight loss.

"Yes, but not for food," Kara said as she rolled Sasha onto her back and kissed her sweetly.

Kara's hands moved silently across Sasha's body and evoked immediate desire from her lover. She knew the precise spots to touch on Sasha's body to send their heartbeats racing, and Kara took advantage of this knowledge to make Sasha soar with arousal. Her lips kissed down Sasha's neck, licking the length of her jugular vein gorged with blood, as her heart pumped wildly to provide oxygenated blood to her growing nipples and clit. Sasha felt the heat and wetness of Kara's excitement as she moved down her body. Kara straddled her right thigh, her lips engulfed a soft breast, and she began to suckle. Her fingertips stroked the sensitive flesh between Sasha's quivering thighs, coating her fingers with her juices. She paused from her suckling to take her fingertips into her mouth and then released the vibrations of her moan onto Sasha's breast.

Kara's hair had fallen around her face, caressing Sasha's skin like strands of velvet, raising gooseflesh across her body. Sasha's moans had turned into low growls as Kara teased her body and she surrendered all control to her lover. Kara's fingers parted Sasha's lips and matched the rhythm of her hips as they undulated on the bed, pressing Kara deeper inside her body. "Oh yes, baby," Sasha groaned as Kara's teeth grazed her hardened nipple and she buried three fingers inside her.

The wind had risen again, howling around the house as Sasha's wails echoed against the bedroom walls. Rain was hitting the windows in sheets as the lightning flashed to illuminate the room and the thunder crashed down upon deaf ears as the lovers were oblivious to anything other than the pleasures being given and received. Sasha's fingers tore at the sheets as Kara's tongue drove in and out of her, sending waves of delight crashing through her body.

Sasha shuddered in climax then pulled Kara up to rest on top of her body as it trembled with the pleasure she had received. Sasha then rolled Kara onto her back and lavished her body with kisses and sensual touches until her exhausted body could take no more. Sasha moved to lie beside Kara and held her tightly in her arms as they listened to the storm rage outside.

After a long nap, Sasha crept quietly from the bed and went to the kitchen to prepare a late breakfast for them. She was pouring glasses of juice when she felt a pair of soft hands encircle her waist. She turned in Kara's arms and kissed her deeply. "I am so happy you are home," she said.

"I missed you too, Sasha," Kara said as her fingers traced the outline of Sasha's full lips.

Sasha shivered under Kara's touch and she knew they would spend the rest of the day in bed. They ate breakfast and then climbed the stairs and sank back into the comfort of their bed.

After a second round of making love, Kara rested her head on Sasha's shoulder. "How do you feel about me staying home with you on a permanent basis?" she asked.

"I would love that," Sasha said as she took Kara's chin in her hand. "Will it be bad for you if you return to work?"

"Well, we haven't checked the paper or the news, but I can almost guarantee the district attorney will not take the blame for the Bellfontaines walking out of court as free men," she said. "I doubt that I would be fired, but any chance of ever being promoted died with Logan."

"It was not your fault that he died," Sasha said. "If anyone is to blame it is Logan himself or the police who let him escape from under their noses."

"I know that and you know that and, truth be known, the public knows that, but they will not rest easy until a sacrificial lamb is offered," Kara said. "I believe the best means of managing the situation is to go in Monday and tender my resignation, which will diminish the drama, and hopefully this whole ordeal will be put to bed."

Sasha understood that Kara was making the correct assumption, knowing how the politics of New Orleans worked, but it was painful to watch her lover give up something she loved so much. Selfishly, she would love to be by Kara's side every day, but she recognized that eventually Kara would tire of the ordinary routine of running Sugarland and her heart would yearn for more excitement.

She could not think of a solution that would allow Kara to maintain her dignity and her position after the peril she had undergone in the name of justice. Sasha found irony in the fact that the very persons who were attempting to obtain justice for crimes committed were the ones ostracized and ridiculed by their profession instead of honored for their valiant attempts. As Kara's tears soaked her shoulder, Sasha formed a plan to exact some justice of her own against those who had damaged Kara's reputation and self-esteem. Some bayou justice was due, and Sasha would be just the person to make it happen.

†

The remainder of the weekend was spent relaxing and planning for the coming Monday when Kara would resign her post. Sasha offered to accompany Kara, but she refused her support, choosing instead to gather the remnants of her pride, to end her career as a prosecutor with as much dignity as she could muster.

Sasha felt the heartache Kara carried with her as she drove into the city, and she wished there was something she could do to lessen the pain for her mate. Her anger fueled a rage burning deep within her every time she thought about the pain Kara was experiencing. She knew her time to act would arrive soon.

†

Kara had used her laptop to draft a letter of resignation over the weekend, and she clutched it tightly in her hand now as she pushed through the crowd of reporters that swarmed her sports car and accompanied her to the front door of the DA's office. Roger was on duty at the desk and he smiled warmly at her as she approached.

"It is good to see you back, Ms. Stewart," he said with a boyish grin.

"Thank you, Roger, but I won't be staying," she said as she signed in and then passed through the metal detector.

In her office, she chatted briefly with Ted and told him she was planning to resign her position. Ted pleaded with her not to leave, but she had already made her decision. She would hold firm to that decision, no matter the argument presented otherwise. She boxed up the few personal items she had in her office and, letter in hand proceeded to the district attorney's office.

Kara left her box at the secretary's desk and knocked before entering the DA's office. The DA saw the envelope in her hand and smiled as Kara approached and extended her hand to him.

"I would like to submit my resignation effective today," Kara said, her voice holding strong while inside her resolve was melting quickly.

"I sincerely hate that events have led to this decision, but I will honor your request," the DA said as he accepted the offered envelope. "There was great promise for you as a prosecutor," he said, unintentionally adding salt to her open wound.

"Thank you for the opportunity," Kara said. She spun on her heel and left his office. Picking up her small box, she held her head high and walked through the doors of the district attorney's building for the last time.

Met by a horde of media as soon as she stepped outside, Kara ignored their storm of questions and politely smiled to them as she continued walking to her car and drove for home. Kara smiled as she passed a sign directing traffic to Tulane. She thought maybe in a few years she would try her hand at teaching. Until then, she would spend her days with Sasha and assist her in any way she could in running Sugarland.

Chapter 16

Days turned into weeks and then months as Kara worked alongside Sasha and learned the ins and outs of running Sugarland. When it was time for Sasha to renew the lease of the cane fields, Kara negotiated an even better price for the lease, making Sasha very proud. After the initial lessons, there was very little challenge for Kara, and as Sasha feared, she began to yearn for something more stimulating to do each day. Sasha operated the business just fine and, though she enjoyed spending time with her, Kara felt she was more of a burden to Sasha when it came to running the business.

After much thought and discussion with Sasha, they agreed that Kara would start up her own practice. She would return to criminal defense as a profession and concentrate on juveniles who had lost their way in hopes that with her assistance she could steer them back from a life of criminal activity. Ted jumped at the chance to practice with Kara and in just a few months, they had an office up and running in a small house in the business district.

It remained painful for Kara to open up the newspaper or turn on the television to see a crime report that so obviously involved the Bellfontaines, and she vowed to do her best to keep as many young men and women out of their powerful grasp as possible. If Kara could not beat them in the courts maybe she could take the fight to the streets, maybe put a dent in the growing number of drug dealers and users who were barely in their teens. The glitz and glamour that dealing could bring to a child raised with barely enough food to eat would be challenging. Kara also knew it would be rewarding if she could convince even one of her clients to play it straight.

✝

Sasha had not forgotten her promise of justice. She began surveillance of the Bellfontaines while Kara was adjusting to work in the city. She would follow Curtis or Ray during their daily routines, learning of their drug houses and watching their business grow. Her rage smoldered as she watched as the youth of New Orleans continually infected by the lure of the drugs made available to them, and the vast amount of money they could make dealing for the Bellfontaines.

Sasha was adept at concealment, but still she secretly wondered why the police were unable to collect the same evidence she was witnessing to put the brothers away. Sasha feared their treatment of Bo Logan months earlier would impede anyone's cooperation with the authorities. They had successfully used his brutal death to intimidate any potential witness against them and further tightened their control on the city. Rumors hinted, and were probably true, that the Bellfontaines had as many cops on their payroll as some of the smaller parishes employed.

Within a few weeks, she was confident she had the routine of each brother memorized and was ready to put her plan into action. Sasha checked the weather report to find that there would be a full moon the coming Tuesday, accompanied by a night of rain and thunderstorms. It would be perfect for phase one of her plan.

✝

Monday night, after Kara had drifted off to sleep, Sasha crept from their bed and dressed quietly before leaving the house. She drove into the city and past the home of Ray Bellfontaine. If Sasha's notes were correct, he would be down in the Quarter spending an evening with one of a half dozen prostitutes they employed. Ray had a healthy sexual appetite. Sasha had tracked him as he indulged his desires on a regular basis. Sasha was disgusted with the way he treated the women. She would make sure she treated his dignity with the same indifference he showed them.

Sasha drove farther down the avenue until she reached Curtis Bellfontaine's home. A family man and father of two children, Curtis was much more settled than Ray and preferred to spend most nights at home with his family. Sasha had the floor plan of his home memorized, from several prior visits, and quietly slipped past the guards to enter the home. She bypassed the children's rooms and walked directly to the master bedroom. Standing at the foot of the bed, Sasha gazed down at Curtis. He had obviously lost weight over the past few months, and Sasha hoped that, in part, it was due to the dreams she used to infect his mind. She wanted Curtis to know how his life would end so she spared him no gruesome detail. Sasha had left several tokens of her nighttime visits to further torment Curtis. Tonight she carried a black rose and laid it on the pillow next to his head.

Curtis sensed her presence and opened his eyes. Paralyzed by the rage in Sasha's eyes, Curtis could barely gasp for his next breath as the terror overwhelmed him. She could hear his heart racing wildly in his chest and she leaned down to whisper in his ear.

"Your time will come soon," she whispered, her voice light and her breath hot on his face.

†

Curtis closed his eyes tightly and when he dared to open them again, Sasha had vanished from his room. He sat up on the bed and saw the black rose on his pillow, and tears began to flow down his face. The woman, whoever she was, had haunted his days and nights for months, and he was slowly feeling his grip on reality slipping away. Curtis was not a man to be easily scared, but this woman terrified him in a way he had never known before. No human could enter his house undetected by the guards or security system and yet she did on many occasions, roaming his house with free will.

Unable to return to sleep after the encounter, Curtis walked down to his office and placed his face in his hands as he continued to weep. If he did not take action soon, this woman would drive him to madness, or worse, fulfill her promise to take his life.

Curtis was not normally a superstitious man, but being raised in the heart of bayou country he knew of the black magic that still held great power over much of the city. He would search out a voodoo practitioner to find out if someone had placed a curse on him. If he found out his suspicion was true, he would make sure the person disappeared in a very unpleasant manner.

†

Sasha watched from outside the window, pleased Curtis was feeling the stress of her psychological torture. What she was giving him was nothing compared to the vile acts he and his brother had committed over the past twenty years. Sasha was normally a warm and compassionate person, but the Bellfontaines had eluded justice once more and the abduction of Kara made it personal, so she felt for the good of the community she must take action.

She walked across the yard quietly and drove down to the Quarter. She drove past several of the homes the Bellfontaines used for their brothels until she located Ray and satisfied that he was on his usual schedule, she drove back to Sugarland.

She slipped into bed beside a sleeping Kara and dreamed of the days to come.

†

The next morning, Sasha decided to go into the city and wanted to know if she could stop by the office and take Kara to lunch.

"That would be delightful, sweetie," Kara said. "What are you going to do in town?"

"Just run some overdo errands," Sasha said as she drank the last of her juice.

"Why don't you pick me up around noon then," Kara suggested as she stood to place her dishes in the dishwasher.

"You have a deal, ma'am," Sasha said with a warm smile.

Sasha finished picking up the kitchen then kissed Kara as she was on her way out the door. Kara was so much happier now that

119

she was back at work and really seemed to be enjoying working with the juvenile cases. In just a few months, Kara had been able to keep several teens out of the system and with careful follow-up, and encouragement, she hoped they would survive the allure of the criminal world.

Sasha went upstairs to shower and dress and then stopped by to see James and Marie. She found them sitting in their kitchen finishing breakfast. "Would you mind if I bought Milly a horse?" she asked.

Both James and Marie looked at Sasha in surprise. They knew how much Milly wanted one, but they were expensive to purchase and maintain. "That is a very generous offer, Sasha," James said.

"Well, she does have a birthday coming up soon," Sasha reminded them.

"Yes, we know, she reminds us every day," Marie said and then chuckled. "She would love to have a horse just like Thunder. I hear her ask for one almost every night when she says her prayers," Marie said. "She even has a name picked out for it."

"Really, what is it?" Sasha asked.

"She wants to call the horse Hera for some reason," Marie said.

Sasha felt her knees go weak. "Hera was the name of my Milly's horse, the one in the portrait," Sasha said with a tremble in her voice.

"That's odd," Marie said. "Why do you think she would come up with that name?"

"I have no idea," Sasha said as she walked toward the door. "But, with your blessing, I will start looking for a horse."

"We would love that, Sasha, really we would," James said.

Sasha drove to New Orleans, stopped off at the local feed store, and inquired about a palomino mare for Milly. She was given numbers for several local horse farms and would call each of them today to see what they had available. Sasha was excited to be able to purchase a horse for Milly, and looked forward to teaching the child how to ride.

Sasha left the store and headed for the Garden District. She knew Ray would be sleeping off a hangover from a night on the town, so she went directly to Curtis's house. As she drove by,

Curtis was getting into his car. She drove further down the block and performed a U-turn just as he was making his first turn. Sasha followed Curtis from a distance and watched with growing interest as he turned onto Chartres Street. When Curtis pulled into a short driveway, Sasha pulled into a parking spot a block away.

She watched as Curtis went to the side door of the home and knocked softly. In his arms, he carried a carton of unfiltered Camel cigarettes and a gallon bottle of Jack Daniels. When Sasha saw the gifts he bore, she chuckled softly to herself. She did not need to see the man who opened the door and ushered Curtis inside to know he was going to see Lady Serena, a voodoo priestess and reported descendant of the famed Voodoo Queen of New Orleans, Marie Laveau. Just a few more houses down the avenue stood one of the homes the Voodoo Queen had lived in, which served now to memorialize her importance to the New Orleans community. Her mausoleum at St. Louis Cemetery was one of the most popular tourist attractions in the city and her legend lived on in the hearts of the inhabitants of New Orleans.

†

One of the tallest and darkest black men he had ever seen met Curtis at the door. He was certain this man could slip through the night undetected and the man's size gave him the chills. Following the man inside, he entered a small dimly lit room, and was given instructions to wait. The smell of incense or some form of herbs filled the house, making Curtis's eyes water from the acrid smell. Never known to place much faith in voodoo in the past, Curtis felt he was dealing with someone with supernatural powers. He suddenly broke out in a cold sweat as he felt someone probing at his mind. He had come to recognize the tingling sensation over the past few months and no longer feared he was losing his mind.

†

Sasha sat in the truck and waited. She found it curious that Curtis would visit a voodoo priestess. Voodoo had come to New Orleans in the eighteen hundreds with the slaves that arrived from

Africa and the Caribbean. Voudon had been an ancient practice in Africa and when enslaved Africans reached the Caribbean and subsequently New Orleans, it became a mixture of Roman Catholic icons and ideologies to become voodoo. Practiced as a religion by slaves and the free black people, voodoo utilized subtle power of suggestion and secret drugs to make up various potions and poisons. There was still a strong belief in the power to mock death with its "zombie" potions.

Sasha recognized that Curtis had come to visit Lady Serena to see if someone had placed a curse on him, and to seek her powerful protection.

Lady Serena would be able to detect that he had been marked for death, furthering his paranoia. She would not be able to name who or how he became cursed, even though she would have great suspicions of Sasha's involvement. Telling Curtis an Immortal was hunting him would only bolster his belief that she was a crazy woman.

✝

The heat in the small room became stifling and Curtis felt a drop of perspiration trickle down his spine. The dark man had disappeared into the house, leaving him to wait alone bearing his gifts. Several minutes later, a small woman appeared in the doorway. As dark as the man had been, Lady Serena was very light-skinned and bore an uncanny resemblance to the pictures he had seen of Marie Laveau. She even wore the 'tignon,' the seven-knotted handkerchief worn around her neck like the voodoo queen. She grinned at him with gapped teeth, and he felt a shiver pass through his body.

Her dark eyes seemed to glower as she looked at Curtis. "Come with me," she instructed as she turned away and led him deeper into the small house. They passed through a beaded curtain into a small room, lit by candles surrounding a small altar to the Blessed Mary. She pointed him to a seat and took the cigarettes and alcohol he offered her from across the small table.

"You come here today a very troubled soul," Lady Serena said. "Let me see your right hand." Curtis reached across the table and she took his large hand in her much smaller ones and turned it over. Her frown increased as she looked at the lines on his palm. What she saw there would only further terrify the man. His lifeline racing across his palm came to a very abrupt stop, and she recognized this as an omen for a premature death.

"You have a very black soul," she said with her thick Creole accent. "During your life you have been a bad man, a very bad man," she said. "I see many lives that you have ruined or taken for your own without any remorse, and now your destiny catches up with you."

"Have I been cursed?" Curtis asked.

"Cursed, no, you have been marked for death by someone who is very powerful, and who has been wronged by you in the past," Lady Serena said.

"Can you tell me who she is?" he asked.

"She, how do you know it is a she?" Lady Serena asked.

"Because she has been entering my house at night and invading my dreams for several months now, a tall dark woman with evil eyes," Curtis said, now sweating profusely.

"I can smell your fear of this woman, but no, I cannot give you her name for I do not know it myself," Lady Serena said. "I can only tell you that she wields a very powerful magic, and she will not rest until the wrongs against her have been righted."

"Is there anything I can do?" Curtis asked.

"You do not have a soul of a spiritual man, but my advice to you would be to put your house in order and do it soon," Lady Serena said.

A wave of nausea struck Curtis full force, and he feared he would pass out if he did not escape the small room quickly. He stood and reached into his pocket, pulling out a hundred- dollar bill and placed it on the table. Curtis looked at the woman once more and imagined he saw a vision of a skull in each of her dark eyes. He was nearly in tears as he walked quickly from the room, mumbling his thanks for her advice.

Lady Serena sighed, relieved to have such a dark soul out of her home. It would take a great potion and many prayers to rid her home of the blackness he had brought with him. So taking a glass from the cupboard, pouring herself a large drink of the Jack

Daniels, opening a pack of the cigarettes and lighting one, Lady Serena began the task of cleansing her home. She burned various herbs and chanted quietly to herself as she imbibed in the dark man's offerings.

Curtis ran to his car, loosening the tie around his neck as he felt he was slowly suffocating. He cranked the car and turned the air-conditioning on full blast to cool his overheated body. He drove wildly down the street and paid no heed to Sasha as he passed by her truck.

Sasha smiled a soft smile. His plan had backfired on him. Instead of finding out her name so he could have her eliminated, Curtis found out he would soon be the one eliminated. She slipped inside his mind to see him terrorized by the news he had received from Lady Serena.

"Crazy old witch," she could hear him thinking, as he drove toward the downtown area.

Sasha looked at her watch and saw that noon was rapidly approaching and she drove to Kara's office.

Chapter 17

Sasha pulled up in front of Kara's office at five minutes before noon and sailed through the front door with moments to spare. She entered the front office and saw Kara's door closed, indicating she was with a client, so she took a seat in the lobby.

"Has she been busy today, Crystal?" she asked.

"She has had three appointments already this morning, and has two more scheduled for the afternoon. Word of her practice has spread like wildfire in the streets," the young teen said.

Crystal was one of Kara's first clients. She was sixteen and already had two children. Arrested for prostitution while trying to raise money to feed and clothe her babies, Kara felt for her terrible plight. Crystal's mother was a crack addict and did very little to raise Crystal, leaving to her own devices, a baby raising babies.

Kara was successful in persuading the judge to withhold adjudication of the charges. Instead, he placed her on eighteen months of probation, with fifty hours of community service, which he mandated be completed in full during the first year. Kara and Ted worked together to get Crystal and her children signed up for housing benefits, welfare and some food stamps. They also managed to get a small amount of child support out of the children's father. Crystal was also eligible for childcare benefits, so part of her agreement for Kara taking on her case was that Crystal would work half days at the law firm as a secretary. The rest of the day Crystal would attend classes preparing her to take the GED exam for her high school diploma. Crystal agreed to pay Kara five dollars a week until she managed to pass her GED test, when her debt to Kara was paid.

Crystal was one of many juveniles in New Orleans who needed someone's guidance and the understanding of someone who could help them with decisions when the need arose. She quickly proved herself an eager learner and chose to stay at the office in the afternoons to study for the exam while answering the phones. Crystal showed a genuine interest in the legal practice and talked with Kara about becoming a paralegal assistant in the future. Kara encouraged Crystal to look into classes once she passed her GED and assured her that she could still work at the office while she attended classes to keep an income coming into her household.

Kara also required Crystal to volunteer two hours each week at a local after-school day care for latchkey kids to complete her required community service hours. The director raved to Kara about Crystal's guidance and counseling of the younger children she worked with. Crystal, honored as Volunteer of the Quarter by the director, was offered full-time employment once she had her GED. Crystal politely thanked her for the offer but promptly told her she would continue working with Kara while she furthered her education. In the three months, she had worked with Kara she had become a more responsible young adult. Once the strain of financial burdens lifted from her shoulders, Crystal had become a doting mother to her two little boys.

Sasha was reading the paper when Kara's door opened and a woman exited with an angry-looking young man in tow. Kara saw her sitting on the couch and once the clients had left the office said, "Sorry I am running late."

"Not a problem, dear, I had time to catch up with Crystal and to read the paper."

"Are you ready to eat or would you like for me to run out and grab something?" she asked.

"I am starved, and I need to get outside for a little while," Kara said. "Can we bring you anything, Crystal?"

"No thanks, Ms. Stewart, I brought a sandwich from home," she said with a bright smile.

"All right then, I will be back in an hour or so," Kara said and followed Sasha out the door.

"How about we grab a shrimp po'boy sandwich and head to the levee?" Sasha asked.

"That sounds wonderful," Kara said as she climbed into the truck.

They drove to the French Market and parked while Sasha ran in to one of the small shops to buy two sandwiches and drinks for them. She glanced back to see Kara lay her head back onto the seat. When Sasha returned and opened the door, she saw Kara, nearly asleep, jump as she climbed back into the truck.

"It's time for more serum for you isn't it?"

"Yes, I think I will take a dose when I get home tonight," Kara said.

"Then you should sleep like a baby tonight," Sasha said.

"Yes, I probably will," she said.

Sasha drove to the River Walk and parked the truck. They took their sandwiches and walked down to the levee to find a small picnic table where they shared their meal. "I need to go out tonight to hunt, so if you wake and I am not with you, you will know where I am," Sasha said.

Because Kara had never tasted the fresh blood of a kill, she was able to survive on the serum alone, but Sasha still had to hunt on occasion. Sasha did not tell her the entire truth. She would be out hunting tonight, just not exactly as stated. There was no way on earth she would feed on the tainted blood of a Bellfontaine and she did not want Kara to have any knowledge of the bayou justice that was about to come to fruition.

They finished their lunch and Sasha enjoyed spending a few minutes with Kara in the warm sunshine. Words were not necessary as the two lovers enjoyed one another's company. Kara was somewhat disappointed to break the moment to return to the office. Sasha felt the drift in Kara's mood and stood to clean up the remnants of their lunch. She took the trash, deposited it in a barrel, and then returned to Kara's side.

"Are you ready to go?"

"No, not really, but I do have appointments this afternoon," Kara said, giving Sasha a brilliant smile.

Sasha opened the door for Kara then moved around the rear of the truck to the driver's side. She felt a tingling and when she looked to her left, she saw the shiny black Cadillac of Ray Bellfontaine as he drove past the levee. *I will see you later tonight,* Sasha projected to the unaware man. Smiling to herself, Sasha climbed into the truck and started the engine.

†

Ray felt a strange tingling in his brain and thought her heard a woman's voice say to him, "I will see you tonight." He looked around the inside of the car even though he knew nobody was riding with him, then shook the thought off as his overactive imagination playing a trick on him.

†

Sasha kissed Kara on the lips when they returned to the office. "Will you be late tonight?"

"I should be home around six."

"I will see you later then," Sasha said as Kara left the truck.

Sasha watched her enter the office and then she quietly pulled the truck away from the curb. She had placed a cooler in the back of the truck along with a bag of other supplies. She grinned wickedly as she left the city and drove south.

†

Sasha had not driven south in some time and enjoyed the leisurely route she took as she headed deeper into the bayou. Cane fields and bogs eventually gave way to a short stretch of highway near the coast and Sasha enjoyed the brief view of the blue water before she turned to head again into the swampland. She followed the route she had burned into her memory and a half hour later turn onto a secluded drive between two fields of cane. Sasha smiled when the storage hangar came into view. Sasha pulled alongside the building and switched off the engine. Yellow crime scene tape blew in the breeze as it hung ghost-like from several trees surrounding the storage building, a reminder of the crime that had taken place there.

As Detective Brody had surmised there was no evidence left behind by Kara's captors, but the Crime Scene Unit had combed the area thoroughly in hopes of just one error. Finding none, the abduction of the assistant district attorney had gone unsolved, but not forgotten in the mind of Detective Brody. He and his staff had tracked down every lead for the last two months, before more pressing crimes took precedence.

Sasha easily popped the lock on the small door leading into the dark hangar. As her eyes adjusted to the darkness, she took in the meager furnishings in the room. The interior was still as she remembered, the cot where Kara was drugged and restrained still sat at the far side of the room. A small table sat in the center of the room. Sasha sat at the table and she could sense a lingering of Kara's spirit. She felt the anxiety and fear her lover had experienced while being held captive. Sasha's anger boiled at the thought of Kara in distress and she slammed her fist onto the small table in anger, the blow echoing throughout the room. Sasha struggled to control the rage she felt toward the Bellfontaines, knowing she would need a clear, calm head to put her plan into place. She took several deep breaths as she looked around the room, memorizing the small space.

She noted there was only one small window in the room as she stood and walked back to her truck. Sasha carried the cooler into the hangar, placing it underneath the small table, then went back for the bag of supplies she would use this night. Sasha wrapped a pair of leg irons around the metal bar serving as a footboard for the small cot and fastened another length of thick chain to the headboard bar. The deep purple of the fingerprint dust lingered like a thick coat on the cool metal and Sasha left it as undisturbed as possible.

From the bag, she took out a large pair of scissors and placed them on the table. She also took out a lantern, placed the large battery in the cavernous compartment, and pressed the switch to ensure it was working properly. The beam burned brightly against the wall and illuminated the room well.

Sasha left the building and pulled the door closed behind her, turning the handle to ensure that the door had locked. She looked up to the sky and smiled at the black clouds beginning to form. She could smell the salt on the breeze that was bringing the clouds in from the Gulf. From across the cane fields Sasha could hear the low rumbling of thunder as the storm began to gather its strength. She walked to her truck as the winds whistled between the stalks of cane waiting for harvest. In just a few more weeks the harvest would begin and then the burning of the cane fields would occur, just as it had for a hundred years to begin a new cycle of life.

Sasha drove past the shoreline and through the bayou back to Sugarland, arriving just as the first drops of rain began to fall. She parked the truck near the stable and went inside to tend to Thunder and the other stock before making a mad dash to the house. Marie was busy in the kitchen, stirring a large pot of red beans that she would spread over rice for their dinner. She had diced up several sweet Vidalia onions and had baked fresh corn bread that filled the kitchen with its aroma.

"Something smells wonderful, Marie," Sasha said as she hung her rain jacket in the back room.

"Red beans and rice tonight. I picked some fresh tomatoes from the garden too, and they are sliced and chilling in the refrigerator for dinner when Kara makes it home."

"Thank you, Marie," Sasha said as she poured a glass of tea and joined Milly at the table, where she was drawing a picture.

"Hi there, Milly," Sasha said. "What are you drawing today?"

Milly turned the paper around so Sasha could see that she was drawing a picture of a horse and Sasha smiled. "Hi Sasha, do you like my horse?" she asked.

"Yes, as a matter of fact I do," she said with a wink to Marie. "Your mom tells me you already have a name picked out for a horse, Milly."

Milly looked up into Sasha's eyes and smiled sweetly. "I will name her Hera," Milly plainly stated.

"That is a lovely name, Milly, but where did you come up with that?" Sasha asked.

"That was the name of Milly's horse wasn't it?" the child asked.

"Yes, it was indeed, but how do you know that?" Sasha asked curiously.

"I'm not sure, Sasha, I just do," Milly said with a grin that reminded her so much of her former lover.

"Well, if the horse will be named Hera, I think it is important for you to know the history behind the name," Sasha said.

Marie sat beside her daughter as Sasha began her story. "Hera was a goddess known as the Queen of the Olympian Deities," Sasha began. "She was wed to Zeus, her brother, and she became the goddess of marriage and childbirth." Sasha saw that both Milly and Marie were listening intently and she continued. "Hera gave birth to Hephaestus, the smith-god who forged iron like no other, then Hebe, the goddess of youth, and finally Ares, the god of war." Sasha smiled at Marie. "Hera lived in a place called Argos where she was loved and worshipped by her followers," Sasha said. "She was known as a fierce goddess, issuing her wrath against goddesses and humans alike that dared fall victim to Zeus's amorous intentions," Sasha added with a chuckle for Marie's benefit, knowing Milly would not comprehend the latter statement.

Sasha looked at Milly who had sat in wide-eyed amazement throughout Sasha's story. "So Hera it shall be," she said with a smile to the child sitting next to her.

Milly smiled back at her and Sasha could see the twinkle in the child's eyes, as she knew Sasha's words were true.

Kara walked into the room and Sasha turned to see her lover's eyes sparkle when they met hers. "No one told me we were having a party tonight," she teased as she sat down at the table with them.

"Welcome home, sweetie," Sasha said. "Marie, why don't you call James, ask him to join us and we will all share dinner together tonight."

"That sounds like a great idea," Marie said as she stood and walked toward the phone.

"Milly, why don't you help me set the table while Kara pours everyone some tea," Sasha said to the smiling child.

"Yes, ma'am," she said as she followed Sasha to the cupboard for plates and bowls.

Moments later, James came rushing through the door, his hair and clothing damp from the rain. "A storm is blowing up and it promises to be a good one," he said as he wiped his face with his sleeve.

"Have a seat and we will be ready in just a few minutes," Marie said with a kiss to her husband's cheek.

They sat around the table while Marie placed steaming bowls of red beans and rice on the table, followed by a platter of sweet-smelling corn bread. Marie then went to the refrigerator to retrieve the chopped sweet onion and sliced chilled tomatoes. Then she joined them at the table and, after a brief blessing, they shared the small feast as the rain began to fall more heavily outside. The lightning drew closer and the electricity flickered several times.

"Looks like we may be in the dark soon," Sasha said as she stood and went to the pantry for two lanterns, identical to the one she used earlier that day, and placed them on either end of the table. She had barely returned to her seat when a lightning bolt struck very near the house. As she predicted, the lights flickered again and the room plunged into darkness. Laughter rang around the table as Sasha and James turned on the lanterns, and they finished the meal by lantern light.

Marie and Kara picked up the kitchen as James, Sasha, and Milly sat around the table talking. When the kitchen was clean, Sasha and Kara walked them to the front door and watched as the small family made a wild dash for their home as the storm came to a brief lull. Sasha watched as the heavens opened up again as James closed the front door behind him and their lantern light disappeared in the small house.

Holding their lantern in hand, Sasha led Kara upstairs to their room. They undressed and climbed into the bed to watch the raging storm. Sasha could hear the faint movement of the tightly wound grandfather clock downstairs and knew the time to initiate her plan was rapidly approaching. She held Kara tightly in her arms as the lightning flashed around the house and torrents of rain pelted the windows.

Sasha gazed into Kara's eyes as lightning lit up the sky and saw the sparkle of mischief in them as Kara's hand slid underneath the covers to rest on Sasha's stomach. Sasha pulled Kara closer until their lips met and they kissed softly at first as Kara's hand caressed Sasha's body with light touches. When Kara's fingers brushed across Sasha's nipples, their kisses intensified as their hunger for each other raced in their veins. Kara rolled on top of Sasha, pinning her lover onto the bed as her mouth moved down to her lover's ear.

Kara's aggression surprised Sasha. Her heart raced as Kara whispered softly into her ear, "I want you so bad tonight," in a voice that growled with desire.

Sasha moaned loudly in response to Kara and made a mental note of increased sexual appetite as a side effect of her lover's failure to take her serum on a regular basis. If Sasha were human, that could be a fatal mistake for Kara to make, as she would surely ravage a human once the blood lust overwhelmed her, but Sasha felt confident she could control Kara.

She felt the heat intensify within Kara's body as her hips ground roughly into her and a trickle of sweat rolled down Kara's face. Sasha could feel the sharp pricks of Kara's fangs as they grazed her neck and Kara sucked greedily at the small river of blood that flowed from her neck.

Kara's body shook violently as the blood of her lover raged through her veins. Sasha took Kara's head in her hands, lifting it from her neck. The feral look in Kara's eyes would have sent a human into cardiac arrest, but Sasha grinned. Overpowering her lover, she rolled Kara onto her back, pinning her smaller hands above her head in one large hand.

Sasha forced Kara's thighs open with her hips and entered her aggressively as Kara cried out in pleasure. Sasha thrust into her repeatedly. Kara's passion echoed in the room, her eyes, and body begging Sasha for more. Sasha's mouth covered Kara's right breast and she suckled it with a ferocious hunger as Kara's hips thrashed uncontrollably onto her fingers.

The heat of their lust burned rampantly within them as their bodies entwined, moving at a blur as they made love with abandon, their passion matching that of the storm raging outside their walls.

Perspiration covered their bodies, mixing with the shiny, slick juices of their desire as they exploded in simultaneous release, crying out as one voice.

Sasha moved down between Kara's trembling thighs, licked her pulsing clit to full erection, and then used her fangs to open small gashes in the sensitive flesh. Sasha's mouth feasted on her body as Kara erupted in a blinding orgasm, her fingers clawing at the bed linens as Sasha's mouth and fingers drove her near madness.

Kara's body collapsed into the comfort of the bed and Sasha moved beside her, holding her in her arms until Kara drifted off to sleep as the rain continued to pour. Sasha kissed her and whispered, "I love you," and then crept quietly out of the bed.

Chapter 18

Sasha ran out into the dark night through the tempest that was raging, cursing her decision to park the truck down by the stable. By the time she reached it, her hair was soaked with the chilled raindrops, which ran into her eyes when she slicked her hair back on her head. She jerked the door open and was glad she had turned the dome light off. She wanted to complete this portion of her plan in total stealth. She could not jeopardize anyone, including James or Marie if they chose to look out the window at that precise moment.

Sasha turned the key to start the engine and listened as the pounding of the rain on her hood drowned out the soft purr. Sasha reached down to the console turning off the headlights and placed the truck in gear as she pulled onto the driveway. When she reached the hard road at the end of the driveway, she turned the lights back on. Even the strongest beam could barely break through the dense darkness that surrounded the truck. The wipers pounded furiously across the windshield to move the rainwater away from her field of vision. Sasha drove slowly and carefully through the storm and was relieved to see the lights of the city when they came into view. The strong winds buffeted the truck as Sasha drove across the river and into New Orleans.

The weather had kept most of the city's occupants inside their homes tonight so the traffic was very light for the midnight hour. Sasha guided the truck through the narrow alleys, dodging windswept debris as she drove into the Quarter. Neon lights cut through the darkness, advertising drink specials and the entertainment promised inside for a minimum cover charge. A good rainstorm would do this place wonders, Sasha thought as the reeking stench of stale urine and spent liquor raced toward the storm drains, flushing the streets clean albeit only temporarily.

Sasha drove in front of each of the homes the Bellfontaines used for brothels, her frown growing as she failed to locate Ray. She turned the truck around in an alley and headed for the Garden District. If he weren't at home for the evening, she would delay her plan for another day. As she drove, a taxi flew past her sending a wave of rainwater across her windshield. Sasha cursed at the impatient driver as he steered his car over in front of her. Sasha gripped the steering wheel tighter and slowed the truck to allow the maniac ahead of her plenty of room to maneuver the slick streets.

Sasha slowed even further when she saw the driver turn on a blinker and prepare to turn into the driveway of Ray Bellfontaine. The rear door flew open a moment later and a young woman raced through the rain toward the front door. The lazy bastard would not get out in this weather, but he obviously had no qualms about one of the working girls getting soaked to the bone while coming to service him. A young woman, barely in her twenties knocked on the door and was pulled roughly inside, and the door slammed shut. Once the taxi had disappeared, Sasha pulled into the driveway and parked outside the large garage.

Sasha entered the house with her mind to find that Ray and the young woman were the only ones inside. Sasha watched as Ray led the young woman into his large den and sat down in a leather chair where he had been smoking a cigar and sipping a brandy. A big-screen television filled the entire wall playing a pornographic movie. Ray pointed to the floor between his feet and told the young woman to blow him as he reached for the thick, sweet-smelling cigar. Blowing the smoke across the room, he glared at the woman who had hesitated to respond to his command. The look in his eyes brought her back to reality and she dropped her coat and purse onto the couch before kneeling between his feet.

Sasha could sense the utter disgust the woman felt for Ray as her hands stroked up the fabric of his Italian suit pants to his crotch. Her hands nimbly unfastened his belt, opened the button of the pants, and slid down the zipper, brushing across the bulge already pressing against the fabric. Ray groaned loudly as her manicured nails scratched across the silk cloth of his boxers as she opened the fly of his pants. "That's it, baby," he growled as the woman slid her hand inside his boxers to fondle his swollen balls.

Sasha reached across the seat and rummaged through the small bag of supplies for the small timer with a remote control device. Slipping quietly from the truck, Sasha entered the garage and located the main power panel. She worked quickly to attach the timer to the central power switch, and with the remote in hand, entered the house.

Sasha had never been inside Ray's house so she moved cautiously from room to room. She could hear Ray's groans coming down a hallway and she followed them until she reached the den. Ray was facing away from her, his eyes transfixed on the television screen as a large man thrust roughly into a small woman, her cries of pain ringing loudly in Sasha's ears. Ray's hands were buried in the young woman's hair as he roughly forced her head into his lap, causing her to gag as his penis thrust into her mouth.

The storm continued to rage outside and Sasha timed the crack of thunder after each lightning strike as the storm moved closer, and she waited for the perfect moment.

Ray's groans were becoming louder. Sasha smiled to herself as a clap of thunder boomed loudly and she pushed the remote, killing the power to the house. "What the fuck," Ray said as the young woman cried out in fright of the sudden darkness.

"Damn storm! Finish me bitch," he bellowed angrily.

Sasha moved quickly across the room, concealed in the darkness. She took a set of cuffs from her rear pocket, snapped the first around Ray's right wrist, and pulled it behind the leather chair. She grabbed his left wrist and pulled it behind the chair, snapping the second cuff in place. Ray was so caught up with his impending climax, that he did not know what was occurring until it was much too late for him to react. Sasha would have easily overpowered him, but the element of surprise made her attack much easier.

"What the fuck! What is going on here?" he cried out.

Hidden by darkness, Sasha told the young woman, "Put his dick back where it belongs, then go and don't stop to look back."

Her voice was gruff, when she spoke. The woman did not hesitate to jump up from her knees, grabbing her coat and purse as Sasha watched her flee the room to escape out the front door. She was certain the woman wasn't crazy about the idea of walking out in this storm, but she couldn't allow the woman to stay in that room any longer.

Sasha chuckled as she heard the front door slam, knowing the woman would not stop running until she reached the Quarter.

"Who are you and what are you doing?" Ray demanded.

"Who I am is no concern of yours," Sasha said with a growl in her voice. "We are going to take a ride." She wrenched Ray up from his seat using the small chain between the two metal cuffs.

Ray cried out in pain as his shoulder sockets stretched to their limit as his captor raised his arms above the high-backed leather chair. She knew Ray wrongly assumed that the police were arresting him when in his arrogance, he shouted, "Go ahead and arrest me, I will be out before you can finish your damned paperwork."

Sasha chuckled at his threat. She could feel his brazen courage escape his body as she leaned close to him and said, "I am not the police, and I am pleased to inform you that you will not be returning here anytime soon." She then covered his head with a black bag with only a hole for his nose to enable him to continue breathing, and tied the strings tightly across the back of his neck. Sasha felt a cold shiver pass through his body as she took his right arm and said, "Let's go."

Ray struggled against Sasha, but her Immortal strength easily overpowered him. She led him through the house, stopping in the garage long enough to retrieve the timer and then exited the house, running into the pouring rain.

She opened the passenger's door and shoved him inside, banging his head on the doorframe causing him to yelp in pain. Sasha ran around the back of the truck and climbed behind the wheel, bringing the engine to life.

"Where are you taking me, bitch?" Ray said, finally admitting aloud that a woman was abducting him.

Sasha lashed out with her right hand and struck Ray's head, making it bang against the metal doorframe again. "Do not call me a bitch again, and as I told you before we are taking a little ride."

Sasha could smell the stench of his fear and knew her plan was working perfectly. Ray remained quiet for a few minutes as Sasha drove toward the river. Nearly ten blocks from his house, Ray and Sasha passed the young prostitute. She had taken off her heels and was running with all her might toward the Quarter. Good girl, Sasha thought to herself as she kept on driving.

Several minutes passed in relative silence. As Sasha slowed to turn onto the bridge to cross the river, Ray made a grab for the door handle in an attempt to flee. "Amazing things, those child locks," Sasha said with a laugh as Ray failed to open the door.

His fingers found the button for the power windows, and despite his repeated attempts, the window would not budge. "Oh, do be a good boy now, Ray, or I will have to drug you to knock you out," Sasha warned.

She did have drugs that would do an ample job of subduing Ray, but she preferred to have him alert and cognizant of everything she did and said. Ray calmed down and sulked for several minutes before he tried to engage Sasha in conversation again.

"Is it money you want?" he asked. "If it is, just let me know and I will make a call and you will have it."

"Money, no Ray," Sasha said. "As you and your brother know, money can buy a lot of things, but it cannot buy me justice."

Ray shivered at the icy tone in the woman's voice. "Curtis, what does he have to do with this?" Ray asked, his paranoia turning to suspicion.

Sasha smiled to herself. Ray had totally misinterpreted her meaning, but his assumption worked well into her plan.

"Do you really believe that Curtis would let you continue being the good-for-nothing, womanizing slacker that you are forever?" Sasha asked, further planting a seed of doubt in Ray's imagination. "He makes all the business decisions and takes all the risks while you ride on his coattails, whoring around in drunken bliss day after day. You have become a disgrace to him in the eyes of your South American contacts," she added, barely able to suppress her laughter.

"So those jungle rats are behind this," Ray said, anger evident in his voice.

Sasha remained silent, allowing Ray time to stew in his thoughts. The rain still lashed against the windshield, but she could now see the moon had risen and was shining brightly on the road ahead.

Ray hung his head and Sasha thought he might have drifted off to sleep until she hit a bump in the road and jarred the truck. "Where are you taking me?" he demanded to know.

"Just for a ride, Ray, so relax," Sasha teased. "It won't be much longer now."

Sasha heard the sharp trilling sound of a cell phone and saw Ray's hands lunge for his left pants pocket in an effort to silence the phone. Sasha carefully pulled the truck off the side of the road and jammed her hand in his pocket to retrieve the ringing phone. Ray struggled against her, but Sasha flipped the phone open and turned the power off, silencing the ringing.

Sasha remembered how they had been able to trace Kara's location by the use of cell phone and she placed the phone in her jacket pocket. She would use this knowledge to her advantage to mislead Curtis in the hunt for his brother once he had determined he was gone. Given Ray's proclivity to overnight binges, Sasha felt she had at least until tomorrow evening before Curtis would become alarmed.

"Those things are so irritating," Sasha said as she rolled down the window and pretended to throw the phone alongside the road, tossing out a partially eaten apple instead.

"You bitch," Ray screamed as he heard the apple splash in water.

Sasha again lashed out with her right hand, this time balled up in a fist, and struck Ray in the temple, snapping his head violently to the side. "Remember what I said about calling me a bitch," Sasha said, issuing her final warning.

"Those things are expensive," he said in a defeated tone.

"No worries, Ray. Where you are headed, there isn't good reception anyhow," she said with a chuckle.

Sasha had looked at the caller ID on Ray's phone before she powered it off. As she suspected, it was Curtis calling. Steering the truck back on to the road to continue their journey, Sasha focused on Curtis Bellfontaine and projected a thought to him.

†

Ray slumped in his seat as he contemplated what would happen to him and he didn't like the thoughts of the South Americans sending an assassin after him. Those men had some brutal ways of dealing with their enemies and he just couldn't see Curtis, his own flesh and blood, going along with their plan. A shiver raced down his spine at the possibility his own brother would allow him to be murdered.

†

Curtis listened to his brother's phone ring several times and then it abruptly stopped. He angrily redialed the number and reached only the stupid voice mail that Ray had recorded. "Damn," Curtis yelled as he snapped the phone closed and slammed it down on his desk in his home office. Curtis had awakened from a dead sleep with an urgent need to talk to Ray. Maybe it was just a nightmare, but Curtis was worried about his brother. He was probably just out on the town partying his drunken ass off, Curtis thought. He downed a shot of Jack Daniels to calm his nerves and headed back to his bed. Still it worried him when he could not reach his brother.

Curtis had barely placed his head back on his pillow when he felt the strange tingling in his head and heard a woman's voice in his head say, *your time will be coming soon.*

Curtis bolted straight up in bed when he heard her message then left his bed to return to his office. He picked up the bottle of Jack Daniels and a large glass, pouring a stiff drink. Taking a deep swallow of the throat-burning liquor, Curtis picked up the phone and dialed Ray's number. He left a message for Ray to call him immediately, and then spent the next two hours drinking and calling his brother's phone.

Chapter 19

Sasha drove for another half hour before she slowed down searching for the secluded pathway that would lead to the hangar. The rain was not falling as heavily as it was when she drove into New Orleans, but heavy, dark clouds promised more to come. The Weather Channel reported that a small tropical wave had formed, and was sitting static in the Gulf bringing the rain inland as feeder bands approached. The rain, forecasted to last at least two days, suited Sasha just fine.

She pulled up next to the hangar with the passenger door closest to the building. She stepped out of the truck and popped the door lock again, and walked inside to turn the lantern on low.

When he heard her return to the truck, Ray briefly considered attempting to run, but in his current condition, he thought better of it. Sasha led him into the hangar the loud clang of the door as the wind caught it and slammed it closed behind them startled him. The hair on the back of his neck stood at attention and his nerves were raw and burning with fear.

Sasha took him to the small cot and sat him down upon it. "Lay down," she instructed.

Ray managed to lie back on the bed and swing his feet onto the foot of the bed. "Roll onto your side," Sasha said, and Ray rolled away from her. She took a key out and unlocked one of the cuffs. Sasha's fist met Ray squarely to his jaw, rendering him unconscious when he attempted to make a break. Sasha laughed at the weak attempt Ray had made against her as she cuffed his hands together in front of him. She easily rolled him onto his back and fastened the cuffs to the headboard with the chain she had installed earlier that day. She then clamped a leg iron to his right ankle and wrapped the chain around the footboard several times before clamping the other iron to his left ankle.

Confident she had him securely restrained Sasha walked back to the truck and changed from her running shoes into leather boots with metal taps. As she stepped back onto the concrete floor of the hangar, the taps echoed loudly in the empty space. Ray would hear her every step as she moved through the hangar, and would know when she approached him. Ray was still unconscious from the blow to his jaw, so Sasha sat at the small table and waited for him to stir.

As she waited for him to regain consciousness, Sasha picked up the scissors and toyed with them, opening and closing their long blades, listening to the sharp rasping sound their movements made. Ray started to stir. She smiled wickedly as Ray fought futilely against the metal that bound him. Sasha watched him struggle for a few minutes then stood and walked toward the bed, the metal taps singing against the concrete. She slowly circled the bed, heels clicking against the rough concrete. Ray struggled against the restraints as he turned his head to follow the sound of her steps.

Sasha stopped at the foot of the cot and leaned down to unlace his Armani shoes, removing them along with his socks, forming a pile of his clothes. She reached behind her body and took the scissors out of her back pocket. Starting at the cuffed hem, Sasha placed the scissors against his clammy skin and began to slice through the fabric of his Italian suit pants. She held him firmly in place as he tried to squirm away from her hands.

"If I were you, I would be careful how I moved. Your clothes may not be the only things that get cut if you continue to struggle," she said with an evil tone to her voice.

Her words paralyzed him with fear, and he barely twitched a muscle as Sasha cut up one leg and then the other. She pulled the thick leather belt from its loops and placed it on the cot beside his body. She made several cuts in the waistband of the fancy pants and then pulled the remnants of the fabric from underneath his body, leaving his lower body covered only by his silk boxers. Sasha ripped open the shirt he was wearing and began cutting up each of the sleeves, until she reached the collar and then peeled the rags off his upper torso. Ray's body betrayed him, his erection pressing against his boxers at Sasha's rough treatment. She picked up the thick belt and doubled it in her hand before lashing it across his bare thighs. His moans were those of pleasure. Sasha's lips formed a snarl and she was tempted to release the fury of her rage on him, however she would not give the pleasure he obviously enjoyed. Ray's body covered with perspiration, and the stench of his fear and excitement filled Sasha's nostrils as she took the clothing and placed them on the pile with his shoes and socks. This would make a nice present for Curtis she thought, as she picked up the pile of rags and placed them in a small bag, removing Ray's wallet and tossing it onto the table.

Sasha looked down at her watch and saw that it was nearly three in the morning. In a few hours, the sun would be rising on the final day of Ray Bellfontaine's life. She knew Ray felt humiliated for being abducted and stripped bare by a woman, yet he was smart enough to maintain his silence.

She sat down at the table again and watched Ray squirm. She knew Ray could feel her eyes on him and felt his terror as he worried what she would do next. She stood and walked over to the cot, dragging the metal chair behind her. The sound of it scraping against the concrete floor sent a visible shudder through Ray as he heard her approach. Sasha sat down beside the cot and placed a booted foot against the bed frame.

"How does it feel to be restrained and blindfolded, Ray?"

"It is not pleasant at all," he answered as calmly as his quivering voice would allow.

"You placed my lover in this very bed, and kept her captive for two days with no concern for how it felt," Sasha growled at him.

"Your lover?" he asked. "Are you talking about that assistant district attorney that was prosecuting Curtis and me?"

"Yes, Kara Stewart, the ex-assistant district attorney, thanks to you," Sasha said, the venom in her voice very evident. "Not only did you hold her prisoner and end her career, but you caused her emotional trauma that will take a long time for her to overcome."

"But, we let her go unharmed," Ray stammered.

"True, there were no physical injuries to her, and you will suffer none by my hand," Sasha said.

She saw Ray relax at this news, and knew he was thinking that Sasha would hold him for a few days and then release him as they had done to her lover. Had he seen the look on Sasha's face at that point, he would have known her plans for him were very different.

"You and your brother have done vile acts against the occupants of New Orleans for the last time. You brag that the law cannot get to you, and it's true, the law has failed to punish you for your crimes, so now you must suffer bayou justice," Sasha said with an evil laugh.

The sound of her laughter caused Ray's bladder to empty, soaking him with urine. She could feel the humiliation burn through him.

"I will leave you now to think about all the horrible things you have done," Sasha said. "I will be visiting your brother tomorrow and will give him any message you wish to send."

"Tell him to do whatever you want him to, to get my release," Ray pleaded close to tears.

"Very well then, I will be back." Sasha walked over to the table to pick up the bag holding Ray's tattered clothing, slipping his wallet in her jacket pocket and went out the door. She could hear Ray crying out for help and smiled as his shouts disappeared within ten feet of the building. No one would hear his pitiful pleas and come to his rescue.

Sasha was pleased with the progression of the plan so far and hoped she would be successful in all her objectives. She mentally reviewed her plans for the coming day as she drove home, which helped to pass the time. The storm had picked up yet again, a large feeder band of rain whipping across the bayou as her wipers worked furiously to keep her field of vision clear.

When she returned to Sugarland, the power had returned, and she took a shower in a downstairs guest room before climbing the stairs to crawl back into bed with Kara. She snuggled into her lover's warm body, and exhausted, slept for several hours.

The weight of Kara sitting down on the side of the bed woke her. Kara was holding two mugs of coffee and offered one to Sasha as she stretched and sat up in the bed.

"Good morning, lover," Kara said with a purr.

"Good morning, tiger," she said, leaning forward to kiss Kara's lips.

"Tiger," Kara said with a laugh.

"Yes, you were quite a tiger in bed last night, my little aggressive lover. Not that I minded in the least," Sasha added with a grin.

"I am not sure what came over me last night, but it felt terrific."

"You were overdue for your dose of serum," Sasha reminded her. "If it has that type of reaction, I may just start encouraging you to hold off for a few extra days."

"Oh, so you enjoyed it that much," Kara teased back.

"I enjoyed it very much indeed," she said as she pushed back the collar of Kara's thick robe to reveal the soft, smooth skin of her right shoulder. Her hair, still damp from the shower, was curly and draped across the top of her shoulders. Sasha let her fingers run through the curls as she smiled at her lover. "In fact, I enjoyed it so much I think I shall have you for breakfast."

Kara took the coffee cup from Sasha and placed them both on the nightstand totally forgotten for the moment. Sasha reached down to untie the belt of Kara's robe and pushed it off her shoulders, watching it fall around Kara's feet. Her right arm encircled Kara's left hip as she pulled her lover down onto the bed and rolled on top of her, smothering her face with soft kisses. "Mmm, you smell good," she said as her tongue licked up Kara's neck.

Kara caressed down Sasha's back and took her ass in her hands as Sasha led them in a slow gyrating dance, their hips moving together in perfect rhythm. Kara could feel her wetness flowing freely underneath Sasha's body and she took her lover's face in her hands. "Are you willing to try something new?" Kara asked as she looked deeply into Sasha's lavender eyes.

"I am always up for something new," Sasha said. "What did you have in mind?"

Kara rolled Sasha onto her back and climbed from the bed to enter the closet. She returned a moment later carrying a leather harness with a strap-on mount and a large dildo. Kara dropped the dildo on the bed and, placing her hands under Sasha's knees, pulled her lover's body over to the edge of the bed. Kara could see the sparkle of excitement in Sasha's eyes as she sat up on the bed and watched Kara raise the leather harness up her legs. When she reached Sasha's thighs with the harness, Sasha stood and allowed Kara to fasten it around her hips. Kara playfully pushed Sasha back onto the bed, reached for the dildo, and slid it onto the mount on the harness.

Kara opened the nightstand drawer and pulled out a tube of lubricating jelly, squeezing some into the palm of her hand. Starting at the base of the dildo, Kara slid her hand upward until she reached the tip of the latex toy. As she pulled upward on the shaft, the harness straps placed pressure on Sasha's outer lips and rubbed across her clit, stirring a desire deep in her loins. Kara went to the bathroom to wash her hands then returned to the bed to straddle Sasha's hips, the dildo resting against the mound of soft curls between her thighs. She leaned forward to kiss Sasha deeply, her hands covering her breasts, kneading them then twisting her nipples between her fingers as her tongue probed deeply in Sasha's mouth.

Sasha could feel Kara's arousal as her juices ran down her thighs and although Sasha was eager to fuck Kara, she allowed her lover to choose the first position of their lovemaking. Sasha was not at all surprised when Kara leaned forward, raising her hips and whispered in her ear, "Open my lips, lover."

She reached down between Kara's thighs and gently spread the soaked lips that concealed the core of her lover's desire. As Kara lowered her hips, Sasha guided the tip of the dildo into Kara's opening, and then placed her hands on her lover's trembling thighs. The feral look had returned to Kara's eyes as she locked her gaze with Sasha while she lowered her body fully onto the dildo. The toy stretched her tight opening, but the sensation was immensely pleasurable for Kara, who was moaning softly. Kara placed her hands on either side of Sasha's shoulders and raised her body, slowly withdrawing the dildo then she lowered it again, impaling her body with the love toy. The faster she moved, the smoother the toy slid into her, each of her thrusts providing stimulation to Sasha's body as well as her own.

Sasha watched Kara's eyes glaze over with passion as she drove her hips onto the toy and rode Sasha's body into a frenzy of pleasure. Kara's gasps mixed with groans of pleasure as Sasha's fingers dug into her skin when her hands pulled Kara's hips down onto her body. Sasha was having a difficult time holding back her climax and was relieved when she felt the first wave of shudders pass through Kara. As their bodies released together Kara's hips ground wildly into Sasha, waves of pleasure crashed through her body and she collapsed onto Sasha's chest.

Sasha lifted Kara off the toy and moved from the bed. She positioned Kara on her knees at the edge of the bed, spreading Kara's thighs wide enough to lower her body to the perfect height. The weight of the toy dangling between her thighs put pressure on her clit as she moved closer to the bed. Sasha reached between Kara's thighs and guided the toy to her entrance, penetrating her with one deep thrust as Kara cried out in pleasure. She could feel the heat of Kara's ass as it pressed against her groin. She remained buried deep inside Kara as her hands reached underneath to fondle her lover's swollen, erect nipples. "You like this don't you?" Sasha said as she painfully twisted Kara's nipples.

"Oh yes, Sasha, please fuck me," she begged.

Sasha released her grip on Kara's nipples and placed her hands on Kara's hips, holding them in place as she slowly withdrew the dildo nearly its full length. Sasha then pulled them back into her loins as she thrust her hips forward, driving the toy deep into Kara. She built up to a smooth, comfortable rhythm, their bodies flowing together in a lustful dance as their cries filled the room.

Each thrust of her hips sent a new wave of pleasure through her, building to new heights for Sasha as she relinquished control of herself to her most primal instincts. Never before had Sasha felt the feelings of power, of domination, of giving and receiving such explosive pleasure and her senses reeled in response. Both she and Kara came with violent spasms and they collapsed in a sweaty tangled heap on the bed.

Sasha carefully withdrew from Kara and rolled onto her back, her heart racing wildly and her lungs struggling for air. She turned her head and found tears flowing down Kara's cheek, the smile on her face telling Sasha they were tears of complete rapture. Sasha reached over with a shaking hand and wiped the tears away with her thumb. "I love you," she whispered.

"I love you too, Sasha," Kara said as she moved closer and placed her head on Sasha's shoulder.

Sasha draped a protective arm over Kara's shoulder and held her close as their hearts raced together.

They fell asleep entwined in one another's arms. When they awoke again, Kara climbed from the bed, removed the harness from Sasha's hips, and led her into a hot shower.

Afterward, Sasha sat on the bed wrapped in a robe and watched as Kara dressed for work.

"Did you hunt last night?" Kara asked.

"Yes, but the weather had everyone locked up tight," Sasha said. "I will try again tonight."

"This weather doesn't look like it is going to change much today," Kara said as she looked out the window. "Everything is going to be soaked for days."

Sasha reached out, circled Kara's waist, and pulled her close. "Soaked isn't always a bad thing," she teased as her hand crept up Kara's thigh.

"Umm, you are so right about that," Kara said as she leaned down to kiss Sasha. "I hope you plan on getting me soaked again tonight," she said as she nuzzled into Sasha's neck.

"You really enjoyed that didn't you?" Sasha asked.

"Just as much as you did," Kara said with a grin.

"You will definitely be soaked again tonight then." Sasha cupped Kara's ass in her hands. "I absolutely loved sharing that with you," she admitted.

"Keep this up and I will not make it in to work at all today," Kara said as she sucked the lobe of Sasha's ear in her hot mouth.

"You had better leave now then," Sasha said, "before I decide to ravish you all day long."

Kara kissed her one final time and then left the room. Sasha watched from the window as she raced toward her sports car and headed for town. Going to the closet Sasha pulled on a pair of jeans and a long-sleeved shirt, slipping on a pair of loafers before she headed down the stairs. She poured a large travel mug full of coffee and headed out into the rain.

Still reeling from the pleasure she and Kara had shared earlier, Sasha pulled onto the hard road and headed north.

Chapter 20

Sasha wound her way through the flooded streets until she reached the interstate and headed north to Baton Rouge. The rain was still coming down in sheets, so the traffic was light and she made good time despite the weather. As she drove, Sasha wasn't exactly sure where she was going, but she knew once she reached the spot she would know, so she let her instincts guide her.

She turned onto a county road just south of Baton Rouge and headed west. There seemed to be more bridges than roadways as she drove deeper into the swamplands. She knew the swampy waters were full of alligators and other creatures that would assist in removing a body as evidence and she grinned at the thought. Sasha slowed the truck when she spied an old barn just off the road and found a small trail that would lead her to the rustic building. She pulled onto the trail, using her truck to bulldoze the weeds that had overtaken the worn, rutted path. It didn't look like anyone had been here in ages, which would be perfect for Sasha's plan.

Sasha pulled up next to the old barn and carefully opened the door, the hinges creaking loudly from disuse. She stepped inside to find that the building was virtually intact, with no evidence of holes in the roof or walls. The faint sunlight filled the room, coming through several small windows from above. She could still smell a trace of the hay that must have been stored in the building at one time, and looking up she could make out a loft with hay still scattered across its floor. A slight breeze wafted through the door she had left open, and Sasha could see particles of dust float through the sunlight and settle on the floor. She approached the ladder leading up into the loft and climbed it carefully, unsure of its strength.

Sasha raised her head to gaze across the open space, grinning and feeling incredibly wicked when she spied a small chair sitting near the loft door. She remembered how the police tracked Kara down using the cell phone given to her by her captors. A devilish grin covered her face as she had planned to use Ray's cell phone to lead Curtis on a wild goose chase. Seeing the chair, though, Sasha couldn't help but play a cruel trick on Curtis. She rummaged around the loft until she found a length of rope that would serve her purpose.

Working quickly, she fashioned a hangman's noose, and after looping the rope over one of the loft's support beams, she tied the rope to a post. She then moved the chair underneath the rope and reached for Ray's cell phone. She flipped it open and found the battery fully charged and was pleased at the strong signal, given the remoteness of the area. Sasha snapped a picture of the empty chair and hangman's noose and sent it to Curtis. There were several voice mail messages showing on the display and each of them flashed Curtis's name. She pushed the redial number, dialing up Curtis's cell phone and waited until he answered.

"Hello," Curtis said. "Ray, is that you?"

No answer came from the other end of the phone.

"Who is this and what have you done with Ray?" Curtis's angry voice demanded.

Sasha couldn't help but let out a soft chuckle.

Curtis's blood ran cold when he heard the laughter. He knew immediately that the woman haunting his dreams made the sound. "You bitch! I will make sure you pay for this," Curtis threatened.

Sasha closed the phone, ending the call, and laid it on the seat of the chair.

The phone began to ring and Sasha opened it again and left it sitting open on the chair. She walked to the ladder and climbed back down to the floor of the barn. As she stepped out into the drizzling rain, Sasha wondered how long it would take for one of Curtis's henchmen to track down the cell signal, though she would be long gone from the area before they did.

†

Curtis left the phone open to maintain contact with Ray's phone as he yelled for one of his bodyguards.

"Get on the phone and have that woman at the police station track down Ray's phone," he sharply said.

"Yes, sir," the man said as he rushed from the room and made his call.

Curtis paced the room while he waited. He knew that whatever had happened to Ray could not be good if that woman was involved. He would have to work quickly to win his brother's freedom back then he would find out who she was and ensure she came to a miserable end. He growled and awaited news from his guard.

When the man walked back into the room, Curtis spun on his heel. "Did she get it?" he asked.

"She is working on it and will call us back with the coordinates as soon as she has a line on his whereabouts," the man said. He shivered as Curtis fixed his icy glare on him and the man turned to leave the room.

"Get the car ready, so we can be on the move as soon as we get her call," Curtis commanded.

"Yes, sir," the man said and gladly left the room, eager to escape Curtis's wrath.

Curtis opened his desk drawer, pulled out a nickel-plated nine millimeter, and checked the clip. Finding it full, he shoved it sharply into the handle of the gun and reached back into the drawer for an extra clip. He would be well prepared in case the woman had an accomplice or several. They would all pay dearly for their actions against the Bellfontaines. His hands shook with rage as he walked over to the small bar and poured a large shot of Jack Daniels and downed it in one long gulp.

Fifteen minutes later, the guard rushed back into the room. "We've got it," he said. "Ray is up close to Baton Rouge."

"Let's get moving then," Curtis said as he picked up the gun and tucked it into the waistband of his pants.

The second guard was waiting in the car in the front driveway and had just finished entering the GPS coordinates into the onboard receiver when the door closed behind Curtis.

"Get moving," Curtis said roughly as he settled into the backseat, mumbling obscenities under his breath.

The second guard wisely took the passenger seat and monitored the tracking on the GPS as they weaved through New Orleans and headed out of town.

†

Sasha pulled her truck back onto the interstate from the county road and turned toward New Orleans. As she drove south, she kept her eyes open for Curtis's limousine, knowing he would not hesitate to use every resource available to find his brother. Nearly an hour later, she felt the tingle of Curtis's presence. Peering across the median of the interstate, she caught a glimpse of the long black car through a grove of trees. She reached out to Curtis with her mind and whispered, *you had better hurry his time is running out.*

"Damn you," she heard Curtis say in her mind. She could almost feel the glare he tossed at the tracking system as he urged his driver faster.

Sasha chuckled and kept on driving as the skyline of New Orleans came into view. She drove through town and crossed the river as the noon hour approached. Sasha had planned to drive down to Grand Isle to check on her captive and feed him a sandwich, while Curtis drove around the state in a panic to find his brother. Instead, she turned around to drive back to Curtis's home, pulling right up the driveway to the front door. She put the truck in park and picked up the bag of tattered clothing, which she carried to the house and left on the doormat. What a nice present Curtis would have when he returned from his wild goose chase.

Crossing the bridge again, Sasha listened to the thump of the windshield wipers as they methodically cleared the rain from the glass. Dark thunderclouds were again forming, promising a night of heavy rains. Sasha drove the remainder of the route, singing along with the upbeat jazz playing on her radio. As she turned off the road onto the path that would lead her to the hangar, Sasha turned the music off and allowed her anger to simmer before she entered the building.

Ray lay motionless on the cot as she entered the room, but turned his head toward the sound of her steps. "Who is it?" he stammered, his voice weak from his cries for help.

"It is just me coming to check on you," Sasha said. "Are you ready for something to eat?"

"Yes, please," Ray said, humbled by her offer.

Sasha sat at the small table and opened the cooler. She pulled out condiments and bologna to prepare sandwiches. She placed the sandwiches on paper towels and walked over to the cot. She pulled a set of keys out of her pocket as she reached for the leg irons. "Do you need to use the restroom?" she asked as she unlocked one ankle cuff and then untangled the chain from around the foot bar. Ray nodded his head. She returned the cuff to his ankle to keep him shackled as she released the cuffs from above his head.

"Sit up and I will lead you to the restroom," Sasha instructed.

Ray sat up on the side of the cot and Sasha helped him to his feet. She led him into the small bathroom and positioned him in front of the toilet. "The toilet is in front of you and the sink is to your right," she said as she leaned against the doorframe.

Ray tried to reach behind his head to remove the sack from his head. "I would not advise that," Sasha cautioned from the doorway.

Ray immediately dropped his hands and used the toilet before sidestepping to the sink to wash his hands. Sasha led him to the table and sat him down before reaching into her pocket and pulling the scissors out once again. She placed her arm around his head as she leaned in and cut a large slit in the sack to allow him to eat the sandwich.

"There is a sandwich in front of you and a cold drink sitting to the right," Sasha said as she sat down opposite of Ray. She watched with pleasure as Ray's hands located the sandwich. He greedily raised it to his mouth and took a large bite. Sasha picked up her sandwich, eating it slowly as Ray devoured the sandwich and downed half the cold drink in one gulp.

"Here is another," Sasha said, pushing another sandwich across the table to him.

"Thank you," Ray mumbled his appreciation.

"You are welcome," Sasha said.

"Did you talk to my brother?" Ray asked.

"Not exactly," Sasha said with a low throaty chuckle, "though we did communicate."

"Your brother is aggressively searching for you at this moment, unfortunately he is headed in the wrong direction," Sasha said. "I did leave him a few little presents that will keep him looking for you though."

"I am not sure I understand what you mean," Ray admitted.

"Of course you wouldn't, Ray, you were not meant to," she said. "Do you remember the clever little trick of leaving a cell phone for Kara to use when you released her?"

"Yes, we figured she could make a nine-one-one call and the authorities could track her from the cell signal," Ray answered.

"Well, I sort of used that knowledge today, except with a few modifications," Sasha said. "I knew I could rely on your brother using his police contacts to track down your cell signal, so we went on a little adventure."

"What are you talking about?" Ray asked confused by what Sasha was telling him.

"Oh, I would say right about now Curtis has tracked your cell phone down and you are several hundred miles south of it," Sasha said unable to suppress her laugh. "You see I drove just outside of Baton Rouge and called your dear brother from there and left the connection open so he could have the signal traced."

"You are such an evil bitch," Ray said.

Sasha saw his flinch when he realized he had called her a bitch.

"Why thank you," Sasha teased. "My only regret is not being there to see his face when Curtis realizes how badly he has been fooled by one of his own tricks."

"What are you going to do with me?" Ray asked the fear very evident in his voice.

"We are going to go for a little ride tonight and then I am going to let you go," Sasha answered him honestly.

"Why not just do it now?"

"Because I have not finished with you yet," Sasha said as she stood and walked around the table. She grabbed Ray roughly by the arm and pulled him from the chair, leading him back to the cot.

Pushing him down on the bed she secured the cuffs above his head again and then his legs to the end of the bed.

"I will be back later and we will play," Sasha said. She spun on her heel and left the room, the sound of her taps clicking on the concrete floor.

†

Curtis and his men followed the coordinates on the GPS to a small barn just west of Baton Rouge. All three men pulled their pistols as they cautiously approached the building. One of the guards snatched open the rusty door and they all rushed into the empty barn, scattering across the space. They squinted in the dim light as they searched the room for any sign of Ray or his captors. The building was empty and silent except for a dull beeping noise. When the men finally heard the sound, they moved toward the ladder leading to the loft and climbed one after another.

Curtis had gone second after one of the guards. He cursed in rage as the empty room came into view, and he realized she had used his own trick to dupe him. He walked over to the chair and picked up Ray's cell, kicking the empty chair across the room.

"This is one seriously sick bitch," Curtis said to his shocked guards. "When I find her she will regret ever hearing the name Bellfontaine," he said as he headed back to the ladder.

"What now, boss?" one guard asked.

"Home for now," Curtis said. "We will have to wait to hear from her to find out what she wants." Curtis was afraid, though, he already knew the answer.

He remembered the words Lady Serena had spoken to him about the strange, powerful one who had him marked for death and his blood ran cold.

†

Sasha drove home and decided to take a short nap before Kara came home for the evening. Marie had supper warming for them. They would eat dinner and enjoy a relaxing evening before she returned to the hangar to deal with Ray for the final time.

157

Chapter 21

Sasha stripped and crawled between the fresh, clean sheets and fell asleep almost instantly. The last few weeks had been taxing on her and she had not realized how little sleep she had actually had until her head hit the pillow. Her dreams were a convoluted mixture of Milly and Kara, both of happiness and sadness. Sasha roamed the bed restlessly and entwined in the sheets.

†

Sasha was sleeping on her stomach, uncovered from the waist up when Kara entered the room later that evening.

Kara had experienced few opportunities to observe Sasha privately, so she sat next to the bed and watched as her lover softly purred in her sleep. She could tell Sasha was dreaming by the smile playing across her lips, and she cautiously slipped into her dreams. Kara had never invaded the privacy of Sasha's dreams and her curiosity got the better of her. She was startled at first as she witnessed Sasha kissing a beautiful blond woman. Kara's instincts told her to flee, and she considered briefly halting her invasion of Sasha's dreams, then as they broke the kiss, Kara saw that she was dreaming of Milly. The beauty of the portrait in the parlor fell short in portraying the absolute beauty of the woman who was now resting in Sasha's arms. For a moment, Kara felt a pang of jealousy. Sasha loved her completely, but Kara understood that a part of Sasha died along with Milly so many years ago.

She sighed as she watched them make love under the ancient oak near the artesian well, a spot that she and Sasha had ridden past on many occasions. They had stopped long enough to water the horses and get a drink of the refreshing water. Now witnessing the dream before her eyes, Kara understood why Sasha never stayed long in that spot. The place held for her precious memories of Milly, and she would not challenge that fact. Turning away from the dream, Kara walked downstairs to the kitchen to allow Sasha the privacy of her most personal thoughts.

Opening the oven door, Kara found the source of the delicious smell that assaulted her nose as soon as she reached the bottom of the stairs. Marie had fried chicken for dinner and the golden crispy-coated meat was warming on a platter next to a half dozen fresh biscuits. On top of the stove was a pot with fresh green beans and a fry skillet full of baked sweet corn. Kara went to the cupboard and took down two place settings, arranging them on the small kitchen table, then took butter and honey from the refrigerator to place on the table. She was putting ice in glasses for the tea when she looked up to find Sasha leaning against the doorframe, watching her, still flushed from her dreams.

Sasha's lips curled into a smile as she said, "Welcome home, darling."

"Hi there, sexy," Kara answered.

"Why didn't you wake me when you came home?" Sasha asked.

"You were sleeping so peacefully I did not want to disturb you," Kara said, her memory of Sasha's dream still fresh in her mind.

"I can't believe how easily I fell asleep this afternoon."

"Well, you are past due for a feeding," Kara said, reminding Sasha that it was indeed time to hunt.

"Maybe I will get lucky tonight," Sasha said as she looked out the window. "Is it still raining out?"

"It was not coming down too hard when I came home, so maybe the weather is beginning to clear some," she said. "There is promise of a brilliant full moon tonight as well, so maybe you will be blessed in your hunt."

Kara was leaning back against the counter as Sasha approached, a gleam of mischief in her eyes. She stopped in front of her and brushed the hair away from Kara's neck as she lowered her mouth to plant a soft kiss on her neck. The mere touch of Sasha's lips on her body sent flames of desire licking throughout

Kara's body and she shuddered under her kiss. Sasha's hands moved upward to rest along each side of Kara's jawline as she slowly kissed her way to her lover's moist waiting lips. Sasha nibbled on her lower lip causing Kara to moan with pleasure as Sasha pressed her against the counter with her hips.

Kara's hands slid down to circle Sasha's hips and pull her lover closer as she parted her lips and invited Sasha's tongue into her mouth. The passion of the kiss grew like wildfire as their hands explored one another's body, caressing, touching, and teasing strokes. Sasha located the zipper on the back of Kara's skirt and lowered it, allowing the fabric to float down her lover's body to the floor. Her fingers manipulated the buttons on her silky blouse and within seconds, Kara's breasts were exposed. Sasha's hands and then her hungry mouth covered the luscious mounds. Opening the blouse further, Sasha reached between her breasts to loosen the fastener on her bra as her lips kissed down Kara's neck. Her hands gently cupped the soft, firm breasts while her fingers stroked across the rapidly growing nipples.

Sasha lifted Kara onto the counter. Her mouth covered Kara's left breast with soft kisses as her hand gently kneaded the sensitive flesh. Kara tossed her head back, her hair flowing down her shoulders, her back arching, filling Sasha's mouth fully with her soft breast. For a fleeting moment, Kara foolishly wondered if Sasha's dream had left her in such an amorous mood, until the sensations her body was experiencing erased all thought from her mind, but the fulfilling of that need.

Kara rested back against the cupboard, her hands on the countertop for support as Sasha's kisses moved lower down her body. Sasha slowly removed Kara's silk panties and lifted her knees to rest upon her shoulders. She knelt down to cover Kara's lower lips with tender kisses as her tongue probed the delicious wetness. Kara shivered as Sasha's hot tongue brushed across her clit and she growled her pleasure as Sasha slowly circled the pulsing button. Sasha breathed deeply of the sensual scent of Kara's excitement as the taste lingered on her lips and tongue.

Sasha's fingers traced the outside of Kara's lips, coating them with her wetness before penetrating her with two long fingers. Her fingers glided through the silky wetness until they were deep inside Kara, then Sasha curled her fingers, the tips stroking the quivering walls within her core. Sasha opened and closed her fingers, as Kara's groans grew louder. She covered Kara's clit with a deep kiss. Sasha watched as Kara's hands covered her breasts, her fingers twisting and tugging at her swollen nipples. Sasha's tongue swirled around Kara's clit as the first quake of orgasm rippled through Kara's body. Her fingers slid smoothly in and out of Kara as the additional moisture created a velvet tunnel for her movement and she increased the rhythm of her thrusts. Kara's body shook violently as she reached her climax, her fingers now buried in Sasha's hair, holding her mouth on her clit as the flood of her juices ran down Sasha's wrist.

Sasha's tongue licked softly as Kara continued to tremor and then her body began to calm. She lowered Kara's legs back onto the counter and wrapped her arms around Kara's waist as she leaned into her lover for a tender kiss.

"That was the most delicious appetizer I have ever had," Sasha said, her eyes sparkling with mischief.

"Oh my God, baby, that was intense," she said, her eyes still slightly glazed.

"Why don't you go upstairs and change into something more comfortable while I serve dinner," Sasha suggested as she helped Kara down from the counter and handed her the skirt and panties she had removed.

She leaned down and kissed Kara before sending her upstairs. She washed her hands and went about the kitchen, setting the food on the table and pouring drinks for each of them. Sasha finished her tasks and sat patiently awaiting Kara's return.

✝

Kara carefully ascended the stairs, her knees still weak from the intense pleasure she had received from Sasha. She dropped her clothing into the hamper and slipped on a pair of Sasha's sweat pants and a baggy shirt then went to the bathroom to freshen up a bit. When she caught her reflection in the mirror, she was not surprised to see a smile spreading across her face.

When she walked into the kitchen, Sasha handed her a vial of serum, which she downed before sitting at the table.

"Thanks, Sasha," she said as she dropped the empty vial in the trash.

"You are most welcome, my love."

†

After their meal, they sat out on the porch in the swing, and listened to the gentle rainfall on the tin roof. Kara rested her head on Sasha's shoulder and snuggled into her lover's body. Sasha rocked them slowly as Kara's body relaxed and fell asleep in the comfort of Sasha's body. She listened to the soft humming sound Kara made as she slept and smiled knowing Kara would sleep well tonight. Sasha carefully lifted Kara into her arms and carried her upstairs to bed. She covered her lover with the bed linens and turned out the light before she turned to leave.

Kara stirred from her slumber as Sasha turned off the light. "Hurry back to me, lover," she whispered.

"I will be back before you know it," Sasha said as she bent down to kiss Kara.

"Good luck with your hunting," Kara said as Sasha turned to go.

"I love you," Sasha said and walked from the room.

Sasha walked to her truck and smiled as she drove south and the rain began to pick up once more.

The full moon rose just as Kara had promised and Sasha watched the dark clouds pass in front of it as she drove. There was no other traffic on the road and she relaxed as she made her way to Grand Isle. When she turned off the hard road, Sasha stopped the truck, opened the glove box, and pulled out the pistol James had loaned her after Kara's abduction. She was sure she would not need to use it, but still she tucked it in the waist of her jeans just in case her plan went awry. She put the truck in gear and drove the short distance remaining to the hangar.

Sasha parked the truck and popped the lock on the door to the hangar. Ray turned at the sound of her steps and asked, "Is that you?"

"Of course it is me, Ray, who else did you think it would be? Did you really think Curtis would have the brains to figure out your location to come and rescue you?" she cruelly asked.

Ray remained silent and could only listen as Sasha packed up the cooler and other supplies and carried them to the truck, placing them in the bed. When she returned Sasha took the leg irons off Ray's ankles and told him, "Roll over onto your side."

She smiled as Ray turned onto his side, knowing he remembered the force of her fist when he resisted her efforts. Sasha released a cuff on one wrist, and then snapped it locked again, securing his arms behind his back. "Are you ready to go home?"

"Yes, I am," he said, whimpering as she sat him up on the edge of the bed.

"Very soon," Sasha said as she pulled him to his feet. "We will see just how good you are at finding your way home." Sasha chuckled.

She led Ray from the building, pulling the door closed behind them and then placed him in the passenger seat of the truck. She could smell his fear as she flipped the child lock on the door and walked around the truck. She slipped behind the wheel and drove away from the hangar. When she reached the paved road, she turned right instead of left, which would have taken her back toward New Orleans, and drove deeper into the bayou.

They drove in silence for thirty minutes until she pulled off the road, onto a smaller path. She drove slowly over the rough, rutted path for nearly twenty minutes. Sasha had been lucky to find this path and it would serve her purpose very well. "Are you ready to play a game, Ray?" Sasha asked the man who sat trembling in his seat.

"What are you talking about?" he asked with a noticeable tremor in his voice.

"Well, as close as I can guess I would say we are about ten miles from the hard road that will lead you back to New Orleans," she said. "Once you reach it, I am sure you can stop a passing car and with your massive wealth buy yourself a ride back to New Orleans."

"So all I have to do is find my way back?" Ray asked, confused.

"Well, it will be a bit more difficult than that," Sasha said with a hard edge to her voice. "You have to find your way back before I find you," she said with a growl. "I will give you a ten-minute head start though, so I figure that is fair."

"What happens if you catch me?"

"I really don't think you want to know that answer, Ray," Sasha said as she watched him shiver. "Are you ready?"

"As ready as I can be."

Sasha read his thoughts as he answered with a false sense of confidence. After all, she was really just a woman and he should be able to outdistance her with a head start.

"Good," Sasha said as she opened her door and walked around to the passenger door. "Let's go then." She pulled him from the truck and through the falling rain led him deeper into the dense woods.

Chapter 22

Dark thunderclouds dimmed the light from the full moon and Sasha could see lightning flashes in the distance. In a few more minutes, she was sure the storm would be on them, further fueling Ray's frustration as he struggled to find his way through the bayou. The crickets and frogs played their nocturnal concert and, in the distance, a bull alligator called out for a mate. The ground, even more soaked by the falling rain, squished underneath their steps.

She reached a cypress knot she had found on a previous venture, and brought Ray to a stop. Sasha untied the bag and lifted it over his head, allowing Ray to see her face for the first time. "Hello, Ray," Sasha said as he looked into her face.

"Uh, hello."

✝

Ray looked around and found himself surrounded by moss-covered cypress. The rain certainly did not help his vision, and he could hear the thunder approaching quickly. This woman was truly evil he thought as he looked down and remembered he was wearing only his silk boxers. Ray looked back into Sasha's face and her eyes glowed with the delight she was enjoying playing her little game with him. Ray was so obtuse he did not realize that Sasha would never have revealed her identity to him if she dared think he would make it out of the bayou tonight. He thought to himself how much pleasure he would take in hunting her down to make her pay for treating him this way once he made it back to New Orleans and could reunite with Curtis.

✝

Sasha looked down at her wrist and saw the indigo glow of her watch as it read eleven fifty. It would be midnight in ten minutes and time to begin her hunt. She walked over to Ray, took a key from her pocket, and removed the cuffs from his wrists. She noticed the gold onyx pinky ring on his finger and an idea came to her to further taunt Curtis, and she smiled to herself. "Time to go, Ray. Remember you only have a ten-minute head start beginning now," she said as she pressed a button on her watch to initiate the timer. "Good luck, Ray," she said, leaning back against the cypress knot.

Ray stupidly took a step toward Sasha. She reached behind her back, pulling out the pistol James had loaned her and waved it at him, stopping him dead in his tracks. "Did you really think I would make it that easy for you?" she asked with a chuckle.

"You bitch," Ray snarled then turned away and started walking deeper into the bayou.

"I will be seeing you very soon," she called after him, grinning wickedly as she watched him disappear from sight, heading in the opposite direction from the road.

✝

The sound of her voice made his blood run cold. His body coated with nervous sweat that mixed with the rain to flow down his near naked body. He tried his best to choke back the panic that threatened to overcome him as he continued to pick his way through the dark night. Each step became a struggle, his feet sinking into the soggy ground, sapping the energy from his legs as the limbs from the surrounding brush tore at his bare flesh. It was not long before Ray's body, covered with welts and small scratches filled the night air with the scent of his blood.

✝

Sasha watched the timer, eager to begin her hunt. She had returned the pistol to her waistband and pulled her ball cap down over her eyes as the rain began to fall harder. She dipped inside Ray's brain and said *your time is almost up and you are heading the wrong direction.*

†

Ray could feel her suggestion in his mind, but he would not allow her to control him any longer. He felt confident that he had moved in the right direction and was sure she was just trying to fuck with his mind. He was silently cursing the evil woman when his left foot disappeared and he fell forward into a bog of quicksand. Ray's initial reaction of panic caused him to flail his arms, causing his body to sink deeper in the bog. When Ray realized the predicament he was in he stopped moving to prevent slipping further into the heavy, thick mud. His eyes came to rest on a cypress root that was a mere six inches from his right hand and he struggled through the thick bog until his fingers brushed against its rough texture. Garnering his strength, he pulled his body slowly from the bog and laid panting, half in and half out of the bog. When his breathing quieted, he heard the distant beeping of the timer echoing through the woods. The sound had to be a trick of his mind. He was sure he had traveled far enough from the woman that he should not be hearing that sound.

†

Sasha gazed up at the full moon barely visible through the dark clouds. Lightning was flashing close now and the rumbling of thunder grew louder with each passing minute. She let the beep of the timer continue for nearly two minutes to allow the sound to reach Ray's ears through the rain and thunder. Her hands had been playing with the cuffs while she waited for the time to pass and now that it had, she snapped the cuffs closed and hung them on a branch.

Each time lightning flashed, she could see the metal glow in the bright light. She decided to leave them hanging there as a memorial to Ray's final resting spot as she slowly walked into the

167

woods. *I am coming for you now, Ray* she projected into the terrified man's brain.

†

Sasha's message urged Ray to pull the rest of his body, covered with the thick, clinging mud, from the bog. He rose to his feet and stumbled blindly away from the bog. As much as he hated the thought, he would have to slow down and be more careful where he was walking to prevent sinking into another bog of quicksand. There were many dangers in the bayou he would need to be cautious of and quicksand bogs became the least of his worries when he heard a large splash in a body of water somewhere off to his left.

He picked up a large branch and used it as a walking stick as he turned to his right to continue his journey. Lightning crackled close around him, blinding him temporarily as he slowly made his way through the bayou. Ray ducked when he saw a large black shadow flying toward him. He felt the flapping of wings pass a foot above his head as a large bird soared past him. Seconds later Ray heard the loud cry of a screech owl coming from a tree not far behind him. Unnerved by the sound he fought against the panic that urged him to run away from the sound as quickly as he could. Instead, he gripped his walking stick tighter and continued on his way.

The rain was coming down hard, and with each step, Ray sank down past his ankles in the mud and water, making a loud sucking sound as he pulled forward for his next step. Ray smelled sulfur in the air just seconds before a bolt of lightning struck a tree twenty yards ahead of him, making his hair stand on end. He felt the ground shudder with the impact as sparks lit up the limbs of the crooked oak like an electrified scarecrow.

He could hear the woman's evil laugh and Ray thought the devil herself had come to claim him. He turned away from the burning tree and ran wildly through a thicket. When Ray stopped running, he looked around and found himself standing on the only piece of solid ground his eyes could make out within his limited field of vision.

168

†

Sasha could not see Ray yet, but she could hear him thrashing about not too far ahead of her, and she could smell the stench of his fear lingering in the air as she easily tracked his path. She did not need her immortal senses to tell her Ray was near, even though she could hear his heart threatening to pound its way out of his chest. Sasha also picked up the faint heartbeat of another human who was approaching from the west. She turned toward that sound, leaving Ray's trail to meet the poor soul who would become her feast this night.

Sasha moved quietly through the swamp until she could see the glow of a lantern ahead. She followed the glow of the soft light until she saw a small flat keel and a man using a pole to propel it down a small inlet leading from the swamp. Only a poacher would be out on a night like this, certain that the Fish and Game Officers wouldn't be out in the weather. She followed his progress as he moved closer to solid ground with each stroke of his pole. Sasha ran several steps and launched herself onto the keel, landing safely two steps away from the shocked man. Sasha's fangs glowed white-hot as she stepped toward the man and his screams resonated through the swamp as she sank her teeth into his neck, ripping it open and silencing him forever. Sasha drank greedily from the man as her blood lust coursed through her veins, satisfying the need burning in her stomach.

†

Ray shook with dread at the sound of the horrifying scream that pierced the air followed by dead silence. He sensed movement to his right and he cautiously turned. He strained to focus his eyes and they flew wide open in terror as he made out the moving shape. Ray was barely two feet away from a roiling mass of water moccasins coiled in a copulating ball. Twenty or more of the aggressive snakes were wound up in the tight mass. Ray was certain there would be others joining the massive orgy as the scent of their mating spread across the air.

†

Sasha finished draining the poacher's body, which hung limp in her arms. The small boat had continued to float as she feasted, and when she turned back toward the lantern, she saw several pairs of red and green eyes glowing just above the surface of the water. She lifted the dead body and tossed it in front of the boat, watching as the eyes began to move toward the offering she had made. Sasha watched as the body disappeared under the water and torn apart by four sets of razor sharp teeth.

†

The loud splash of the something striking the water forced Ray from his frozen stance he turned away from the mass of snakes. His second step left him in a smaller ball of the mating snakes. They immediately struck out at the invader, several sets of fangs penetrating his ankle before he could react. Ray cried out in agony as he reached into the swirling mass, grabbing the ball and tossing it away from his body. Another set of fangs latched onto his forearm and broke off in his flesh as Ray flung the snake as far as he could. He stumbled forward, willing his feet to move him away from the horror of the snakes.

Unfortunately, for Ray, the venom of the moccasin was not immediately fatal and it would be a short while before he would die from the bites. Praying he could make it to the road and seek aid before that occurred, Ray took off at a full run, oblivious to any further danger the swamp had in store for him. Ray felt the poison of the venom burning in his body, and his ankle and forearm swelled to the point of cracking through his skin in a matter of minutes. His vision began to blur as he ran and soon he was stumblingly blindly through the swamp.

†

Sasha jumped back to the shore and returned the way she had come. She could hear Ray's cries for help as she moved closer to his location and when he finally came into sight, Sasha's enhanced eyesight allowed her to see the red, swollen flesh where the snakes had attacked. She moved within ten feet and climbed onto a cypress stump to witness his struggle.

"Do you know how ironic this is?" she asked Ray.

Ray could make out her voice, but he was unable to trace its location. "Please, help me," he begged as hot tears flowed down his swollen face.

"Even if I could, Ray, I would not help you," she said. "Justice is served. One snake taken down by many," she said then laughed.

"Are you sightless yet, Ray?" she cruelly asked. "Once the venom makes it into that thick skull of yours, Ray, you will begin having visions. I hope they are comparable to the evil you and your brother have shed on the city for the past twenty years."

Sasha watched as Ray tried to locate her position with his ears, but he remained facing the opposite direction from where she sat.

The sound of her laughter rang in his ears and Ray howled his rage at the woman who mocked him.

He dropped to his knees and groped about him in search of something he could use for a weapon. Ray gasped in horror when he found the pain and swelling from the numerous bites was paralyzing his fine motor control. His hand rested on a nice branch that would have made a wicked good club, if only he could close his fingers around it. He heard Sasha laugh as he realized his body was shutting down.

✝

Sasha caught a glimpse of the ring shining on Ray's left hand. She stepped down from the stump and walked over to him. The black onyx ring with a gold B emblazoned on it was no doubt a cherished piece of family jewelry she thought as she reached down and pulled the ring from his hand.

"This will make a nice gift for Curtis," she said and then returned to her seat above Ray.

"Curtis," she heard him say weakly.

"Don't worry, Ray, your brother will be joining you soon," Sasha said with a wicked laugh.

Sasha watched as Ray's body collapsed on the ground and began to convulse with seizures. The locations of the bites split open with his movements and blood began to weep from his body. The thrashing of his body had alerted the carnivorous creatures of the swamp to his presence. Now they moved closer as the scent of his blood reached their nostrils, carried by the rainwater that washed his body. The more humane side of Sasha hoped Ray's life would expire before the three alligators that had him surrounded would move in for the kill.

Sasha watched as they crept closer. She listened as Ray's heart raced uncontrollably until it went into arrest and he ceased to move. No longer perceived as a threat the large carnivores raced to his body. Sasha watched the largest drag him back into the water followed closely by the other two. In a matter of minutes, Ray Bellfontaine was no more. Sasha climbed down from the stump, sliding his ring into her pocket and walked back toward the truck. There was one more task to complete and then she could join Kara in their warm bed.

Sasha followed the light of the bright full moon no longer obscured by the dark clouds as it lit up the woods. She returned to the cypress tree that held the cuffs. They hung there like a hangman's noose dangling in the soft breeze. One day someone would run across the cuffs, but Sasha knew no poacher or bayou resident would touch them as Ray's evil still clung to their metal bands. Sasha smiled as the rain had also ceased and in twenty short minutes, she was back in the truck and headed back to the hard road.

Sasha turned the radio to a soft jazz station, which kept her company on the long drive back to New Orleans. It was almost two in the morning and she hoped to make it home before the sun began to creep above the horizon.

Chapter 23

Curtis had returned to his home from his escapade to Baton Rouge, more angered than ever before at the dark-haired woman. He knew she was behind Ray's disappearance and his rage boiled over when he returned to find his brother's tattered clothing sitting on his doorstep. Curtis sent his wife and children away for the night and had barricaded himself in his office with a fresh bottle of Jack Daniels.

†

Sasha passed very little traffic on her way back to New Orleans and since the rain had blown through, she made excellent time. She parked the truck across the street from Curtis's home and entered the house with her mind. There were additional guards inside the home tonight. Curtis was obviously worried for his safety. There were two guards inside the office, sitting across the room from him playing cards, and two more just outside the door. This left the front of the house unguarded. Sasha slipped easily inside the home and walked undetected to the empty master bedroom.

She reached into the pocket of her jeans to retrieve the ring and then pulled out Ray's eel skin wallet from her jacket pocket. She placed the wallet and the ring on Curtis's pillow and quietly left the room and then the house, no one the wiser for her visit.

†

Curtis drained another large shot of Jack Daniels as he searched his brain for ideas to find and rescue his brother from the dark-haired woman. He had learned from his trip to Baton Rouge that she enjoyed toying with him and he could only hope that she would contact him with ransom demands for Ray's return. Curtis knew he was only fooling himself thinking in this manner. This woman could care less about money, her goal was vengeance, but for what wrong they had done, Curtis could not determine. He feared he would never see his brother again, a fact that, unknown to him, was soon to be confirmed.

†

Sasha drove out of the Garden District and pulled off the road just as she had crossed over the river. She sent her thoughts out to enter Curtis's mind. Curtis raised both hands to his head as he felt the tingling deep in his brain that signaled he was about to receive a message from the woman. *I left a present for you on your pillow, and I will be back for you very soon.*

†

Curtis almost tipped his chair over as he rushed from his desk out of the office, nearly running over the two guards stationed outside the office as he crashed through the door. He ran up the stairs to the master bedroom, the four guards in fast pursuit. Curtis came to a dead stop as his eyes came to rest on the two objects lying on his pillow. He did not have to open the wallet to know it belonged to his brother. The black signet ring lying next to it told Curtis everything he needed to know. His brother was dead and he would be next if he did not take immediate action.

Curtis ran to the closet and tore the doors open as he growled at the guards. "Get that damn pilot of mine to the airport now and get the car ready," he barked as he located a large suitcase and opened it on the bed. Curtis stuffed the suitcase full of clothes and then went to his nightstand and pulled out his pistol and several loaded clips. A guard picked up the suitcase as Curtis tucked the pistol into the waistband of his pants and slipped the clips into his jacket pocket.

"Carlos," Curtis shouted to his most trusted bodyguard and close friend.

"Yes, boss," he answered.

"Go home and pack a bag and meet me at the airport as quick as you can," Curtis instructed.

"Yes, sir," Carlos said as he ran from the room and out of the house.

Curtis was in a panic and knew he had to escape the city until he could make plans to rid his life of the evil woman who had taken his brother from him. He decided to leave his family behind. The woman had passed on plenty of opportunities to hurt his wife and children, but had failed to do so, so he felt they were safe for the moment at least. He would double the security at the house. Curtis understood her fight was with him and now that Ray was gone, him alone. A cold drop of sweat ran down his back causing him to shiver as his imagination feared what she had done to Ray.

†

Sasha laughed as they scurried like rats around the house searching for her and she drove the rest of the way home wearing a huge smile. She knew Curtis was preparing to flee, but no matter how far he ran, she would follow to fulfill her promise of bayou justice against the older Bellfontaine brother.

†

There was just one more detail to wrap up tonight. Sasha drove down to Bourbon Street. She parked the truck on a side street and walked toward the Bellfontaines' whorehouse. There was one witness to her abduction of Ray and she would have to deal with that now.

The woman was certain to have gotten a good look at her, and though she did not know her name, her description was a detail Sasha could not leave dangling in the wind. Sasha reached the small two-story house and searched the rooms only to find that the woman she was looking for was not inside the house. Sasha wondered if the woman was working the streets. She walked back toward the District, a block away, and sat on a small brick wall to wait.

The wait did not prove to be a long one. Sasha looked up to see the woman stumbling down the sidewalk in her direction. Sasha searched the woman's mind and discovered she had not shared Sasha's identity with anyone, yet Sasha could not take that risk. As the woman approached, Sasha stepped from her concealed spot and ushered the woman into a dark alley. The startled woman gasped. Sasha covered her mouth with her hand and pressed her roughly against the brick wall.

"Hush now," Sasha said. The woman nodded her head in agreement. Sasha pulled her hand away from the woman's mouth, and she wisely remained quiet. Sasha looked her square in the eyes and asked, "Do you know who I am?"

"I do not know who you are, but you are the woman that took that snake Ray away."

"Have you told anyone what you saw that night?" Sasha asked.

"No, I haven't and no one knew I was summoned to service Ray that night."

"That is very good," Sasha said as she pressed her palm against the woman's forehead and entered her mind. You have never seen my face until tonight, and if you should suddenly remember where we met earlier and talk to anyone, I will be back for you.

Sasha smiled at the woman and removed her hand, knowing the woman would have no memory of what happened at Ray's house. The woman slumped down in her arms and Sasha was quick to catch the woman. She helped the woman back to her feet and propped her against the wall once more.

"What happened?" the woman asked, the alcohol still very evident on her breath.

"You stumbled and fell," Sasha said. "I happened to see you fall and came to help you."

"Well, handsome, my room is just down the street, if you would like to come in and let me thank you appropriately," the woman said.

"Thanks, honey, but I am already running late for a date as it is," Sasha said. "Can you make it the rest of the way home?"

"Yes, I can, but do come by and see me sometime," the woman said as she straightened her skirt and walked back onto the sidewalk.

Sasha watched the woman as she did, in fact make it up the front steps of the house and disappeared behind the front door before she stepped onto the sidewalk and returned to her truck.

†

Physically and emotionally drained, Sasha closed the door behind her after entering her home. She walked into one of the guest rooms and stripped the still damp clothes from her body as the shower heated. Ray had been easy prey, but Curtis would present much more of a challenge for Sasha, one she would welcome when the time was right.

The shower did little to refresh her body and spirit, but the object lying on her pillow when she returned to their bed gave Sasha her second wind. The strap-on rested on her pillow with a note from Kara that simply said, "Wake me."

Sasha placed the harness around her hips tightly and used the lube to coat the latex toy before she crawled onto the bed. Kara was fast asleep, lying on her left side. Sasha moved next to her, the sex toy resting against the cheeks of Kara's ass as Sasha's arm encircled her lover's body. Sasha pressed her breasts against Kara's back as her hand covered her lover's breast, her thumb stroking the sleeping nipple. Sasha used her left hand to brush the hair away from Kara's neck then nuzzled her face between her neck and collarbone.

Kara stirred slightly as Sasha began to lick from her neck to her ear. She moaned softly in her sleep as Sasha gently squeezed her breast. Her tongue traced the outer edge of Kara's ear and her warm breath blew softly across her cheek. Sasha pressed her knee between Kara's thighs, parting her legs slightly as she slid the latex between her lover's thighs. Sasha slowly rocked her hips as the ridges of the toy rubbed across Kara's lower lips, teasing them with promises of the pleasure to come. Kara's clit awoke from its slumber, rising above its protective covering to receive slow strokes from the tip of the toy.

Kara opened her eyes and Sasha watched the corners of her mouth lift into a smile as her hand moved down between her thighs to press the toy harder against her as Sasha rocked her hips. Kara moaned loudly and turned her face to Sasha, her eyes begging for a kiss. Sasha leaned into her lover for a soft, slow kiss, her hand stroking Kara's side and down her hip. Sasha lifted Kara's leg and hooked her elbow under it keeping it raised slightly as Kara guided the head of the toy into her opening. She then took Sasha's tongue into her mouth, sucking roughly down its length as she pressed her hips back against Sasha. Sasha twisted her body to a semi-seated position that would allow her to rock her hips against Kara as the toy slid smoothly into her lover's entrance.

Sasha pressed her hips into Kara's ass, driving the sex toy deep inside and began rocking in and out of her lover in short strokes. Kara reached behind Sasha and pulled her hips deeper into her so that she penetrated her completely with each powerful thrust of her hips.

Kara broke the kiss and gasped for breath. "Oh yes, baby, that's it," she groaned as Sasha plunged the sex toy in and out of her. Sasha gritted her teeth to hold back the orgasm that threatened to rip through her. She stopped the movement of her hips just long enough to roll Kara onto her stomach and shove a pillow beneath her before entering Kara again. She thrust deeply into Kara as her wails of pleasure echoed in Sasha's ears, driving her body wild with lust. Sasha could hold back no longer and with a final grunt, she thrust into Kara and they both came with a shuddering climax.

After a few minutes, Kara released the harness from around Sasha's hips and tossed the toy to the end of the bed. She reached down and pulled the covers over their sweat-soaked bodies and snuggled into Sasha as they wound their way into dreams and finally to sleep.

†

Curtis Bellfontaine and Carlos waited on the small jet for the pilot to return from filing his flight plan. Curtis had reached his breaking point and Carlos knew better than to leave Curtis to his thoughts at this point. He sat across from the man who had ruled the drug trade in New Orleans with an iron fist and watched his hands tremble with fear as he attempted to raise a glass of Jack Daniels to his lips.

Never before in his life had Curtis run away from a fight, even when it was the most ruthless territorial battle, but the dark-haired woman had him terrorized and he knew he must flee or lose his life. He would spend some time down in South America, renewing his friendship with the local cartel and planning how to deal with the woman when he returned.

It was unfortunate for Curtis that he had not seen the reporter from the local paper who snapped several photos as he and Carlos boarded the private jet. With a small amount of snooping, the reporter discovered the flight plan to Colombia.

✝

Kara crept from bed and quietly prepared for work. She slipped from the room while Sasha slept deeply and walked from the house into a beautiful, bright day, picking up the newspaper from the porch.

She opened the paper to see the headline. The front page of the newspaper carried one of the pictures the reporter had taken with a caption that read, Curtis Bellfontaine flees to Colombia while his brother Raymond is reported missing. No article followed, but Kara smiled as she glanced over the caption again. She was tempted to wake Sasha up with the news.

Sasha had been sleeping so peacefully when she left that Kara chose not to call and disturb her lover's rest. She would deliver the news personally, when she returned home from the office.

When Sasha woke, it was nearly noon and she was alone in the house. She showered and dressed in jeans and a sweatshirt before going downstairs. She looked at the clock and saw that it was already after one. Sasha glanced out the small kitchen window and knew that Milly would come running down the driveway soon after stepping off the school bus. Today was the big day, and Milly would be bursting at the seams with excitement. In just a little over two hours, she, and Sasha had an appointment at one of the horse farms Sasha had visited earlier and Milly would pick out her Hera.

She took a leftover chicken leg from the refrigerator and drank a glass of tea before leaving the house to walk over to James and Marie's house to wait for Milly.

Marie greeted her at the door and welcomed Sasha into the kitchen where she and James were just finishing lunch.

"Can I fix you something?" Marie asked.

"No, Marie, I just finished a piece of chicken from last night's dinner," Sasha said.

"Good afternoon, Sasha," James said as he laid the newspaper down on the table. "Did you hear about this yet?" he asked as he tapped at the picture of Curtis.

Sasha sat next to him and picked up the paper. Her smile widened as she read the caption. "One down and one to go," she said and looked up to find James grinning back at her.

"Well, all I know is New Orleans will be a much nicer place without of two of them around," Marie said as she sat a cup of coffee down in front of Sasha.

"You won't get an argument from us on that one, my love," James said.

"Unfortunately, though, there are many others out there more than willing to replace the Bellfontaines, but at least it will take years for them to build that kind of power again," Sasha said as she lifted the cup to her lips.

"I would love to know what got after Curtis to make him leave the country like that," Marie said with a chuckle. "He looks completely exhausted and terrified in that photograph."

"Maybe it was just his own guilt finally catching up to him, mama," James said.

"You may be right, but I would have preferred seeing him shipped off to Angola instead of flying off to a foreign country to live like a king," Marie said.

"By the way, Sasha, Milly hardly slept last night waiting for today to come," James said with a chuckle. "She is so excited to go look at horses today."

"Well, if we are lucky, she will find the one that fancies her and she will soon be the proud owner of her own Hera," Sasha said.

"We can't thank you enough," Marie said as she placed her hand on Sasha's shoulder.

"It will be nice to have a riding partner again," Sasha said and then fell silent for a moment as she remembered the many days she and her Milly had spent riding together.

James stood and left the kitchen, returning a moment later carrying a small leather saddle.

"We couldn't afford the horse, but Marie and I picked this out for her."

Sasha took the child's saddle in her hands and let her fingers run across the ornate leather tooling. "You have done well selecting this saddle. It will serve Milly well for years before she outgrows it," she said with a smile. "Are you sure you and Marie won't go with us today?"

"No, Sasha we think this is something you and Milly should do together," Marie said. "I am sure we will have plenty of opportunities to see her ride once she gets her horse."

On cue, Milly came bursting through the front door and ran into the kitchen, skidding to a halt when her eyes landed on the saddle James was holding. "Is that for me?" Milly asked.

"Happy birthday, baby," James and Marie said together.

Milly walked over and let her small hands play across the leather just as Sasha had done. The saddle was nearly as big as she was and when Milly looked at her, she had tears in her eyes. "Thank you, Mother and Father," she said politely and she hugged each of them tightly.

"Are you ready to go find the horse that goes with that saddle?" James asked.

"Yes, Father, I thought this day would never come," Milly said as she turned toward Sasha and then turned back to James, taking the saddle from his lap, filling her arms.

Facing Sasha, Milly waited expectantly. "I guess that is my cue to get moving," Sasha said with a soft chuckle. "We will be back later," she said as she followed Milly from the house.

Milly struggled slightly with the weight of the saddle, but carried it proudly to the truck. Sasha took the saddle from the small girl and carefully placed it in the back of the truck. Milly smiled and ran quickly around the truck and was in her seat, buckling up before Sasha had opened her door.

"All set?" Sasha asked as she smiled to Milly.

"Yes, ma'am," Milly answered.

Sasha started the truck and they slowly pulled down the drive to see a man about a horse.

Chapter 24

Kara was busy reviewing a file when her intercom buzzed and Crystal announced that a Detective Brody wished to speak with her. "I will be right there, Crystal," Kara said as she tucked away the file and straightened her desk.

When she walked out into the reception area, Kyle Brody stood and reached his hand out to her. Kara took it and said with a smile, "It is so good to see you, Detective."

"Likewise, Ms. Stewart, and you are looking very well," Kyle, said.

Kara started walking toward her office and asked, "What can I do for you today?" She closed the door behind them and pointed Kyle to a chair.

"Actually, this is strictly a personal visit," Kyle said. "I assume you have seen the front page of the paper this morning?"

"Indeed I have," Kara said.

"Then you know the Bellfontaines are out of business, at least for a while," Kyle said.

"Yes, do you know what is going on with them?" Kara asked.

"Rumor has it that a voodoo witch has cursed both of them," Brody said. "Word on the street says Ray has been missing for several days and since Curtis is fleeing south, one would assume he received news of his brother's death." Kyle sat back on his seat and drew a deep breath. "You wouldn't happen to know any other details would you, Ms. Stewart?" he asked.

Kara could not stifle the laugh that erupted from her. She covered her mouth and raised her hand in apology to Kyle. When she could speak again she said, "I am so sorry, but, Detective Brody, that was the last thing in the world I thought you would ask of me." Taking a breath to stifle a giggle, Kara said, "I would prefer to see them rotting away in Angola or some other nice state facility."

"I understand, Ms. Stewart, but given your past history with the Bellfontaines, I felt I needed to ask, purely on a social level mind you," he said.

"I assure you, Detective, I had nothing to do with the disappearance of Ray or in chasing Curtis out of the country," Kara answered honestly, fighting to regain her composure.

Smiling, Detective Brody stood and again offered his hand to Kara. "Good riddance to a pair of poisonous snakes then," he said. "I will be sure to drop by if I find out any additional information and I hope if you learn anything worthwhile, you will give me a call."

"I certainly will, Detective," Kara said as she followed him back into the waiting area.

✝

The handsome young detective nodded to Crystal and then stepped back into a glorious New Orleans afternoon. Kyle knew the young attorney was telling the truth and was a trifle disappointed that she did not know what came of the Bellfontaines. He would not have much time to research the issue as the power struggle to take over the Bellfontaines' territory would soon begin and the homicides would mount until the strongest faction won. "Never a dull moment in the Crescent City," he said to himself as he returned to his unmarked police cruiser.

✝

Ted walked into the reception area just as Kara broke out in a fit of laughter. He looked at Crystal who was also staring at Kara and then back to his partner. He sat on the edge of Crystal's desk and they waited for Kara to tell them what was so hilarious.

Kara finally took a deep breath and said, "Detective Brody wanted to know if I had anything to do with Ray Bellfontaine's disappearance and Curtis's sudden need for a vacation."

Ted surprised her when he said, "Well, you do have motive, but opportunity and means, just doesn't seem likely."

Kara looked at him with a shocked look on her face. Crystal and Ted broke out in laughter, soon joined again by Kara.

Their fit of hysterics ended with the second surprise visit of the day.

✝

The door to the office opened and Milly pulled Sasha through the door. "I guess we made it just in time for the party," Sasha said as the three adults wiped the tears in their eyes.

"Was that Detective Brody, I saw leaving?"

Ted began to snicker and Sasha gave him a curious look. "I am sorry, Sasha, but Kyle stopped by to ask if I had anything to do with the disappearance of the Bellfontaines, and I just find that terribly funny."

"You, little mild-mannered Kara Stewart," Sasha said with a smile. "That is funny." They all erupted in another fit of laughter. Even innocent little Milly who had absolutely no idea what was so funny, joined in the laughter.

When the laughter broke, Sasha told Kara, "Milly has something to ask you."

Milly took her cue and looked up at Kara. "Sasha and I are going to look at horses and I want you to come with us," Milly said. "Can you?" she asked so sweetly.

Shocked by Milly's request, Kara turned to look at a smiling Crystal.

"Only one appointment this afternoon," Crystal said.

"One that I can easily take," Ted said with a grin.

"Well then, let's go buy a horse," Kara said and Milly squealed with excitement. "I will see you two later," she said as they left the office.

Milly climbed in between Kara and Sasha and belted herself in. Sasha had been surprised when Milly suggested they stop by Kara's office and ask her to go with them, but she eagerly complied with the child's request.

Now that they were merrily on their way again, Sasha smiled as she listened to Kara and Milly chatter away. When she turned down a long drive, several young palomino colts rushed to greet them. Sasha could see Milly's delight as they ran alongside the truck, following them all the way to the horse barn.

Mr. Thompson was there to greet them as promised. He took Milly by the hand, and led her inside the barn and showed her two different horses in separate stalls. When she saw the smaller horse in the second stall, she knew she had found her Hera. She turned to look at Sasha, her eyes brimming with joy and said, "This is the one, Sasha."

Mr. Thompson attached a lead to the young horse's halter and led her out to a small riding paddock for the three of them to have a better view. The horse had smaller than normal features, but she had a glow about her that was hard to resist. When Milly walked up to her, the horse gently nuzzled her neck as Milly threw her arms around her. It was love at first sight.

"Are you ready to ride her?" Sasha asked.

"Yes, please," she said. Sasha returned to the truck to retrieve the saddle while Mr. Thompson went to the barn to get a bridle.

Sasha took a small blanket and placed it on the horse's back before laying the saddle across her and leaning down to tighten the cinch. She then picked up Milly and placed her in the saddle, adjusting the length of the stirrups to fit Milly as Mr. Thompson placed the bridle on the horse and handed the reins to Milly.

Sasha took the lead and slowly walked the horse around the paddock with Milly on her back. Once Milly felt comfortable, Sasha removed the lead and told Milly to nudge the horse with her heels to get her moving. The three adults watched as Milly rode the horse around the paddock several circuits before nudging her into a slow trot. Milly bounced a bit in the saddle, but Sasha would soon have her riding like a pro.

"I do believe you have made a sale, Mr. Thompson," Kara said as they watched Milly and her Hera slowly circle the paddock.

Sasha handed the man a check for the purchase and he agreed to deliver the horse the following morning. Sasha had agreed that she would teach Milly to ride when she came home from school and they would ride together on weekends over the property.

Milly rode over to where the adults were standing and the smile on her face was so brilliant it sent a throb of pain straight to Sasha's heart as it reminded her so much of her Milly. She reached up, helped the child down to the ground, and then removed the saddle from the horse's back.

"I shall see you in the morning then, Mr. Thompson," Sasha said and they shook hands to seal their bargain.

Milly hugged Hera's neck then took the saddle from Sasha as they walked back to the truck.

Sasha placed the saddle and blanket back into the bed of the truck and looked down at Milly. Milly held her arms out to hug Sasha and whispered, "Thank you, Sasha."

"Happy birthday, Milly," Sasha said as she returned Milly's embrace.

"Why don't we stop by the feed and seed and let Milly pick out a bridle for her new horse," Kara suggested.

"Good idea," Sasha said as they climbed into the truck.

A half hour later, they left the store with a new bridle, halter, and lead for Milly to use with her Hera.

†

The afternoon had completely faded away when they returned to Kara's office to retrieve Kara's car. Milly did not move from the middle seat when Kara left the truck, remaining instead seated next to Sasha. Milly placed her hand on Sasha's thigh as they rode and Sasha felt an all too familiar tingling where the child's hand touched her, but she shrugged the feeling off.

When they returned to Sugarland, James had pulled the grill out and was busy grilling steaks for Milly's birthday dinner. Sasha took the saddle and blanket from the back of the truck and handed it to Milly and they walked to the barn. Sasha pointed out a small saddle rack for Milly to store her saddle and then she took out a hammer and a couple of long nails to create a hook for Milly's bridle and halter to hang outside of the stall that would be Hera's. They fed and supplied Thunder with fresh water before returning to the picnic table James and Marie had set up. Milly could hardly eat the fantastic meal as she told her parents about Hera and the wonderful ride she had taken.

Night fell quickly and James lit torches around the picnic table. They shared cake and ice cream before an excited Milly left to bathe before bed. The small child hugged each of the adult's necks and told them she loved them before she disappeared into the house. Kara and Marie cleared the table and then took coffee out to Sasha and James as the four adults enjoyed the dancing of the fireflies across the front lawn. They appreciated the peaceful moment on a relaxing fall evening in silence until the bayou chorus came to life and the stillness of the night was broken.

Kara stretched and suggested they retire for the evening and after saying their good-bye's she and Sasha walked into Sugarland.

Chapter 25

Sasha held Kara in her arms until her lover fell asleep and then her mind went into gear as she began planning how to track down Curtis Bellfontaine. Once Hera arrived tomorrow and settled into her new home Sasha would take a ride to town. She wanted to see if she could glean any information from Curtis's wife or children that would lead her to his location. If she were lucky enough to pinpoint a location, she would begin to plan in earnest. She did not want to wait too long to take care of Curtis and was eager to be done with the completely messy business of bringing justice to pass.

She curled her body around Kara's and drifted into peaceful dreams. When Kara stirred the following morning, Sasha crept quietly from the bed and went down to get them a cup of coffee. Kara stretched and sat up against the headboard as Sasha returned with the coffee.

"Good morning, my darling," Kara said.

"Good morning, love. I trust you slept well," she said.

"I always sleep wonderfully when I fall asleep in your arms, Sasha," Kara said as she took the offering of coffee from Sasha.

"Some nights better than others," Sasha teased.

"Indeed. You do have a rather delightful way of putting me to sleep," she added with a mischievous smile.

"Do you have a busy day today, love?" Sasha asked.

"Ted and I will be interviewing several potential new clients today," Kara said. "What are your plans for the day?"

"Mr. Thompson will deliver Hera at nine and I will make sure she is all settled in, and then when Milly gets home from school we will begin riding lessons," Sasha said.

"Admit it, Sasha, you are almost as excited as Milly is," Kara teased. Kara had ridden a few times with Sasha, but she did not have the love for riding that Sasha did.

"All right, I do believe I am," Sasha admitted. "It will be nice to have a riding partner again."

After they finished their coffee, they showered and dressed before going downstairs.

"Would you like some breakfast?" Sasha asked.

"I would love to have some breakfast with you, my love," Kara said.

"I think I am in the mood for an omelet, how does that sound?" Sasha asked.

"You have my mouth watering already," Kara said as she poured them more coffee.

"Ham and cheese good for you?" she asked.

"Perfect," Kara said. "I will make some toast and pour some juice when you get close to being done."

Sasha took out the ham and started cutting it into small cubes and then took eggs from the refrigerator and whipped them into a bowl. Kara hopped up onto the counter and watched as Sasha created the first omelet, perfect in every way. She reached over and dropped the toast as Sasha folded the eggs in half and slid off the counter to pour their juice. She carried two large glasses to the table and dropped more toast as Sasha began the second omelet.

"Go ahead and get started while it is still hot," Sasha said as she turned back to the stove.

"Mmm, this is so good, Sasha," Kara said after her first taste.

The toast popped up and Sasha buttered it quickly as she waited for the cheese to melt, then slid her omelet onto a plate and joined Kara at the table.

Kara leaned over and kissed Sasha. "Thank you for cooking for me."

"Anytime," Sasha said, returning her kiss.

After breakfast, Kara left for the office and Sasha walked down to the stables to prepare for Hera's arrival. She fed Thunder and put down fresh wood chips in the stall that would be Hera's new home. "You are going to have a new stablemate, Thunder," Sasha said as she scratched behind the large stallion's ears.

Thunder perked his ears, alerting Sasha to the sound of a horse trailer as it turned into the long driveway and pulled up to the stable. Sasha picked up the new halter and lead, and left the stable. James and Marie walked out to meet Sasha and waited for the truck to come to a halt.

"Good morning, Mr. Thompson," Sasha said.

"Good morning, Ms. Thibodaux," he answered.

"James and Marie are Milly's parents," Sasha said as she introduced them.

"I sure hope your daughter enjoys this pretty little mare," he said as he walked to the rear of the trailer and pulled the door open. He stepped inside and slowly backed Hera from the trailer. Sasha quickly exchanged halters, placing the one, Milly had picked out on the small horse and handed the old one to Mr. Thompson.

"She is a beauty," James said as he and Marie walked up to stroke Hera's shoulders.

"I can see why Milly fell in love with her," she said, as she looked the horse in the face.

"I appreciate doing business with you, Sasha," Mr. Thompson said, shaking her hand before taking his leave.

Sasha walked Hera around a bit so James and Marie could get a good look at her. "I hope you have the movie camera charged up," she said.

"Oh yes, and two brand-new rolls of film," Marie said with a chuckle.

"Great," Sasha said. "I am going to place her in the stall and then drive into town for a little while." She looked at James. "Would you mind checking in on Hera every now and then until I get back?"

"It will be my pleasure," James said as he walked with Sasha to the stable.

"I will be back long before Milly makes it home from school," she promised as she led Hera into the stall and released the snap on the lead. She hung the lead next to the stall and watched as Hera and Thunder make their acquaintance by nosing each other through the stall walls. "I will be back soon," Sasha said as she left the stable and headed to her truck.

Sasha drove across the river and turned toward the Garden District. She had planned to stop by Curtis Bellfontaine's house first to see if she could pick up any information on his location from his wife. Sasha passed the house then completed a U-turn and parked across the street from the Bellfontaine home. She entered the house with her mind and found a guard in the hallway and Curtis's wife in the kitchen as she baked cookies for her children.

Sasha easily entered her mind and discovered that she had recently talked with Curtis and her memory of their conversation was fresh on her mind. Like reading a book, Sasha learned that Curtis was the guest of Marco Bolivar in Colombia. He and his sister Regina live in a fortress compound deep in Cali, the heart of the cocoa growing country. It was here that Curtis and Carlos had fled when they left New Orleans and it would be there that Sasha would find him to exact her revenge.

Satisfied she had enough information to begin planning Sasha returned to Sugarland and began her research on the Bolivars and the small area of Cali. It would be a dangerous venture to travel to South America in pursuit of Curtis, but Sasha felt he would stay down there for months and she wished to be finished with the brothers Bellfontaine once and for all.

Getting to South America would be the easy part of the journey. Cali was a very fertile valley, surrounded by dense jungle that Sasha would have to travel through in order to reach Curtis without detection. She would also have to wind her way through Bogotá and avoid the narco-terrorists that preyed on foreigners who dared travel in their world. Aside from outright murders, kidnapping Americans for ransom had become a valuable source of revenue, second only to the movement of cocaine through the country. Sasha had no doubt that the Bolivars would have many of these mercenaries working for them, so getting to Curtis would prove much more difficult than Ray had been.

She was deep in thought, developing her plan when Milly came running down the driveway, squealing with excitement. Sasha closed the Internet and walked outside to meet her.

"Go change into your jeans and boots," Sasha said as Milly came running up to her.

She watched as the young girl ran quickly into the house and only minutes later joined Sasha on the front steps. "Okay, Sasha, I am ready," she rattled off in her excitement.

Sasha stood and they began walking to the stables. "I guess the first thing we need to work on is the basic care you will need to give Hera," Sasha said. She knew that Milly was dying to be riding, but Sasha felt it was important to start with the basics.

Sasha took Milly to the feed bins and showed her the sweet feed mix and the oats. "Each morning before school, you will need to place two scoops of sweet feed into her feed bin and at night two scoops of oats with a block of hay," Sasha said. "The automatic watering system is already hooked up, but you need to check to make sure she has fresh water at all times."

Milly listened intently to Sasha's instruction as she was oriented to the stable. "Your saddle and blanket should always rest on this rack, to allow it to dry and air out properly," Sasha said. "Until you grow a bit more, you will need help to saddle and bridle Hera, but you still need to know how."

Sasha took the bridle down and she and Milly walked inside the stall. Milly watched as Sasha removed Hera's halter and then gently slid the bit between the horse's teeth and placed the top of the bridle behind the horse's ears. Sasha ran the strap through the buckle underneath Hera's jaw and showed Milly how to secure it tightly. She then walked Hera from the stall, looped her reins over a hitching post, and went back inside to pick up the saddle and blanket. Sasha used a soft brush across Hera's back before picking up the saddle blanket. "You always need to make sure there are no wrinkles in your blanket, to prevent chafing," Sasha said as she smoothed the blanket over Hera's shoulders. "It is also wise to hook your right stirrup and girth strap onto the saddle horn so it does not slam into her side when you place the saddle across her back," Sasha said and demonstrated.

Sasha and Milly walked around the front of the horse and Sasha lowered the girth strap and stirrup. Returning to her left side, Sasha reached beneath her belly and took the girth in her hand. "Make sure it is straight and not twisted. If you make that mistake and it becomes painful you will probably end up on the ground," Sasha said with a chuckle. She tightened the strap, tied it off, and turned to look at Milly. "I think we need to ask your dad to cut a stump that you can use to mount Hera until you get a little bit taller and can reach," Sasha said with a grin. "Until then," she laced her fingers together and instructed Milly to place her right boot in her hands and she lifted until Milly could place her left foot in the stirrup and could swing her right leg over Hera's back and come to rest in the saddle.

"Get comfortable while I saddle Thunder and then we will ride," Sasha said. She walked back into the stable and returned moments later mounted on the large stallion. "Soft hands are very important to a good rider, Milly, do you know why?"

"No, ma'am," Milly said.

"Because your hands and knees are the most important body parts used in riding," Sasha said. "You steer and guide your horse with your hands and knees, and if you do not do it right, you can hurt or confuse your horse, so always be gentle. Are you holding your knees tight to her?"

"Yes, ma'am," Milly said.

"Good, the strength of your legs will keep you in the saddle and the pressure you put on her shoulders will tell Hera many things," she continued.

"Like what?" Milly asked.

"Like how fast you want her to go and in which direction. You guide her head with a gentle pressure of her reins against her neck, like this," Sasha said as she pressed the reins against the left side of Thunder's neck to ask him to turn right and just the opposite for left. "And when you want her to stop or to back up, you pull the reins softly back toward your belly button." She demonstrated as Thunder backed up ten feet. "It is important that you never jerk hard and that you learn to communicate to Hera with your body," Sasha said. "Does all this make sense to you Milly?"

"Yes ma'am, it does," Milly said with a huge grin.

"So you think you are ready to ride?" Sasha asked.

"Yes, Sasha, I am."

Sasha nudged Thunder forward and leaned down from her saddle to open the gate into the small corral.

"Loosen up your reins and nudge Hera with your knees," Sasha said.

She watched as Milly followed her instruction and guided the small mare into the riding ring.

"Very good," Sasha praised Milly.

James and Marie were sitting on the fence rails, movie camera and photo camera in hand. James was videotaping Milly on her first big ride and both parents watched their child with pride as she straightened her back and listened to Sasha's instructions.

Sasha was very impressed with Milly and within two hours, Milly and Hera were cantering smoothly next to her and Thunder. Milly was learning to ride just as quickly as her namesake had and she smiled widely at the young child.

Kara returned home and walked up the fence. She watched as Milly and Sasha circled the ring, smiled, and waved when she caught their attention. "It is hard to tell which one of them is having more fun," she said to James and Marie.

"They have been riding for over two hours," James said with a broad smile.

"Don't be surprised then if Milly is a little sore tomorrow," Kara said.

"I am sure if she is, she won't mention it for fear we would make her slow down," Marie said with a chuckle.

Sasha slowed them to a walk as they cooled the horses and then they rode back to the hitching post and dismounted. James, Marie, and Kara walked over to join them. "James, I have a project for you," Sasha said.

"What would that be Sasha?" James asked.

"I need you to find a tree that has broken off and cut a section to use as a mounting block for Milly," Sasha said.

"I think I know the perfect one," James said. "I will do it first thing in the morning."

Sasha removed the girth from around Hera's underside and lifted the saddle from her back, handing it to Milly and then removed the saddle from Thunder. They carried the saddles back into the stable and placed them on the saddle racks. Sasha picked up two brushes and handed one to Milly before stopping to pick up a bucket.

She placed the bucket next to Hera to allow Milly to climb onto it and be able to reach the horse's back and shoulders. "You always want to brush your horse down good after a ride," she told Milly, demonstrating the proper technique.

"What are we having for supper tonight, Marie?" Kara asked as she watched Milly brush Hera.

"Red beans and rice with a big skillet of corn bread," Marie said.

"Will you three join us then?" Kara asked.

"Sounds good to me," James said and Milly shook her head yes.

"I think I will go change clothes and chop some onion then," Kara said as she left the stable.

"I will walk with you and set the table while they finish up with the horses," Marie said. "James, will you take the cameras back into the house?"

"Of course, dear," James said.

Sasha and Milly finished brushing down the horses and took them back into their stalls. They removed the bridles and placed the halters back on the horses and then fed them their oats for the night. Sasha handed Milly a block of hay and lifted the child high enough to drop the hay in Hera's bin. They rinsed off the bits and hung the bridles on the outside stall walls.

"I think that is it for tonight. I don't know about you, but I worked up an appetite," she said to Milly.

"Me too, Sasha," Milly said as she reached up and slipped her hand inside Sasha's larger one.

Milly's action surprised Sasha, who smiled as the warm hand slipped inside hers. Milly had never held her hand and there was something comforting about holding the small child's hand as they walked to the house. James met them on the front porch and they entered the house together.

"Today was the best day," she said as James held the door open for them.

As soon as they finished sharing the tasty meal, Milly asked to leave the table.

"Go ahead," James told his daughter, knowing she would be headed straight for the stable to check on Hera.

"You have certainly made this a memorable birthday for Milly," James said to Sasha.

"We have indeed," Sasha quickly corrected James. "I cannot believe how fast she is learning to ride."

"She looks so natural on the horse," Marie said as she started to clear the table.

"That she does," Kara agreed as she dipped out a large bowl of beans for her and Sasha to warm up for tomorrow night's meal.

The four adults sat around the table and talked for a short while, allowing Milly to spend some time with Hera.

✝

When James and Marie left the main house, James walked down to the stable and found Milly sitting on the top rail of the stall door with Hera's head in her lap. The sight of his daughter and her horse was priceless and he wished he had a camera in his hand. He walked up behind Milly and placed an arm around her shoulder.

"She is really a fine horse isn't she?"

"She's the best, Father," Milly said as she softly stroked down Hera's face.

"It is time to tell her good night, so you can get your homework done and get ready for bed," James told his daughter.

"Yes, sir," Milly said and hugged Hera's neck before she climbed down and walked to the house with James.

✝

Kara and Sasha had moved out to the swing, and they waved good night to James and Milly as they walked into the house. "That is one happy little girl," Kara said with a smile.

"Yes, she is," she said as they rocked slowly in the swing. After a few moments Sasha said, "I am going to need to go out of town for a week or so."

"Oh really?" Kara said. "Where to?"

"I have some Network business I need to take care of," Sasha said. She hoped Kara did not notice that she had flinched when she

197

told the white lie. As far as she could tell, she did not. Sasha did not like lying to Kara, but she did not need to know what she was planning to do.

"When will you be leaving?" Kara asked.

"I will try to make arrangements for this weekend and be back as soon as I can."

"I have several court dates this coming week or I would offer to go with you," Kara said.

"That is no problem," Sasha said. "I will finish up and get home as quick as I can."

"Very well, just know that I will miss you every minute you are away then," Kara said as she rested her head on Sasha's shoulder.

"As I will be missing you," Sasha said, kissing the top of Kara's head.

†

The rest of the week was uneventful as Sasha made plans for her trip and continued Milly's riding lessons. Sasha asked James if he and Marie would handle the bed-and-breakfast business in her absence. She also asked him to drive her to the airport early Saturday morning. When her alarm went off, Sasha crept from the bed and quietly prepared for her trip. She kissed Kara softly and walked out to place her bag in the truck. James joined her a few minutes later.

"I hope you will continue to work with Milly on her riding while I am gone," Sasha said as she and James talked on the way to the airport.

"Do you really think Milly could wait until you get back to ride again?" he asked.

Sasha chuckled, knowing James was right. "Just keep her working in the ring until I return," Sasha said.

"Do you know how long you will be gone?" James asked.

"If all goes well, I hope to be home next weekend, but I will call to let you know for sure," Sasha said as they pulled up to the departing flight drop-off.

"Be careful and come home as quickly as you can then," James said as Sasha stepped from the truck.

"I will be back before you know it," Sasha said. Taking her bag from the back of the truck, she disappeared inside the terminal. Her route would take her from New Orleans to Houston and from there to Panama City. Once she arrived in Panama City, she would board a small commuter and continue her journey into Bogotá. From there, Sasha would rent a jeep to travel deep into the jungle. However, before leaving Bogotá, Sasha planned to meet with Sera, an Immortal with whom she had been in contact, to arrange for the purchase of supplies.

Sasha walked to her departure gate and located a seat to wait for her call to board. She opened up her backpack and pulled out several topographical maps of the Cali area, studying them closely until it was time to board. It would take all of a day to drive to Cali from Bogotá, on the less-than-perfect jungle roads. Sasha hoped she could avoid a confrontation with the narco-terrorists who roamed the countryside.

The first leg of her journey passed smoothly, but on the flight to Panama City, the jet encountered a vicious storm and the turbulence had several passengers scrambling for the lavatory. Sasha just closed her eyes and rested her head against the back of the seat until the worst of the storm was over.

Occasionally, she would look out of the window and watch the flashes of lightning in the clouds as they flew through them.

When the flight reached Panama City, Sasha located the gate and clutching her small bag close, climbed onto the smaller propeller plane. She was glad to see clear skies, knowing that a storm like the one they had flown through could be devastating to a plane this size. The small plane was overcrowded, and the heat of so many bodies stuffed inside the plane and inadequate ventilation had everyone sweating profusely. Sasha breathed a sigh of relief when they were airborne and the air-conditioning system finally kicked into gear. Two hours later, Sasha felt the plane begin to descend. She looked beyond the passenger seated next to her to see mile after mile of deep green jungle.

Chapter 26

Sasha passed through customs with as much patience as she could muster. They questioned her intensely on her reason for traveling alone and her ruse of a fishing trip caused many glances, but the officials bought her story. The small bag she had packed contained nothing that would tip them off to her true reason for being in the country.

Ignoring the armed guards posted throughout the small airport, Sasha made her way quickly to the small rental car agency. She hoped the jeep assigned to her would help her blend in with the local traffic. Still covered with mud from a previous rental, it also had multiple dents in its body. Sasha paid the man in cash and pulled out her map that would lead her to Sera. Thankfully, Sera lived on the outer edge of town, so Sasha did not have to drive through the metropolitan traffic during rush hour. As the sun began to sink, Sasha pulled away from the airport.

†

Thirty minutes later, Sasha pulled into a small residential neighborhood and located the address Sera had given her. She could feel her fellow Immortal's presence as she stepped from the jeep and walked toward the house.

The front door opened and Sasha looked at one of the most beautiful women she had ever seen. The tall woman's long dark hair fell halfway down her back. Her cinnamon-brown skin was flawless and her dark eyes glowed as she smiled at Sasha. She raised her arms and hugged Sasha before saying, "It is so nice to meet you, my sister, please be welcomed to my home."

"Thank you for your hospitality, my sister," Sasha said as she followed Sera into the small, yet comfortable home.

Sera motioned for Sasha to take a seat. "May I offer you something cool to drink?"

"That would be wonderful," Sasha said and watched Sera disappear into a small kitchen.

Sera returned carrying two glasses of sangria and handed one to Sasha then sat down across from her. "When we talked earlier, you mentioned a hunting trip,"

Sasha smiled at Sera, knowing the woman was searching for additional information. "In New Orleans there were two brothers who were very evil men. They escaped punishment from the law many times for a vast number of brutal crimes. In one of their efforts to escape prosecution they chose to endanger my mate. I promised them that they would suffer bayou justice for their actions. The time for that is now."

"Yes, I can understand that, Sasha, but why are you here?"

"I have taken care of one of the brothers, but the eldest of the two has fled here. He has taken refuge with his drug smuggling partners and I have come to hunt him down, to finish what I have started," she explained.

"There are some very dangerous men in this wild country, Sasha, so you will need to be very careful," Sera warned. "Not just from the drug smugglers, but from the narco-terrorists, as well. There has been a recent rash of kidnappings of Americans and other foreigners for ransom. I seriously doubt your presence in our country has gone unnoticed." Sera placed her glass on the small table between them. "For a long time I have suspected that the narco-terrorists have received information from the custom agents when a foreigner enters the country, and I would not be surprised if you were followed as you left the airport," Sera said.

"I will be very careful, Sera. I hope that I did not place you in jeopardy, by coming here," Sasha said.

"No, not at all," Sera said. "Visitors to my home are very common, and once the narco-terrorists realize they are a guest of mine, they have a tendency to be left alone after that," Sera said with a chuckle. "It only took a handful of them to come up missing to encourage them to stay out of my business," she said with a wicked gleam in her eyes. "But, be cautious when you leave and keep vigilant for a dark vehicle following you on your journey," Sera warned.

"I will keep all my senses open," Sasha promised. She felt very comfortable with Sera and was surprised to find such a beautiful woman living alone.

Sera read her thoughts. "My partner, Victoria, has gone out for a little snack and to make sure if anyone was following you, that they take a detour," she said with a smile.

"Very well," Sasha said, returning Sera's smile.

"So is your partner well after her ordeal?" Sera asked.

"She suffered bad dreams for a while, but is moving on with her career and life," Sasha said, smiling as she talked of Kara.

"How long have you been mated?" Sera asked.

"Just a few years. I lost the one who created me after sixty odd years to the AIDS epidemic in the eighties," Sasha said, sadness evident in her tone.

"I am very sad to hear that. I can tell from your energy she was very loved by you," she said. "It is hard for anyone to replace your first."

"That is so very true," Sasha said. "How long have you and Victoria been mated?"

"For almost ten years now," Sera said. "She wasn't the first I created, but the first I have taken as a mate, and I think I shall keep her for a while." Sera chuckled.

They heard Victoria enter through the back door. She came into the small den where the two women sat talking.

"Speaking of my love, Sasha, may I introduce Victoria," Sera said.

Sasha stood and hugged the tall blond woman who had entered the room. She saw why Sera had chosen her for her mate, her beauty complemented Sera's completely. "It is very nice to meet you," Sasha said.

"Likewise," Victoria said with a slight German accent. "There were two men trailing you a few blocks down the street, but you don't have to worry about them any longer," she said with a grin. "They made quite a tasty snack."

"I appreciate your assistance," Sasha told Victoria.

"My pleasure, do either of you need a refill?" she asked, seeing the half-empty glasses on the table.

Sera looked at Sasha who smiled and nodded her head. "That would be lovely, darling."

Victoria returned with a pitcher and refilled both glasses before filling her own. "Will you be staying with us for the night?" Victoria asked as she licked the sweet liquid from her lips.

"There really is no need for you to be on the road tonight," Sera said. "It is much safer to travel during daylight hours and we would love for you to spend the evening with us."

"I would like that too, if it is not an inconvenience for you."

"Not at all," Sera assured her. "Victoria has a nice roast in the oven and we would like to hear what else is going on in the world these days."

"Very well then, let me get my bag. I will be pleased to be your guest for the evening."

Sasha returned to the house and Sera led her to a guest room where Sasha placed the bag on the bed before going to the kitchen.

Victoria had set the table, and once all were seated, served a fantastic meal.

"This looks fabulous," Sasha said as she surveyed the food on the table.

"My Victoria is a marvelous cook," Sera said as she leaned over to kiss her lover.

"Thank you, Sera. So Sasha, you are from New Orleans?" she asked.

"Yes, I have lived there most of my life, except for a brief period when I was studying in Europe and was made by my first," Sasha said.

"Ah, Europe," Victoria said. "Where and what were you studying?"

"I was studying piano in London and was fortunate to tour in Paris, Ireland, Spain, and throughout Britain while I was there," Sasha answered.

"I lived in Berlin, until I traveled to this beautiful country and met Sera," Victoria said. "I do miss Germany and Europe, but haven't been able to convince her to travel yet."

"Why not, Sera, it is so beautiful there?" Sasha said.

"The whole hunting ordeal is such an inconvenience," Sera said.

"You have not been introduced to the Network then I take it?" Sasha asked.

"The Network?" Sera asked.

"In Atlanta, there is a team of scientists who are also Immortals. They have created a serum, that replaces the need for human blood," Sasha said.

"You have got to be kidding," Sera said.

"No, I am serious. As a matter of fact, Kara, my lover, has never had to feed off a human since she turned."

"That is amazing," Victoria said. "How does it work for you?"

"I use the serum every two weeks, but I still have to feed on humans every month or so," Sasha said. "I wish now that I had brought some with me," Sasha said. "I would love for the two of you to try it."

"That would have been great, but I am sure it would have been difficult to explain when passing through customs," Sera said with a chuckle.

"When I am finished here, I will have some shipped to you, for you to sample. Then you would have no excuse to not travel, Sera," Sasha said as she shot a wink to Victoria.

"Oh, so you two are going to gang up on me now?" Sera asked.

"We just know how much you would enjoy Europe once you get there, my love."

"Is that so?" Sera said.

"Very much so," Sasha said. "Europe would make your time invested in travel well worth it."

"Well then, maybe I will have to rethink my position on traveling, if this serum is as good as you say, Sasha."

"I do not think you will be disappointed in its results. If nothing else it will reduce your need to hunt as often."

"Speaking of hunting," Sera said, "why don't you follow me and you can check out the supplies you ordered while Victoria picks up the kitchen."

Sasha followed Sera into the garage and watched as she opened a large duffel bag. Sera removed a twenty-five automatic handgun equipped with a silencer. "Small but deadly," she said as she handed the gun to Sasha. It felt very light in her hand compared to the gun James had loaned her, but this would be very easy to conceal and the silencer only took seconds to attach. Several sets of dark clothing and combat boots with a bundle of clean dry socks were also included. Sasha inspected the climbing gear and several lengths of varying sizes of ropes. Sasha had been able to tap into satellite images of the compound, but could not zoom in close enough to gain data on the height of the walls that protected it.

Sasha rummaged amongst food supplies and water purification tablets to find several boxes of ammunition for the pistol and was satisfied Sera had provided everything she would need to breach the walls of the complex. She returned the pistol to the bag, zipped it closed, and stood to pull cash from her pocket.

"Don't even think about it," Sera said. "Just go get the bastard and come back safely. Bring back the supplies you don't use in case someone else needs assistance in the future."

"I cannot ask for a better deal than that," Sasha said as she hugged Sera warmly.

"Would you care for some coffee?" Victoria asked from the kitchen.

"That sounds good to me, darling," Sera answered, and then walked with Sasha back into the small den.

"So, what do you and Kara do for a living in New Orleans?" Victoria asked as she walked into the room carrying a tray of coffee.

"I own a sugar cane plantation and a small bed-and-breakfast and Kara is a criminal defender, specializing in trying to keep juveniles out of the system," Sasha said with pride. "She was previously with the district attorney's office, but after the debacle with the Bellfontaine brothers, she resigned and opened her own practice, I think it has been a great change for her and I know she is much happier with her own practice."

"I would imagine she takes a great deal of pride when she is able to save a teenager from the mean streets of today's world," Sera said.

"Very much so," Sasha said. "The young woman who was her first client is now working in her office and attending college on a part-time basis. We are very proud of her."

"What do the two of you do to keep yourselves busy?" Sasha asked.

"I am a part-time travel agent," Victoria said with a chuckle.

Sera smiled at her lover and then looked at Sasha. "My family grew Brazilian hardwood forests and then shipped the processed woods across the world, so I have an inheritance that allows me to play housewife to Victoria. I dabble in things such as fine art trading when the mood strikes and I need to get out of the house for a while."

"Milly, my creator and first love, was a painter from France," Sasha said.

"Would that be Milly Vansant, by chance?" Sera asked.

"Yes, it would," said a shocked Sasha.

"Come with me," Sera said as she stood and took Sasha's hand. Sera led Sasha into the master bedroom. Hanging above the large bed was a picture Milly had painted when she was in France.

Sasha would have recognized the bold strokes of Milly's work, and would have known it to be hers without having to see the tight signature that graced the lower right-hand corner of the framed art.

"I came across the piece almost a year ago and knew immediately that I must have it," Sera said. "There is something that draws me to the picture every time I enter the room."

"That was one of the paintings that Milly did on commission for a gallery in London. The gardens in the painting were just as beautiful in real-life Paris as they are on that canvas," she said.

"Paris. I wondered where this was," she said. "Victoria, my love, you win, we are going to Paris just as soon as we can get started on the serum."

Victoria squealed and rushed into the room to hug Sasha's neck. "You have made tonight such a wonderful night for the both of us," she said. "How can we ever make it up to you?"

"You just did, by sharing this painting with me and by Sera agreeing to take you to Paris," Sasha said as they returned to the den.

They drank the remainder of the coffee and then retired for the evening. Sasha did not realize how tired she had become, and when she slept, she had wonderful dreams of her and Milly in Paris.

Chapter 27

Sunday morning Sasha awoke to the ringing of church bells as they called worshippers to Mass. She could also smell bacon frying as it wafted throughout the house. When she crept from the bed and made her way to the kitchen, she found Sera cooking breakfast and Victoria sitting at the table reading the paper and drinking coffee.

"Good morning," Sera said when she saw Sasha walk into the kitchen.

"Good morning, you two," Sasha said as she stretched in the doorframe.

"Breakfast is about fifteen minutes away, so you can shower and dress, or join Victoria for coffee," Sera said.

"Coffee sounds heavenly, right now," Sasha said.

Sera chuckled and handed her a heavy ceramic mug. "Make pretend you are at home then," she said to Sasha. "Did you sleep well?"

"I had a fantastic night's sleep, thank you," Sasha said.

"Great, it may be the last one you have in a comfortable bed for a few days," Victoria reminded her.

"Don't remind me," Sasha said with a chuckle. "I do not look forward to nights spent in the jungle."

"Climb high and try your best to stay dry," Sera said as she took the last of the bacon from the frying pan. She stirred the potatoes she was frying and turned to ask Sasha, "How do you like your eggs?"

"Any way you wish to cook them, my friend," Sasha answered.

"How about scrambled with some onion and cheese blended in?" she asked.

"My mouth is watering already," Sasha said as she sat down next to Victoria.

Sasha caught the photograph of a crime scene splashed across the front page, but could not read the Spanish print that described the story. "Another busy night in the streets?" she asked.

"A major clash between two rival drug gangs. Nearly two dozen killed and several others wounded. Pretty routine for the weekend here," Victoria said with a sigh.

"It is a shame that the lure of drugs and the wealth that can be obtained from them makes human life so cheap," Sasha said.

"The irony of the whole deal is that the men who give their lives in these gang wars reap barely more than minimum wage while the drug lords rake in millions each year," Sera said. "Even the police on the payroll make more than those who risk their lives every day for the drug traffic."

"I know there have been many attempts to quell the flow of drugs from South America, but for every drug lord that is taken down, it seems three more rise to take his place," Sasha said.

"In a country as economically poor as Colombia, cocaine is the main source of income for the greater majority of the people who live here. There is little in the way of legitimate enterprise that will even attempt to compete with the drug trade," Victoria said. "This is such a beautiful country and it has so much to offer tourists, but with governments warning their citizens to steer clear of Colombia, it has never been fully appreciated."

"It did not used to be that way, and that is what makes it so sad to see," Sera said from the stove. "There are fishing villages and beautiful mountainside villas that are crumbling from within that used to be filled with foreign tourists and money flowed freely, but those days are gone and will probably not be revisited even in our long lifetimes."

"That is incredibly sad," Sasha said as she drank her coffee.

Sera carried bowls of fried potatoes and eggs to the table, joined by a platter of bacon and toast. "Eat hearty, my friend," she said as she returned to the refrigerator for chilled orange juice.

Sasha ate a huge breakfast. After helping Victoria clean the kitchen, she headed off to shower and dress in her traveling clothes. Sera passed by her room as Sasha was packing up and said, "Leave your dirty clothes and I will wash them for your trip home, and it will be less you have to carry."

"Thank you both for all your assistance and hospitality," Sasha said as she picked up the large duffel and headed for the front door. She hugged Victoria and Sera and with good luck wishes from them, she stepped out into a bright sunny morning.

"Remember to watch your back," Sera said as Sasha walked to her rented jeep.

Sasha had studied her route intensely, but she still pulled the maps out and placed them on the seat beside her. She also made sure the pistol was handy and the silencer attached, just in case she needed a quick defense. With a final wave to Sera and Victoria, Sasha made a U-turn and headed off to start her journey.

Twenty minutes later, the paved road began to deteriorate and Sasha began to weave her way through the dense jungle that she had observed from the plane the previous day. Maneuvering around the potholes in the road became very tedious. Sasha understood how easy it would be for strangers to fall victim to abduction as they attempted to traverse the horrific jungle roads. Sasha frequently glanced in her rearview mirror watching for anyone following her. She breathed easier each time she saw the darkness of the jungle unobstructed in her view.

For two hours, Sasha saw no sign of any human inhabitants until she saw a small bus come teetering toward her from the opposite direction. The closer the bus approached the more detail Sasha could see. The bus looked crammed with passengers and there were crates of animals and vegetables loaded on top. The driver expertly wove around the biggest of the potholes. Sasha held her breath as she passed the much larger vehicle on the narrow road. The driver smiled and waved to her, and she felt many pairs of eyes watching her as the two vehicles passed.

Sasha could feel the slow incline of the road as she drove higher into the mountainous region. After a severe twist in the road, the horizon opened up to a small town and Sasha took advantage of the stop to top off her fuel, stretch her legs and purchase some fruit from a local vendor. Her body was taut from the stress of the drive and the brief walk did much to settle her jangled nerves.

She pulled out her map, spread it across the hood of the jeep, and calculated she was about one third of the way to her destination. After driving the treacherous roads, she was thrilled that she had taken advantage of Sera and Victoria's hospitality. She had absolutely no desire to be driving this road after dark. Thinking of the journey yet ahead of her, she climbed back into the jeep and headed south. The only other traffic she passed that morning was another bus, loaded just as the first had been, obviously filled with farmers taking their wares to the larger city to sell.

For another four hours, she drove higher into the mountains then began following a small river as it twisted along with the road. Had the roads been in better condition, she could have enjoyed the scenic drive, but the ruts and holes required every ounce of her concentration. She began to catch a glimpse of rich, fertile valleys and knew she had arrived in Cali.

She spied a small trail that took her from the road and when the trail led to a clearing, Sasha pulled the jeep to a stop. Several miles down in the valley there appeared to be a large compound of some sort, and she felt she had arrived at her final driving destination. As the sun began to set, Sasha pulled the jeep into the dense jungle. Using the machete she chopped limbs from the surrounding trees to conceal the jeep from any prying eyes that may venture her way.

As the sun slumped against the horizon, Sasha took out the leftover potatoes and bacon from the morning's breakfast and downed a bottle of water as she gazed across the valley. The lights of the compound came to life as Sasha slowly chewed the last of the home-cooked food. The place looked huge from this view and Sasha decided she would move closer the following morning.

For tonight, she would sleep in the jeep and then head for the compound at first light, wearing the duffel bag like a backpack as she stalked closer to the compound. She figured she was a good five miles away at this point and the trip down into the valley promised to be exciting. Lucky for her, the river wound its way across the far side of the compound, so that would be one less complication she would have to deal with.

Content with the concealment of the jeep, Sasha climbed inside and listened as the jungle mist came with the falling of the night. She laid the pistol on the seat beside her and reclined the driver's seat as far back as it would go. The seat, while not the most comfortable of beds, would surely be more comfortable than the tree she would sleep in tomorrow night.

Sasha glanced at her watch, still set on New Orleans time. Kara would probably be heading up to bed by now and she reached out with her mind. *Good night, my love,* she softly whispered in Kara's mind.

I miss you and hope you come home soon, Kara replied.

Very soon, I promise, my love. Sweet dreams, Sasha said.

You too Sasha, I love you, Kara said.

I love you too, Sasha said, and then slipped from Kara's mind.

Sasha tuned her ears to the sound of the jungle and closed her eyes to rest.

Chapter 28

The sharp cry of a howler monkey woke Sasha just as the sun was cresting the horizon. The shrieks echoed from miles away. Sasha presumed that two or more of the loudly vocal primates were engaged in a territorial battle and were using their calls to warn one another of boundary encroachments. Primarily leaf eaters, the howlers strictly guarded their feeding zones, becoming highly aggressive toward any intruder they perceived as a threat to their food source. The howlers lived high in the canopy of the rain forest, and the presence of a human would not intimidate them. They could however, prove problematic for Sasha if their shrieks alerted the compound of her presence in the jungle.

She would have to take her chances and travel as quietly as she could through the jungle that she was certain held much more dangerous creatures than the noisy primates. Hoping to reach the compound before dark, Sasha hefted the duffel onto her shoulders and, marking the location of the jeep on her GPS, started into the jungle.

The canopy of the tall trees blocked the majority of the morning sun, but the humidity in the jungle soon had Sasha's skin covered with perspiration. The more she walked, the more thankful Sasha was for the thick-soled boots that were relatively light in comparison to the protection they provided against the roots and thorny vines that grabbed at her ankles as she walked.

Each time she reached a clearing, her eyes would seek out the compound. She would smile when it looked closer each time she caught a glimpse of it nestled in the dense jungle. Amazed by the vastness of the cocoa fields, they stretched in every direction, well beyond the scope of Sasha's enhanced vision. That must represent billions of dollars in street value she thought as she gazed across the fertile valley. Sasha drank a bottle of water and kept her eyes open and ears tuned for any source of water to refill her supply.

Two hours later, her ears picked up on the trickling of a small spring. Sasha refilled the bottle she had emptied earlier, dropped a purification tablet into the bottle as a precaution, and slipped it inside her pack. Sasha marked the location on the GPS and continued to descend into the valley.

Alerted to the sound of a helicopter overhead, Sasha found a clearing in time to see a small helicopter flying over the fields. Looking more closely, Sasha could see a hundred or more workers stripping the cocoa leaves from the stalks as they processed the foliage for the next crop of drugs. Surrounding the workers were armed guards that would not only insure their safety as they harvested, but would also guarantee that the workers hoarded no product for personal gain.

Sasha continued picking her way through the jungle until her eyes spotted the compound. At her elevation, she was still several hundred yards above the compound and had a very clear view into the interior. She watched a buzz of activity as people moved quickly between several large buildings. She observed fifty or more heavily armed men patrolling the grounds as several large trucks were loaded with bales of bundled cocoa leaves. She spied a large tree that had a wide, flat area approximately twenty-five feet up where branches forked off in several directions. The spot was perfect for Sasha to view the compound. The location provided a comfortable place for Sasha to rest and observe the compound and be safe from prying eyes. Sasha shouldered the pack and began to climb the tree. When she reached the fork, she opened the duffel and set up a small camp. As the sun started to set she pulled out bottles of water, the last of the fresh apples she had purchased, some beef jerky, and a pair of binoculars. She also pulled out a small tarp she would use to cover her body to keep the dampness of the morning dew from soaking her as she slept. She changed into clean, dry socks and moved out on a limb to survey the compound. Workers continued loading the trucks until a full hour after darkness fell. Then she watched as armed guards escorted them from the compound. Sasha munched on an apple and then chewed on some of the jerky as she carefully watched the movements inside the walls.

Gazing across the compound, Sasha felt the tingling sensation that told her another Immortal was close by. Even more curious, Sasha picked up the binoculars and began to scan the people moving through the compound. She watched as a dark car pulled up in front of the main house and three passengers departed. Sasha focused on them and saw Curtis Bellfontaine talking to a man and woman who must surely be Rico and Regina Bolivar. As Sasha's eyes came to rest on Regina, the tingling became stronger. She watched as the woman turned toward the jungle looking for the source of the tingling she too was experiencing. Sasha was relieved when the three began walking and disappeared into the large house.

Sasha leaned back against the tree. She had not even considered the possibility of an Immortal inside the complex, much less one of Curtis Bellfontaine's protectors. She was not sure how this development would work into her plan, and she would have to move even more cautiously to prevent detection. The jungle's nighttime chorus was in full swing as Sasha crawled back to her campsite. She gazed up into a beautifully lit night between the leaves of the dense canopy. The nocturnal creatures called to one another from trees high above the forest floor, and Sasha could hear the movement of small animals as they searched for food and mates in the humid night.

Sasha reviewed the plan in her head. She intended to breach the compound the next night to abduct Curtis. She was considering spending another night observing the compound when she again felt the tingling. She climbed back out onto a broad limb and watched as Regina stepped off the covered porch and walked across the compound toward the jungle. Sasha could feel the woman's mind searching for her presence as she walked toward the perimeter wall. The woman knew she was there and Sasha was contemplating contacting her when Regina sent out a message.

I can feel your presence in the jungle, Regina said. Who are you?

Sasha knew answering her would not give away her location, but it would confirm that she was indeed near the complex. Daring to trust the stranger, Sasha opened her mind.

I mean you no harm, my sister, Sasha said.

Then why are you stalking my home? Regina asked.

Because inside your walls you offer protection to one who has endangered the one I love. His life became forfeit when he chose to act against her, Sasha said.

I assume you mean the American, Regina said.

I do, Sasha said. He and his brother held my mate captive for several days to allow themselves to slip through the grasp of justice. After her release, I vowed to provide her that justice. I have traveled here to fulfill my promise. I have already dealt with his younger brother and have now come for Curtis.

Sasha waited while Regina thought about the words she had just projected to her.

The man you talk of is despicable and has been nothing less of a bad influence on my brother, Regina said. Since his arrival, all he has done is drink up my brother's stock of fine liquor and lounge around the manor like a sloth during the day. I would not be at all disappointed to see him disappear myself.

Sasha was surprised to find a possible ally within the complex.

I do not intend to interfere with any activity within your complex, but I will take Curtis into the jungle and deal with him there, Sasha said.

When did you have in mind to proceed with your plan? Regina asked.

Initially, tomorrow night, but I had not planned on the compound being so tightly patrolled.

Regina laughed softly inside Sasha's mind. Tomorrow night will be perfect, she said. Rico and his men will be leaving the compound to transport the next shipment of leaves for processing midmorning tomorrow and will not return until late the following day. Security will be much less after the trucks and guards move out, and if you will allow me to assist, I can get you into the compound without risk of detection.

I would like that very much, Sasha said.

Just give me a time and I will meet you at a small private gate behind the main house and make sure Curtis has had a few drinks in his system, Regina said.

An hour after dark then, Sasha suggested.

Very well then, my sister, until we meet tomorrow night, Regina said and as she turned and walked back into the house.

Sasha scanned the house for any evidence that Regina had shared her presence with anyone and found she had not. She climbed back down from the limb and leaned back against the duffel she would use as a pillow. Pulling the tarp across her body, Sasha willed herself to sleep. Tomorrow she would be busy initiating her plan and needed to be fresh and rested. Listening to the calls from the jungle, Sasha drifted off to sleep.

The dripping of the morning dew on her forehead woke Sasha just as the sun was beginning to rise. Looking across the valley the fields were shrouded in fog and the jungle was relatively quiet for the time of day. She climbed out on a limb. She could barely see an outline of the compound as several figures moved ghostlike through the dense fog. She knew it would be hours before the sunlight made its way through the thick clouds. That would delay the departure of the shipment and delay the return to the compound. Sasha smiled as she folded her tarp. She removed food and water for the day from her duffel and then lowered it to the ground. Moments later, Sasha scrambled to the ground. Picking up the duffel, she switched on the GPS and started the climb back to the location of the spring.

Sasha had decided she would return to the spring this morning and hide her duffel and the supplies she would not need for tonight's adventure. She would take a roll of duct tape, a pair of handcuffs, the pistol and silencer, and an extra clip of ammunition, though she hoped to not need the gun at all. With Regina's help, she should be able to slip in and out of the compound without detection.

With the sweat trickling down her spine, Sasha followed the trail she had traveled the previous day. She would have to take into account the more physically demanding climb when she returned later that evening with Curtis in tow. When the trickle of the spring reached her ears, Sasha veered off the path twenty yards until she located a large tree that would serve her purpose well. She opened the duffel, took a section of rope, and placed it behind the tree. She then took the remainder of the supplies from the duffel and concealed it behind a clump of brush.

Sasha drank a bottle of water, refilled it and dropped a purifying tablet in it before starting back down the trail. She was becoming familiar with the jungle path and made her way back to her perch before noon. She climbed the tree and saw the trucks were pulling out the compound gate, destined for somewhere south of Cali where the drugs would be processed and prepared for shipment.

Sasha leaned back against the tree and ate a light snack. She was as prepared as she could be and now would rest and wait patiently for the sun to set. Sasha watched as a troupe of howlers moved above her high in the tree canopy, calling to one another as they played and foraged for food. They were quite comical as they danced between the branches, chasing the younger primates as they taunted their older siblings. Sasha had to keep herself from bursting out with laughter at their antics, but it helped to pass the time.

Sasha napped for a while in the afternoon and when she woke, the sun was fading from the sky. She reviewed the plan one more time and ate the remainder of her food. If all went as planned, she would be back at Sera's home to prepare for the journey home in two days.

Chapter 29

Just before nightfall, Sasha climbed down from her tree and slipped quietly through the jungle. She carefully circled the compound until she arrived at the small gate Regina had told her would be unguarded. She waited under the veil of darkness for her accomplice. She allowed her mind to slip inside the compound and found Curtis in his guest room heavily involved with a bottle of single malt scotch. She searched for Carlos and found him in the guardhouse playing cards with several others. Curtis, alone in the house with Regina, was drinking his memories into oblivion.

Soon you will have no memories to drown away each night, Sasha thought to herself. After tonight, you will have no worries whatsoever. You will rejoin your beloved Ray very soon, so you may burn in hell together.

Are you ready? Regina asked.

Yes, Sasha replied from the jungle.

I will meet you at the gate in just a moment, Regina said, and you will be alone in the house with Curtis. I will go to the guardhouse and make sure you are not disturbed while you make your exit with Curtis.

Thank you for your help, Regina, Sasha said.

You are doing me a big favor by taking care of that nuisance for me, Regina said.

My pleasure then, Sasha said.

A few moments later, Sasha saw the small gate swing open and saw the form of Regina standing in the darkness. She stepped from the protection of the jungle and walked toward the gate. When she crossed over, Regina smiled at her and whispered, "Hello, I am Regina."

"I am Sasha," she said as she offered her hand. "I will be in and out in just a few minutes, I promise."

"No worries, take whatever time you need and promise me that you will make his end a memorable one," Regina said.

"That I can guarantee," Sasha said as they walked back toward the house together.

"Thank you again."

"Good luck," Regina said and walked across to the guardhouse.

Sasha watched Regina enter the guardhouse and then she slipped into the house and went in search of Curtis. She followed her senses through the house and found the door to his room open. Curtis had his head lying on a small teakwood desk with his back to the door. Sasha entered and stepped across the room to stand behind him. She reached behind her back for the cuffs and quickly snapped one over his right wrist then wrenched his arms behind his back and secured the second cuff.

"What the hell," Curtis mumbled as his alcohol-soaked mind caught up with his speech.

He tried to stand and Sasha pushed him back into the chair roughly. She tore a length of duct tape from the roll and placed it across his mouth. Curtis looked up to see her, his eyes went wide with terror, and he struggled against the cuffs and tried to scream. A hard slap to his face helped to calm his terror. Sasha pulled him from the chair and dragged him across the room to the door. She locked the door behind them to prevent anyone from discovering his absence until tomorrow at the earliest and marched Curtis from the house. They walked through the gate as Sasha pulled it closed quietly behind them and led him into the jungle.

Good-bye, and thanks again for your help, Sasha projected to Regina.

You are very welcome and safe travels, my sister, Regina answered.

Curtis stumbled through the jungle, his feet dragging in his stupor. Each time she roughly pulled him to his feet. "We have a long hike ahead of us," she growled as she moved him forward as quickly as she dared.

They followed the jungle trail, aglow with moonlight, for nearly two hours before Sasha reached the chosen spot. She pressed Curtis roughly against the tree as she reached for the rope and secured Curtis to the trunk of the tree. She wound the scratchy hemp around his shoulders, down across his waist and across the top of his thighs before securing it tightly on the backside of the tree.

Curtis was breathing hard from the exertion of the climb. His failure to fight against Sasha was evidence that he had given up hope of escape. She went to her duffel bag, took out a bottle of water, and drank half its contents as she watched Curtis. His eyes fixed on hers, and she could see tears rolling down his cheeks. She was disgusted by his weakness; after all Ray had not cried until after he was bitten by the snakes and laid on the ground pleading for her help.

Sasha returned to the duffel, pulled out a large slab of the jerky, tore a bite off with her teeth, and slowly began to chew. She had burned many calories while she dragged Curtis along and she needed a boost of energy. Sasha squatted on the ground in front of Curtis, watching him closely as she chewed the peppery meat. Sweat was pouring down his face as he watched her in terror as she fixed her glowing eyes on him. She swallowed and raised the meat again to her mouth for a bite, this time allowing Curtis a view of her fangs as she ripped off a chunk of the meat.

Curtis's eyes grew wider as he saw the sharp fangs tear through the meat with ease.

Sasha stood and ripped the duct tape from across his mouth. He cried out in pain and watched as she returned to the spot in front of him and settled into a comfortable position.

"Do not bother trying to scream," she said. "You are miles away from anyone who could hear you and I will not hesitate to replace the tape. Do we have an understanding?"

"Yes," Curtis said weakly.

"Good, you will be dead in a short time and I wanted to give you an opportunity to speak your mind before it is time," she said.

"Who and what are you, and why are you doing this?" he blurted out.

"My, my so many questions and all at once," Sasha teased. "I am Sasha Thibodeaux, an Immortal, or you would call me a vampire. I am from New Orleans as you probably know and I am weary of the evil you have spawned on the streets of my beloved home. I was tolerant of your behavior until you and Ray made it personal by kidnapping my mate and holding her captive."

Recognition dawned on his face. "The lawyer from the district attorney's office?" he asked.

"Her name is Kara Stewart, and yes she is my mate."

"But, we caused her no harm," Curtis pleaded.

"No, you just kept her drugged, restrained, and blindfolded for several days," Sasha said. "No physical harm, but I believe when you meet your brother again, he will tell you much differently," Sasha said with a chuckle.

"So it was you who killed Ray?" Curtis asked.

"No, not exactly," Sasha said. "Do you really want to know what happened to Ray?"

"Yes," Curtis answered.

"I took Ray from his home one night and we traveled down to the very hangar where Kara was held by your thugs," Sasha said. She rocked back on her heels and looked directly into Curtis's eyes. "I blindfolded and cuffed him and then restrained him just as Kara had been restrained. Then I used a sharp pair of scissors and cut that beautiful Italian suit from his body and well. You know where the clothes ended up."

Curtis glared at Sasha.

"Then I used one of your tricks," Sasha said. "I knew you would be able to track down Ray's cell phone using your police connections, so I took you and your boys on a wild goose chase." Sasha stood and walked toward Curtis. "Oh, how I would have loved to have seen the look on your face when you climbed into that loft and realized you had been duped. I took great effort in tying that hangman's knot and was very proud of setting up that little scene for you, all the while sending you off in the wrong direction."

"You are a sadistic bitch," Curtis said with a snarl. "What did you do to Ray?"

"Your brother and I played a game after a few days," Sasha said.

"What kind of game?" Curtis asked.

"Ray and I took a ride deeper into the bayou then I released his hands and removed his blindfold," she said. Stepping closer,

Sasha could see Curtis recoil from her gaze. "I gave Ray a generous head start and told him if he could find his way back to the main road before I found him, he would be a free man.

"I was very disappointed in Ray," Sasha said honestly. "I would have thought someone with so many street skills could have navigated better than he did, but he let his arrogance overtake his common sense." Sasha paced in front of Curtis. "Ray was certain he could outmaneuver a woman and when his plan began to fail him, he began to panic, and that was his undoing."

"Ray never did have much respect for women," Curtis said.

"No, he did not, and even when I tried to correct the error of his path, he laughed and continued in the wrong direction," she said. Sasha bent down and took a drink from the bottle of water. "I never had to lay a hand on your brother."

"How did he die then?" a confused Curtis asked.

"Ray blundered into a nest of mating water moccasins and received several bites. As you probably know, their bites do not kill quickly," she said as she watched Curtis flinch. "Ray struggled to find the road until the venom from the bites seeped into his brain and he began to go blind and become delusional." She watched Curtis shiver as she placed the visual in his mind. "The bites swelled until his skin broke open and the blood began to weep onto the rain-soaked ground and the scent of his blood called to the carnivores of the bayou."

Curtis continued to shiver at the visuals Sasha shared with him.

"He was surrounded by several large alligators as the seizures began, causing his body to begin thrashing on the ground with convulsions. His erratic movements and groans of pain kept them from approaching, until his heart went into arrest and failed. Once his body became still, the alligators attacked and feasted on him to conceal any evidence that Ray Bellfontaine had ever been in the bayou." With an evil grin, she continued, "So, legally, I did not kill Ray, I simply enabled his own stupidity to become his undoing."

Sasha felt him grow nauseated as he listened to her story, his imagination racing with fear of what she planned for him. "What are you going to do with me?" he asked.

"Well, since you have been so clever and devious in escaping justice from the authorities, I have taken it upon myself to deal with you. You shall be made to pay for your crimes with your life, but I promise it will be much quicker and there will be less pain than Ray suffered." With a wicked grin Sasha added, "I have grown tired of dealing with you and your brother."

Curtis watched Sasha approach him again. She took a long strip of duct tape and placed it across his mouth. She walked back to the duffel, dropped the tape inside, and took out a long machete. She walked in front of Curtis so he could see the glow of the moonlight on the shiny blade. Sasha held the blade so the moonlight reflected off the blade into Curtis's face. "It is not as sharp as the cane blade that was used on Bo Logan, but I am fairly certain my Immortal strength shall make up for any dullness in the blade and make it a clean cut," Sasha taunted.

Curtis's bladder released and Sasha could smell the acrid urine that soaked the front of his pants. "Good-bye, Curtis," Sasha said and with a powerful swing of the machete she severed his head. His head tumbled onto the floor of the jungle and came to rest. The blade buried in the flesh of the tree. Sasha pulled to release it and then plunged it into the ground beside Curtis's headless body. The blood continued to squirt from the base of his severed neck until his heart, starved of oxygen, slowed and then stopped beating. Sasha bent down and picked up his head by the hair and positioned the head onto the handle of the blade, just as Bo Logan's had been placed on the metal fence stake at Jackson Square.

"That was for Bo Logan's widow and fatherless child," Sasha said. She turned away and, shouldering her duffel, hiked back to the jeep.

When Sasha located the jeep, she pulled away the concealing branches and tossed the duffel in the backseat before she collapsed exhausted into the reclined driver's seat. Sasha thought she would feel a sense of relief when Curtis received punishment, but instead she had an empty feeling that only one woman could satisfy. She had fulfilled her promise to seek justice against the brothers, but the rage that had consumed her thoughts for so long left her exhausted and in need of Kara's gentle loving touch.

Sasha rested her head against the seat and slept until the sun crept up across the horizon. She then cranked the jeep and began the arduous trip back to Sera's, winding the jeep around potholes as fast as she dared on the treacherous road. She was halfway there when she looked in her rearview mirror and saw an ominous black sedan approaching. Regina would have sent her a warning if Curtis's disappearance had raised an alarm so quickly, so she worried over the intention of the vehicle stalking her. She let off the gas and watched as the car quickly gained on her. She searched the tinted glass of the windshield for any visible signs of the vehicle's passengers. Pulling the jeep carefully off the side of the road she held her breath until the vehicle kept moving and raced beyond the jeep to disappear in a cloud of dust. She could feel eyes fixed on her through the dark tint as the car went by and Sasha knew she would need to be extra cautious as she drove on.

Taking a deep breath, Sasha pulled back onto the road, keeping a careful eye ahead of her as well as behind her for other traffic. When she reached the small town she had stopped in earlier, she again topped off her fuel and went inside for apples and a cool drink. When she stepped outside her blood ran cold. The same black car was parked across the street at a small café. Still unable to see inside the car, Sasha hoped the passengers had stopped off for breakfast and were not stalking her. She walked calmly back to the jeep and crawled inside, her heart racing as she turned the wheel and pulled the jeep back onto the road. Her eyes fixed on the rearview mirror as she drove away from the small town. As she watched, the black sedan pulled onto the road behind her.

They had obviously seen that she was female and traveling, sensing her to be easy prey. Sasha watched their approach in the rearview mirror. She reached into the backseat to pull out the pistol as her mind raced to form a plan.

Chapter 30

Sasha kept her speed steady as she scanned the road for a side trail to pull into. The black sedan maintained its distance, slowly stalking her. She searched with her mind and found that there were two men inside the sedan. Sasha smiled when her eyes came to rest on a small side road and she slowed and turned away from the hard road. As expected, the sedan also slowed and followed Sasha's jeep deeper into the jungle. Several hundred yards off the road, there was a clearing off to the right. Sasha pulled into the middle of the field, turning the jeep to face the oncoming traffic and waited for the sedan to approach.

The sedan stopped twenty yards in front of her and two dark, heavyset men stepped from the car. One had drawn a pistol as they began to walk toward the jeep. Sasha opened the door and stepped out to meet them. The gun convinced her that she was dealing with a pair of narco-terrorists who had intentions to do her harm. Sasha stepped from the jeep with the pistol concealed behind her. Sasha walked briskly toward the men as she raised the gun and fired a shot, dropping the first man. The startled second man reached to draw his gun. Sasha smiled at him as he managed to squeeze off a round before Sasha placed a bullet between his eyes.

The bullet struck her left shoulder and she felt the burning sensation as the bullet tore through her skin. She pumped another bullet into the first man's head to stop his groaning and writhing on the ground. The second man was dead before he reached the ground. Sasha rolled him onto his back with her foot to check his lifeless body.

The pain in her shoulder increased as the flesh healed rapidly from the inside out, driving the invading bullet from her body. Sasha dropped to her knees and reached for her shoulder just as the fragment of the bullet worked its way out of her skin. The metal fragment still burned from the explosion from the gun and was warm as Sasha rolled it between her fingers. She watched as the wound disappeared completely, leaving a small red dot and the hole in her shirt as the only evidence of her injury. Sasha slipped the fragment into her pocket and turned to walk back to the jeep, leaving the lifeless men sprawled across the ground. She hoped the remainder of the trip would go by without further interruption and she could leave the killing behind in the jungle.

The last few hours went by without further incident and as Sasha emerged from the jungle, she pulled the jeep off the road and drove down to the river's edge. She picked up the pistol and walked to the river, tossing it as far as she could out into the water. Reaching deep into her pocket, she pulled out the bullet fragment and tossed it into the murky water as well. With no further evidence that could trace her back to the two dead men in the clearing, Sasha climbed into the jeep and drove to Sera's home.

When she pulled in front of Sera's home, she could feel the tingling of Sera as she entered her mind. *Welcome back, Sasha, come on in.*

The sun was setting as Sasha shouldered the duffel for the last time and walked quickly into the house. Sera took the duffel from her and returned it to the garage as Victoria ushered Sasha to the den and went in search of a cool drink for all of them.

"Did you have a successful hunting trip?" Victoria asked.

"Very successful," Sasha said as she leaned back into a comfortable chair. "I am proud to announce that Curtis Bellfontaine has breathed his last."

"Did you have any difficulty getting into the compound?" Sera asked as she sat beside Sasha.

"Surprisingly enough, I had some inside help," Sasha said.

"Oh really, how did that happen?" she asked.

"Well when I was surveying the compound, I felt the tingling of another Immortal," Sasha said. "As it turned out, Regina Bolivar is one of us and she was more than eager to assist me in removing Curtis from their home. With her assistance, I waltzed in, took Curtis, and was out of the compound in a matter of minutes. If all went as planned, they are just now discovering

Curtis is nowhere inside the compound and hopefully I will be on a plane out of the country before they find what is left of him."

Sera pointed to the hole in Sasha's shirt. "It looks like you had a bit of trouble somewhere along the line," she said.

"I made a slight detour when a couple of your friendly narco-terrorists with less than honorable intentions decided to tail me," Sasha said. "I was hoping to return the pistol to you without firing a shot, but they had to be dealt with."

"I trust you concealed the evidence," Sera said.

"It is safely at the bottom of the river," Sasha said. "Everything else except the food supplies, a length of rope and the machete is returned to you in the duffel."

"Very well," Sera said.

"I cannot begin to thank you enough for your assistance," Sasha said with a smile.

"It has been our pleasure," Sera said. "You look like you could use a hot shower and a hearty meal before a good night's rest."

"Why don't you shower and put on some clean clothes while Sera and I finish dinner," Victoria said.

"That sounds like a wonderful idea," Sasha agreed. Finishing her drink, she excused herself to the bedroom. The shower soothed Sasha's aching muscles and she felt her body relax as the tepid water cascaded down her body. The task of dealing with the Bellfontaines had been more emotionally exhausting than she had anticipated but Sasha had felt a burden lift from her shoulders with the task completed. Tomorrow she would be on her way home to Kara and she would not waste another thought on Curtis or Ray.

Sasha stepped from the shower and patted her body dry. As she looked in the mirror, her eyes came to rest on the bullet wound on her shoulder that had already begun to fade to a dull pink. In another day or two, there would be no sign of the brief encounter at all except in her memory and Sasha was sure those too would fade in time.

She dressed and returned to the kitchen to find Sera and Victoria waiting patiently for her.

"You look much more relaxed than a couple of days ago," she said as Sasha took the seat offered to her.

"A distasteful chapter of my life has ended and I hope there are only pleasant ones ahead. I know in the larger scheme of life, the deliverance of the Bellfontaines to their Maker will have little effect on the corruption and crime in New Orleans, but I can rest well knowing they paid a huge price for interfering in the lives of two Immortals."

"To justice then," Victoria said as she raised her glass of wine and they toasted Sasha's accomplishment.

"So what is next for you my friend?" Sera asked.

"I will fly out in the morning, make a stop in Atlanta at the Network to get you set up for the serum and then return home to Kara," Sasha said. "Hopefully life will return to normal and we can spend our lives at Sugarland. Maybe do some traveling in the future," she added.

"Maybe we can meet you in Europe," Victoria said with a chuckle.

"I would really like that. I know that once you get Sera over there, she will absolutely fall in love."

"I will see what I can get set up for next spring then," Victoria said with a smile to Sasha.

"Just keep us posted and we will gladly meet you."

They spent the remainder of the evening talking about Europe and travel in the United States. Near midnight, Sasha excused herself to retire for the evening and again thanked her friends for all their help.

She stripped off her clothes, slipped between the soft sheets of the bed, and drifted quickly away into a deep sleep filled with pleasant dreams.

✝

Sasha awoke the next morning rested and after a hearty breakfast said good-bye to Sera and Victoria. Two hours later, she was in the air, on her way back north to the woman she loved. Sasha reclined her seat and closed her eyes as the small jet cut through the turbulence. She reached out with her mind and found Kara. *I love you and will be home tomorrow,* she said.

I love you too Sasha and can't wait until you return, Kara answered.

With her lips curling into a smile, Sasha let her mind relax and she dreamed the sweetest of dreams.

Chapter 31

When Sasha landed in Atlanta, Katrina and Elise greeted her at the airport.

"It is so good to see you, my friends," Sasha said as she hugged the two women.

"You are looking terrific," Elise said as she took Sasha's small bag.

"It is good to see you too, my friend," Katrina said as she hugged Sasha again. "I just hate that Kara is not traveling with you."

Sasha grinned at Katrina. "I had some nasty personal business to tend to that I did not want to involve her in," Sasha said.

"That sounds mysterious," Katrina said as she guided Sasha toward the parking garage. "I cannot wait to hear this story. Are you hungry?"

"No, I am good thank you," Sasha said.

"Well, you had better change that soon," she said. "I have some juicy, thick steaks planned for dinner."

"Mmm, red meat, you sure know your way to my heart, Elise," Sasha said, grinning.

"Yes, yours and Katrina's," Elise said with a soft laugh.

Katrina closed the car door behind Sasha and slipped in the front seat beside Elise. "Tell us about this mystery trip of yours," she said as she turned to face Sasha.

"It will be a long story. Why don't we wait until we get back to your place and I can share it with you over a bottle of nice wine," she said.

"Oh, you are going to keep us steeped with anticipation I see," Katrina said.

"No worries, dear, we have a nice bottle of red waiting for us at the house," Elise said as she pulled out of the parking garage.

"So how are things with the two of you?" Sasha asked. "Is business still good?"

"We are doing quite well, thank you," Elise said. "We have just celebrated another anniversary and business continues to thrive."

"Congratulations to you both. Kara and I will be celebrating an anniversary too very soon," she said with a smile.

"Is Kara doing well?" Katrina asked.

"She is. In fact, she has her own private practice now and is doing very well," Sasha said.

"Private practice? I thought she was with the district attorney's office," Katrina said.

"She was, but that is all part of the story," Sasha said.

"You are going to kill me with all this suspense, Sasha," Katrina said.

Sasha chuckled. "You will know soon enough, I promise."

Elise pulled the car into the parking garage and they rode the elevator up to their penthouse. Katrina took Sasha out to the covered balcony while Elise went to the kitchen for wine. She stepped out onto the balcony as Katrina was pointing out highlights of the city as dusk faded and the city lights came alive.

"Such a beautiful city," Sasha said as they turned to join Elise on the oversized chaise furnishings surrounding a small table.

Elise poured them each a glass of deep red wine, handing the first to Sasha as they made themselves more comfortable. "Thank you, Elise," Sasha said as she accepted the offered glass.

"You are very welcome," Elise said with a seductive smile.

Sasha saw the desire burning deep in her eyes and knew it was time for Elise to feed. There was no denying the look when the lust for blood was present. Sasha felt the urge rise up in her also as she realized the time for her to feed was rapidly approaching.

Katrina watched the exchange between the two women as she reached for a glass of wine. "So tell us what grand adventure brings you our way again," Katrina said to break the fixed gaze between her lover and her friend.

"Life for Kara and I was progressing well," Sasha started. "Her transformation proceeded smoothly and she was able to land a job with the district attorney's office rather quickly." Sasha took a drink of the sweet wine and settled the glass back on the arm of the chair. "She had successfully prosecuted several cases, and was rising quickly within the ranks of the assistant district attorneys when a murder occurred that would change our lives forever."

"Did it involve an Immortal?" Elise asked.

"No, thank goodness, though New Orleans has a large population of Immortals," Sasha said. "An enforcer for a pair of drug kings became sloppy and murdered a low-rent drug pusher. A pair of diligent bar bouncers caught him in the act. It was shaping up to be a simple open-and-shut murder case, until the enforcer was convinced to turn State's evidence on his employers," Sasha explained.

"I bet this is where things began to turn ugly," Katrina interjected.

"Indeed. The Bellfontaine brothers had grown very powerful in New Orleans and had escaped the long arms of justice for many years as they tainted the streets with drugs, prostitution, and murder." Sasha sighed deeply. "The few times charges were actually brought against them, they easily bribed a judge or made witnesses disappear and the charges were dropped." She paused in her story and took another sip of wine.

"So Kara was assigned the position of prosecuting them?" Elise asked.

"Be patient, my dear, and allow Sasha to tell her story," Katrina chided.

"Yes, Elise, ultimately Kara was assigned the case and the star witness was taken into protective custody. His family was placed in the witness protection program for their safety as a term of his deal," she continued. "It was an opportunity of a lifetime for the district attorney to purge the streets of two vile drug lords. He put his best assistant on the case." Sasha smiled, thinking back on how excited Kara was when given the assignment. "The district attorney had political aspirations and he was certain the publicity of this case would win him a seat in the upcoming elections."

"There always seems to be a crooked politician in every story now days," Katrina said with a chuckle.

"The problem was, that no one took into consideration the measures the Bellfontaines would take to maintain their freedom, including kidnapping a beautiful, young, assistant district attorney," Sasha said.

"You have got to be kidding," Katrina nearly shouted. "They had the audacity to take on an Immortal?"

"They were very clever men," Sasha said. "They had no clue of her real abilities, but kept her heavily sedated for several days until they could hunt down the witness and dispose of him. After they had accomplished this goal, Kara was released and found her way home to me."

"You could not use your powers to locate her?" Elise asked.

"Not if they were keeping her drugged, my love," Katrina said.

"Exactly," Sasha said. "The very few moments Kara's mind was lucid were barely enough to let me know she was unharmed, but did not allow for enough of a connection to trace her location."

"With the witness gone, there was no case against the brothers, right?" Katrina asked.

"Exactly," Sasha said. "There was no evidence to prove that they had kidnapped Kara, so they were released, even though everyone knew they were behind her abduction."

"I know you had to be furious," Katrina said.

"Once Kara was returned to me in good health, my rage began to grow and I promised myself the brothers had escaped justice for the last time." Sasha's anger flashed in her eyes. "Kara was used as a scapegoat for the district attorney's failure to prosecute the pair and the police force's pitiful attempt to protect the witness and she resigned her post." A smile grew on her face as Sasha continued her story. "I waited a short time and began to seek out justice, first with the younger brother and now most recently with the elder who fled to South America when his brother disappeared."

"I hope you made them both pay miserably for their treatment of Kara," Elise said with Katrina nodding in agreement.

"They both paid dearly," Sasha said with a smile.

"During my trip to Colombia, I received assistance from three Immortals, and I would like to repay their kindness by setting them up with the Network for the serum," Sasha explained. "They have no such resource and have to rely on hunting humans as their source of survival."

"If you will leave their information with me, I will take care of that tomorrow," Katrina said with a smile.

"Thank you, my friend," Sasha said. "My trip would have been much more hazardous without their assistance."

"Then they shall be rewarded highly for their kindness to our sister." Katrina reached for the bottle of wine and refilled their glasses. "To justice served," she said and lifted her glass.

Elise and Sasha lifted their glasses and they shared the toast. "Justice," they said in unison and took a sip of their wine.

Katrina cooked the steaks and they shared a delicious meal together. Sasha would be flying out early the next morning so she refused their offer to accompany them to the club that evening to snack. Instead, she took a dose of the serum and climbed into a warm, comfortable bed. As Sasha rested her head against the pillow, she allowed her mind to open and search for Kara.

Hello, my baby, Sasha projected.

Oh Sasha, I miss you so, my love.

I miss you too, my darling, and will see you tomorrow, Sasha promised. Elise and Katrina send their love.

Tell them hello and give them a big hug from me.

I sure will and I will see you for lunch tomorrow, my love, Sasha replied.

I love you, Sasha.

I love you too, Kara, Sasha projected, ending their mental conversation.

Sasha closed her eyes and allowed her body to succumb to sleep. Her dreams came quickly combined with a mixture of images of Milly and Kara. Sasha tossed restlessly as the dreams haunted her and left her confused. Sasha had no idea why Milly had surfaced again in her subconscious and invaded her dreams at every possible chance. Granted, Milly had been her first true love, but since her transformation, Kara had filled her days and nights with endless love. Still, Sasha was confused to dream of Milly in a manner she could not explain.

†

Sasha stepped out into the early morning sunlight and joined Katrina on the balcony for coffee. "Good morning," she said as she sat next to Katrina.

"Good morning, my friend," Katrina answered. "Would you care for some coffee?"

"That would be great," Sasha said.

"Elise has run out for fresh baked bagels, but should return shortly," Katrina said.

"Sounds great," Sasha said.

Katrina noted a slight frown on Sasha's face and asked, "What has you worried, my friend?"

"Have you ever dreamed of a previous lover, Katrina, one that you know can never return to you?" she asked.

"Milly?" Katrina asked in return.

"Yes. Milly is invading my dreams more and more, and for the life of me I cannot figure it out," Sasha said with a sigh.

"Milly was a very important part of your life for a long time," Katrina said to remind Sasha of the bond they had shared. "I do think it is odd, though, I do not have any words of experience in the matter to guide you, my friend." She smiled sweetly at Sasha. "Does Kara meet your every need?"

"Oh yes, Katrina, and very well I might add," Sasha said with a grin.

"Well, then if that is true, I certainly have no clue why Milly has cropped up in your subconscious after so many years. Listen to your dreams and try to make sense of them. There is obviously a reason behind them."

"Thanks, Katrina, I will," Sasha said.

"I wish I knew more, my friend, but as I said, I have no experience of which to guide you," she said as Elise stepped out onto the balcony with a plate of bagels filled with cream cheese.

"Ah, perfect timing as usual, my love," Katrina said as she took a bagel and passed the plate to Sasha.

Sasha took a bagel from the plate. She bit into it and the cream cheese squirted out the sides of the still warm bread. "This is totally sinful," she said as she wiped the cheese from her chin.

Elise laughed as she bit into her bagel and the luscious filling squirted out. Sasha's worries about her dreams faded with their laughter. In just a few short hours, she would again be home and in the arms of the woman she loved.

Chapter 32

Sasha walked out into the bright sunlight of a muggy New Orleans midmorning, lowering her dark sunglasses to give shelter to her eyes. She was relieved to be back on the soil of the city she loved and within the hour she would see Kara again. A broad smile played across her face as she picked up her bag and went in search of James.

James hailed her from fifty yards down the curb and rushed to Sasha, taking her bag.

"It is so good to have you home, Sasha," he said as he hugged her neck.

"It's great to be home, James," Sasha replied. "I trust everything is well."

"Now that you are safely home again, the world is perfect," James said as he placed her bag in the bed of the truck.

Sasha opened the door and climbed into the cab. "If you don't mind, James, please drop me off at Kara's office," she said.

"I don't mind at all, Sasha." He pulled away from the curb. "I know she will be anxious to see you. Milly was also excited to hear of your return," James said. "She and Hera have been working very hard to impress you with her skills. She is eager to show you what she has learned in your absence."

"I bet she is," Sasha said as she settled back into her seat. "Has she been riding every day?"

"Are you kidding? We have to drag her off that horse to get her to come in for supper," he said. The pride he had for his daughter was evident in his tone. "Hera has turned out to be a perfect gift for Milly. Martha and I were worried at first that maybe she was too young for such a responsibility. But, as it turns out, Milly is usually up before we are in the morning and goes to feed Hera before she gets her own breakfast."

Sasha was also proud of Milly becoming responsible for Hera at such a young age. "You have a fantastic young lady on your hands, James," Sasha said. "Her artistic talent is growing rapidly and she is very mature for her age."

"A great deal of that is due to you and Kara being involved in her life," James said. "You, in particular, are such a strong influence on Milly. She literally worships the ground you walk on."

"Well, I don't know about that, but she does look up to me," Sasha said with a slight blush.

"She adores you, Sasha, there is no doubt of that," James said as he maneuvered the truck through the narrow city streets.

Silence fell between them as James drove to Kara's office. Sasha could feel the beat of her heart increase as they neared their destination. When James pulled to the curb, she could feel Kara reaching out to her mind.

Welcome home, darling, Kara projected.

Thank you, my love. I will send James home and be inside in just a moment, Sasha answered.

Hurry, Kara responded.

"Just drop me off please, James, and I will ride home with Kara," Sasha said. "Tell Milly I won't be late and we will ride when I get home."

"Will do, Sasha," James said and he watched as she left the truck and stepped inside the door of Kara's building.

"Hello, Crystal," Sasha said.

"Hi, Sasha, I do believe Kara has been waiting on you," Crystal said as she pointed to the office door.

"Thanks, Crystal," Sasha said as she walked across the room. She opened Kara's office door and stepped inside to find her lover on the phone. She closed the door behind her, knowing there would be no need to press the lock behind her. Kara's eyes lit up as she watched Sasha cross the room and she ended her call.

She stood and took Sasha in her arms, and when their eyes met Sasha felt the most incredible love. She leaned in to kiss Kara's lips and felt her body begin to tremble. Pulling her lover close, Kara whispered, "I have missed you so."

"I missed you as well, my love, and promise to never leave you again," Sasha whispered into the sweet smell of Kara's hair. She took Kara's face in her hands and kissed her again, slowly this time, her tongue enjoying the taste and softness of Kara's lips. Sasha could hear their hearts pounding in her ears as they beat strongly together as one pulse.

When the kiss ended and Sasha stepped back, she could see the fire of desire burning brightly in Kara's eyes. "I hope you do not have plans to work late tonight," Sasha said.

"I have one more file to finish up and I will be done for the day," Kara promised with a grin.

"I will leave you to your work then. When you finish you will find me walking on the levee. I need a chance to stretch my legs a bit and walk on the rich soil of my home," she said. Sasha kissed Kara softly again. "I love you."

"I will see you later, Crystal," Sasha said as she left the office and headed toward the harbor area and the mighty Mississippi River. The Big Muddy flowed as swiftly as she remembered and she took comfort from the seductive movement of its water. Sasha always seemed to end up here on the river's banks whenever she felt a need to reconnect and today was no different. When she stepped off the jet earlier that morning, she knew a dark chapter of her life had ended. She had vowed justice for the wrongs done to her lover, and with the demise of Curtis Bellfontaine, her mission was complete.

As Sasha walked down the levee, she spotted a cloaked figure bent over and plucking leaves from a small bramble of bushes growing wild along the river's edge. As she drew nearer, the dark figure turned toward Sasha. She stared into the mysterious face of Lady Serena, the voodoo practitioner Curtis had visited. As their eyes met briefly, Sasha felt Serena's message.

Hello, my sister, Serena said.

Greetings, Serena, Sasha answered.

Have we met? Serena asked.

Not exactly, Sasha answered.

How is it then that you know my name? Serena asked.

A man who feared for his life visited you not long ago. He was a very vile man and you sent him on his way quickly when you realized the darkness of his soul. I am the dark woman who haunted his dreams, Sasha said.

Does he still have dreams of you? Serena asked.

He will dream no more, Sasha said with a smile creasing her face.

Very well then, my sister, may you go in peace along your journey, Serena said.

Thank you, Serena, Sasha said as she walked past the mysterious woman.

Sasha felt the weight of her heavy thoughts lift from her shoulders as she continued to walk away from Lady Serena. The smile on her face grew with each step as Serena served to validate the rightness of Sasha's actions and reduced the guilt weighing on her conscience. The sun warmed her skin as she strolled down the river walk and her nose took in the heady aroma of Cajun spices mixed with the sea salt blowing in from the Gulf. Home never felt quite so good, Sasha thought as she turned in search of Kara.

✝

Kara pulled her sports car into a vacant parking spot and walked up the embankment onto the levee, walking briskly to join the woman she loved. Her smile broadened when she saw Sasha walking toward her a few hundred yards ahead. She could feel the tingle of Sasha's presence reverberate through her body as she walked on to meet her lover. Sasha's brief absence from their bed had stirred a hunger within Kara, one she intended to sate later in the day. She could feel the pulse jumping in her neck as her mind remembered the pleasures Sasha's body gave her and her skin began to flush.

Very soon, my love, Sasha projected to Kara. I feel your need and will quench your desire later this evening.

I have missed you so, Sasha. Promise you will never leave me alone like that again, Kara said.

Never again, my love, Sasha said as she raised her arms and embraced Kara.

"Take us home," Sasha whispered softly.

Kara turned and placed her hand on the inside of Sasha's elbow as they walked back toward Kara's car.

†

Sasha sat back in the deep, comfortable seat and watched the scenery pass by her window. The shops and restaurants blurred into the Big Muddy and then turned into the subdivisions that were crowding the river's edge. When Sasha saw the first stalk of sugar cane come into view, she knew she was close to the home she loved and finally allowed her body to relax.

When Kara turned the car into the drive, they could see Milly already riding Hera in the arena. Kara turned to look at Sasha and found her smiling as she watched her young student practicing her skills. Sasha felt Kara's eyes on her and looked over at her.

"You know you need to spend some time with her, don't you?" Kara asked. "She has missed you almost as much as I have, but for different reasons."

"Would you mind if Milly and I went for a ride then?" Sasha asked.

"Of course not," Kara said. "Milly can have you this afternoon and I will have you tonight," she said with a devilish smile.

"That sounds very promising," Sasha said.

"You go ride while I check on dinner. Then we can have a nice relaxing evening at home and you can tell me about your trip," Kara said.

Sasha returned Kara's smile and knew a large part of the detail of her trip would not be included in the story she told her lover. It was not a matter of trust. Kara's integrity would be intact if ever questioned about the disappearance of the Bellfontaine brothers. Because of her abduction and then the loss of her job at the district attorney's office, Kara had motive for seeing the brothers disappear and could be a prime subject in an investigation. Sasha would not allow that. She kissed Kara softly on the lips and left the car to join Milly in the arena.

†

Kara closed the car door behind her and heard Milly squeal "Sasha" as she caught sight of her mentor. She smiled with the knowledge of how much Sasha loved the little girl and walked onto the porch and inside Sugarland.

✝

"Welcome home, Sasha," Milly said, her blue eyes sparkling brightly as she steered Hera over to the fence where Sasha stood watching them.

"Thank you, Milly," Sasha said as she felt a shiver run through her body. Milly's eyes seemed to look right into her soul, disturbing Sasha by the familiarity she felt from that gaze. She shook off the feeling and reached up to stroke Hera's neck.

"Your father says you have been practicing hard while I have been gone, so why don't you show me what you two can do," Sasha said.

Milly smiled brightly and turned Hera away from the fence. She took Hera through her paces until she reached a soft canter. It was uncanny how horse and child moved as if they were one entity. Sasha found herself impressed by how quickly Milly's riding skills had developed.

"Beautiful," Sasha said when Milly brought Hera to a sliding stop, both horse and tiny rider landing several feet away. "Do you think you are ready to leave the ring?"

"Oh yes, please, Sasha," Milly answered.

"Let me saddle up then and we will go for a short ride," Sasha said and disappeared inside the stable.

Chapter 33

Sasha walked into the barn and brought Thunder out to saddle him for their promised ride. As she bent down to fasten the girth, she felt the hairs on the back of her neck rise, just as they do when lightning is about to strike close. She finished her task and turned around to find Milly and Hera watching her from the entrance to the stable. Sasha returned Milly's smile, and with a slight air of discomfort, placed a booted foot in the stirrup and pulled herself atop the large stallion. The odd sensation passed as quickly as it arrived, but left a lingering sensation in the back of Sasha's mind.

"Are you ready to ride?" she asked as she approached Milly.

"Oh yes, Sasha, I have been waiting for days for you to ride with me," Milly said.

"Excellent, why don't we start off with a walk down the lane and once we reach an open field we can speed it up a bit," Sasha suggested.

Milly was ecstatic just to be riding outside the arena with Sasha and would have been very satisfied by anything her mentor suggested. She kept looking up at Sasha, a smile beaming on her face as they rode.

"How is school going for you?" Sasha asked.

"It is going pretty well and I really like my classes, but I can't wait for the next break so I can spend more time riding," Milly answered.

Sasha chuckled at Milly's response. "Just remember there is more to life than riding a horse. Do not forget you have a tremendous artistic talent as well that needs practice," Sasha reminded her.

"I know, Sasha. I can draw and paint after it gets too dark to ride," she said with a smirk.

"I can see I have created a monster," Sasha said and they both laughed.

At the end of the lane, they turned right and Sasha looked at Milly. "Ready?" she asked.

Milly's wild grin would have been enough of an answer, but she nodded her head yes in response to Sasha's question. Sasha used her knees to urge Thunder first into a trot and then a soft canter, quickly followed by Milly and Hera. As they rode, Sasha looked over at the young child, her blond hair blowing in the wind, and a saw a look of total glee on her face. Milly turned her head to look Sasha directly in the eyes, penetrating her with her ocean-blue eyes. Sasha's mind flashed back to the memory of riding together with her Milly and the joy they had shared together on horseback and she couldn't hold back a smile. Thunder's gait faltered over a section of uneven ground, bringing Sasha back to reality. When she looked over at Milly, she found the young child smiling back at her warmly, the moment of Milly gone, once more stored neatly away in her memory.

Sasha slowed the pace and returned them to a brisk walk. Both horses were excited from the exertion of the canter and eager to stretch their muscles for an extended run. Sasha knew Thunder was up for a full-out run, but she knew Milly was probably not strong enough yet to take on that challenge so she nudged him into a slow canter again across an open field, with Milly and Hera keeping pace right beside them. There was no fear in the child's bright eyes as they quickly crossed the expanse leading to the first of the many miles of cane fields.

Sasha slowed down to a walk again to allow the horses to catch their breaths and to traverse the road traveled so frequently by the large equipment used to tend the cane fields. "You must always be careful when riding, Milly," Sasha warned. "One misstep on this uneven ground and Hera could snap an ankle."

"Yes, ma'am," Milly said to heed her warning.

"The open fields are fairly level and are good for a faster pace, but still be careful where you ask Hera to go," Sasha instructed. "A horse has a good set of senses about him and he will not be forced to go where he feels fear. So never try to force Hera to go somewhere, as there will be danger if you do."

Milly listened intently to Sasha, her attention hanging on every word that came from Sasha's mouth.

"There are also creatures you will need to be wary of if you encounter them during a ride," Sasha said. "In a straight line, a gator can outrun a horse; but a horse can outmaneuver a gator." Sasha looked over at a wide-eyed Milly. "Living on the bayou you will encounter gators, so you need to know how to deal with them." It was clear Milly had not given this issue any thought from the wide-eyed look she was giving Sasha.

"If you run across a gator while on Hera, or worse yet when you are on foot, remember he can only run in a straight line. If you run in a zigzag motion you will outrun him and he will tire of the chase." Sasha saw the all too serious look on the young child's face. "Do you know what happens if he catches you?"

Milly shook her startled head, unsure she wanted to hear the answer.

"If he catches you, you become gator bait," Sasha said and then roared with laughter.

Milly laughed along with Sasha, but was not one iota interested in becoming gator bait at any cost. Concern was all over her young face when she stopped laughing.

"You will see gators, Milly, I will guarantee that, but Hera will instinctively freeze in her tracks and most likely the gator will be on its way, but if it chases remember to zigzag," Sasha said as she wove her hand from side to side. "Most importantly, trust Hera's instincts as nine times out of ten they are better than ours."

"Yes, Sasha," Milly said.

They rode for a while in silence, both enjoying the warmth of a late fall day. Sasha could feel a bead of sweat trickle between her shoulder blades. She instinctively rode toward the artesian well for a cool drink for horse and human alike. When they arrived, she and Milly dismounted and Sasha took the aluminum cup from the nail where it rested and filled it with cool water before handing it to Milly. Milly took the cup and sipped from it as Sasha dipped out a bucket of cool water for the resting horses. An osprey cried in the distance and Sasha turned to watch his flight as he approached their small clearing and then perched on a large branch as he searched the area for prey. When she turned back around, Sasha found that Milly had sat the cup down and was standing in front of the large oak tree in the center of the clearing. Again, memories of the older Milly returned as Sasha thought back to the many times they had shared a picnic and then made love on the very spot where the young child was now standing.

Sasha dipped out a cup of water and after taking a sip, walked toward the tree. Milly heard her approach and turned to look at Sasha. "This is a very special place for you, isn't it?" she asked.

Sasha forced a smile to her lips. "Yes, it is Milly." Tears threatened to well in her eyes, but Sasha managed to hold them at bay. "Milly Vansant, the woman you were named after, loved this very spot. She and I shared some very special times together here." She smiled at the stories that tree could tell if it had a voice. Her attention returned to the present when Milly spoke.

"You really loved her didn't you?"

Floored by the young child's comment, Sasha wondered what a child so young could know about the kind of love she and Milly had shared. "Yes, I really did and still do love her," Sasha answered softly.

Milly reached over and touched Sasha's hand. "I hope I feel a love like that one day," she said.

Her eyes brimming with tears, Sasha said, "One day you will," and before the tears could erupt, Sasha turned and walked back to the horses.

✝

Milly could feel the sadness seeping from Sasha and stayed silent while they were taking their water break. She reached out, touched the tree, sensed the vibration of life running through the powerful oak, and smiled before spinning on her heel to join Sasha.

Sasha lifted Milly into her stirrup and she quickly scrambled into her saddle. She picked up her reins and watched as Sasha easily mounted Thunder and they turned to head for home. They cantered for nearly a mile before walking the remainder of the distance back to the stable.

They unsaddled the horses and hosed them down, towel drying them before leading them into their stalls for their evening meal. Sasha lifted Milly so she could drop a block of hay into Hera's bin and made a note to buy a small stepladder for Milly to use until she was tall enough to reach into the stall. After hanging the wet towels to dry and checking the horses one last time, Milly and Sasha left the stable.

Milly slipped her warm hand into Sasha's as they walked. When it was time to part, Milly said, "Thank you for taking me for a ride today."

"You are very welcome," Sasha said. "I know Thunder enjoyed being able to stretch his legs a bit too."

"Good night, Sasha," Milly said. "Will I see you tomorrow after school?"

"I will be here," Sasha said. She watched as the young girl turned and ran onto the porch.

Sasha could see the light on in the kitchen and knew Kara would be making the final preparations for dinner. She hoped there would be just enough time to take a quick shower to rinse off the effects of the ride before dinner.

She walked into the kitchen to find Kara stirring a pot of sauce to go with the spaghetti she was about to boil. "Do I have enough time for a quick shower?" she asked.

"Only if you make it a quick one," Kara teased.

"I will do my best to hurry then, my love," Sasha said and ran up the stairs two at a time into their bedroom. Kara had placed new candles around the room and their soft glow lit the bed, making it look so enticing. Sasha had rinsed in the shower and was toweling herself dry, when she heard Kara call to her from downstairs.

"Two more minutes, darling, and everything will be done," she called out.

"I am on my way, baby," Sasha yelled back as she pulled on a pair of sweats and a T-shirt. She ran a brush through her thick, damp hair and with a final longing glance at the freshly made bed, headed to the stairs.

†

Neither Sasha or Kara were hungry for food and after a perfunctory attempt to eat the meal, they put away the leftovers and headed upstairs to the bedroom. Kara lit the candles around the bathtub and drew a steamy bath while Sasha turned down the covers on the bed. She slipped into the hot water behind Kara and wrapped her arms around her lover.

"It is so good to be home," Sasha whispered to Kara.

"I missed you terribly," she said her lower lip on the verge of a pout as she turned her head to the side to look at Sasha.

She grinned and took Kara's chin in her hand, lifting her face as she brushed her lips softly across hers. Sasha's tongue traced the outline of her lips. Kara sighed and parted her lips, allowing the tip of Sasha's tongue to glide past them. Their tongues met in a slow, sensual kiss as Sasha's hands traveled up and down Kara's body, smoothly stroking her soft skin. Kara's moans grew louder as Sasha progressed further down her body and her hands spread Kara's thighs. Sasha's fingers danced beneath the water as her fingers teased the silky opening of her lover's wetness. She circled the soft folds of skin gently until Kara's bud became gorged with blood. She drew tiny circles across the top of her clit as it throbbed with anticipation. Sasha's tongue searched deeper in Kara's mouth as two fingers slid into the welcoming wetness below. Her thumb remained fixed atop Kara's clit, stroking it as her fingers rocked slowly in and out of Kara's body, the water rushing in and out of Kara's body with each movement of her hand.

Kara felt the fire burning inside her growing fierce with each stroke of her lover's hand. She began to rock her hips in rhythm with Sasha's movements. Sasha sensed Kara's rapidly growing need and increased the speed and depth of her thrusts as Kara gasped for air to fill her lungs. Sasha lifted her head and watched the mist of desire form in Kara's eyes and when her body began to tremble with the beginning of her orgasm, she could see the absolute bliss her lover was experiencing.

Sasha removed her fingers slowly and held Kara close while she recovered from the intense climax. When the tremors subsided, Sasha guided them out of the tub. After patting Kara dry, she wrapped her in a thick robe and walked her to the bed. Sasha dried herself and joined her lover in the bed, snuggling close to share the warmth of her body.

After several minutes, Kara opened the front of her robe and moved on top of Sasha, their skin pressed together as she covered Sasha's mouth with her own. Kara's hips rolled slowly between Sasha's thighs as she kissed her way down Sasha's face and neck. She nibbled lightly at the hardened nipples she found awaiting her mouth and the scent of their excitement filled the bed. As Kara moved down Sasha's body, she left a silky trail as her mouth and hands teased her lover into a frenzy of passion. Sasha bit her lip to keep from crying out when Kara parted her lips and her tongue disappeared deep inside her. Kara's tongue probed and tantalized as she drank the juices of Sasha's excitement. When Sasha could hold back no longer, her body released a fury of spasms that shook the bed. Kara slowly licked up to Sasha's swollen clit and wrapped her lips around the sensitive flesh, tugging and stretching it, adding to the duration of Sasha's climax. When Sasha cried out for the second time, Kara slowly kissed her way back up Sasha's body and rested on top of Sasha until the spasms subsided. She laid her head on Sasha's chest to listen to the strong beating of her heart, which sounded like an echo of her own heartbeat. Forever one, Kara thought as she tenderly stroked the outline of Sasha's smiling face.

"Welcome home, baby," Kara whispered as her fingers reached Sasha's lips.

Sasha could taste the evidence of her excitement on Kara's fingers and it sparked her hunger for the taste of her lover. Without speaking, Sasha rolled Kara onto her back and began to suckle first one breast and then the other as her fingers glided gently over Kara's soaked lower lips. From time to time, Sasha would draw tiny circles around Kara's nipples with the wetness covering her fingers. She would moan with the taste of her lover that assaulted her senses as her tongue eagerly licked Kara's nipples. Thirsting for more, Sasha moved between Kara's thighs and began slowly licking across the top of her lips, savoring the sweetness of her taste as she teased her lover's body.

Kara spread her thighs wider, opening her lips in invitation, but Sasha chose instead to take Kara slowly, increasing her arousal to new heights. Whenever Kara came close to peaking, Sasha would slow her motion, her tongue barely whispering across her most sensitive parts until Kara feared she would go mad with need. Sasha ignored the movements of Kara's hips as her body begged her for release. When Sasha was ready, she covered Kara's clit with her hot mouth and slid two fingers deep inside. Kara's hips bucked wildly against the thrust of Sasha's fingers and her clit throbbed deep inside Sasha's mouth as her climax rolled over and over her body in waves of pleasure.

Exhausted and covered with a mixture of sweat and their juices, Sasha moved up beside Kara and took her lover in her arms. Sasha stroked the top of Kara's head as her body swelled with each new breath. Moments later, Sasha realized Kara had drifted off and pulled the covers across their sated bodies. She held Kara close, continuing to caress her lover's soft skin, until Sasha's eyes grew heavy and she joined her lover in sleep.

Three hours later, Kara stirred in her arms and Sasha opened her eyes to find her lover awake and watching her closely. "Hey, baby," Sasha said as she turned on her side to face Kara.

"You still wear me out," Kara said with a grin.

"I think that is mutual," Sasha said as she leaned in to kiss Kara.

Kara realized that since Sasha had been home, they had spoken very little. "Tell me about your trip."

"Well, Katrina and Elise send their love and hope you and I will come for a visit soon," Sasha said.

"So you went to Atlanta?" Kara asked.

"Yes, in a roundabout way," Sasha said.

"Hmm, very well, continue please," she said.

Sasha nuzzled her face into Kara's neck. "I had some business to attend to in South America. While I was there I met several fellow Immortals who knew nothing of the Network or their work on the serum," Sasha said. "So, to thank them for their assistance, I promised to visit Atlanta and get them set up for delivery of the serum."

"What business did you have in South America?" Kara asked inquisitively.

"Just some unfinished personal business," Sasha replied as she kissed Kara's neck.

Kara knew Sasha was trying to avoid the conversation by attempting to distract her lover. If Kara's needs had not already been sated, her ploy may have worked. Instead, Kara pulled back from Sasha and propped herself up on an elbow. She looked Sasha directly in the eyes and asked, "Did your business have anything to do with Curtis Bellfontaine?"

"Now why would you ask that?" Sasha said, hedging a direct answer.

"Could be that Ray's disappearance and Curtis's flight from the country had something in common with your mysterious adventures of late," Kara suggested.

"Mysterious adventures," Sasha said with a chuckle. "Why my lady, I know not what you mean." Sasha said coyly.

"Late nights hunting, when you have no need to hunt and your latest trip to who knows where," Kara said.

Sasha leaned down and kissed Kara's lips. "Those," she said, "those were made to rid your dreams of the demons that haunt them." Sasha was very well aware of the dreams that plagued Kara's sleep, waking her in a cold sweat. "Man's justice could not be met, so bayou justice was given its due." Sasha pulled Kara into her arms. "You will dream of those demons nevermore and your sleep will have only peaceful dreams," Sasha promised as she stroked Kara's hair. Sasha watched as Kara's eyes grew heavy. "Nevermore," Sasha whispered and with a smile on her face, she closed her eyes to join Kara in her dreams.

The End

About the Author

Ali Spooner

Ali Spooner is a native of Florida, currently living and working in Memphis, TN. Home for Ali is Pensacola, Florida where she has a partner of twenty years, one son and a grandchild that has her wrapped completely around her little finger. Her other children are all four legged, three dogs and two cats, and my dearest companion in Memphis, Rascal, a rescued tiger kitten named after my favorite country group.

A true daughter of the South, Ali enjoy spinning stories about the South, the strong, but gentle women and creatures that make it a wondrous place to live.

As an "Indie" author, Ali has been writing for many years as a hobby, and after a cancer diagnosis in 2010, she decided to take a leap and start self-publishing and has published over a dozen stories. Ali's characters range from cowgirls and psychics, to a healthy dose of supernatural beings. She has written stand-alone titles and series. Ali frequently writes several stories at a time, depending on which characters are bouncing around loudest in her head.

Ali is an avid reader and her other hobbies include photography, outdoor activities and watching college sports.

Other Books from Affinity eBook Press

Sugarland—Ali Spooner Sasha Thibodaux travels to London from New Orleans to continue her studies as a concert pianist at King's College. While exploring her new home she befriends Milly Vansant, artist and instructor.

When their friendship blossoms into romance, Milly reveals her true nature as a vampire to Sasha, who joins her in love for eternity.

Their love survives the tragic sinking of a luxury liner during the Great War, a killer hurricane, and the Spanish Flu pandemic.

They decide to leave the chaos of war-torn Europe, traveling to the States, and eventually purchasing a plantation called Sugarland.

Will this be their home for eternity, or, will catastrophe continue to plague their quest for a peaceful life together?

Out of Retirement—Erica Lawson Melanie Stokes was a doctor—a very good one, or so she hoped. She was calm and cool under pressure, and very little fazed her. Until…

Caitlin Joseph ran a small retirement home for older women in need. The fact that everyone in the house was gay was a coincidence, although it did cut down the number of women agreeing to live there.

Mel took up an offer to do some relief work for a local community center when their regular doctor was away on holidays. As soon as she arrived at the home she knew something was different about the place. Was it the little old lady chasing the paper boy down the street or the sign saying "Dykes Retirement Home"?

But there was something about the place that also appealed to her. Sure, Caitlin was cute as a button, but it was more the fact that she took very good care of her charges, despite their rather bizarre behavior.

The older women seized the opportunity to introduce a woman into Caitlin's lonely life, using any means possible to keep Mel coming back. Their plans were boosted by the introduction of another woman into the house, who set hearts a fluttering and blood pressure rising. Now if she was a lesbian it would have been perfect…

Requiem—JM Dragon & Erin O'Reilly In the final book of the When Hell Meets Heaven Series, Olivia and Amelia reluctantly join forces with Parker and Remington to save their lives and those of the ones they love. The only problem—will three alpha females and an ex-nun be able to work toward a common goal and not kill each other before they complete their mission.

The four women are up against the formidable strength of DOCO along with a corrupt politician, bent on mass destruction. Can they complete their mission knowing that a requiem will be the harbinger of their end should they fail.

Beginning of the End—Alane Hotchkin What happens when life doesn't go exactly as you planned and you must protect others from your own fate? Escaping a horrific childhood, Nikki longed to find happily ever after in adulthood. What she found was Hell. Or did it find her? Finding the courage to break the cycle of betrayal, she opens her heart one last time. Alex lived a childhood others dreamed of. Her father never once denied the young rebel a thing. All her life she dreamed of protecting others; to follow in her father's footsteps. Soon though she learned sex and fists made the most powerful of weapons. Alex controls the women in her life through fear and sex, will breaking the cycle be too much to overcome? Will loving Nikki be enough to change her, or is Alex beyond help?

Alex would give Nikki the world, but at what price? When a person's tightly controlled reality snaps what then…? This is the Beginning of the End for one of them and the ultimate sacrifice for the other. But who is who in this game of life?

Galveston 1900: Swept Away—Linda Crist On September 7-8, 1900, the island of Galveston, Texas, was destroyed by a hurricane, or 'tropical cyclone', as it was called in those days. This story is a fictional account of Mattie and Rachel, two women who lived there, and their lives during the time of the 'great storm'. Forced to flee from her family at a young age, Rachel Travis finds a home and livelihood on the island of Galveston. Independent, friendly, and yet often lonely, only one other person knows the dark secret that haunts her. Madeline "Mattie" Crockett is trapped in a loveless marriage, convinced that her fate is sealed. She never dares to dream of true happiness, until Rachel Travis comes walking into her life.   As emotions come to light, the storm of Mattie's marriage converges with the very real hurricane. Can they survive, and build the life they both dream of?

This second edition of one of Linda Crist's best-loved novels maintains the original story, while incorporating some reader-pleasing passages that were cut from the first edition. As an added bonus, the short story "Something to Celebrate" is included at the end of the novel, detailing further adventures of Rachel and Mattie.

Rapture: Sins of the Sinners—A. C. Henley & Fran Heckrotte   A serial killer is targeting young lesbians throughout the state of Texas.

Texas Ranger Cochetta Lovejoy is assigned to the case. Convinced she knows who is committing the murders, Ranger Lovejoy is willing to do whatever it takes to put the perpetrator behind bars--even if it means stretching the limits of the law by manipulating the judicial system.

Detective Agnes Kelly-Elliott is one of Ft. Worth Police Department's finest investigators.

When Ranger Lovejoy appears on the crime scene of a recent murder, Agnes fears a dark secret that, if revealed, could destroy her family ties, and end her career.

This is a dark, gritty, graphic tale of desire gone awry, and flawed characters looking for redemption in all the wrong places.

Till There Was You—S. Anne Gardner   Julia is a woman used to power and is not afraid to use it or impose her will to get her way. She appears to have the world but a part of her is empty and cold as a frozen tundra. Julia rides in the mornings to clear her head and to make plans for what she is about to set in motion.

Theodora, known as Teddy, is trying to put together a marriage filled with uncertainties. She felt once upon a time that she would have a great love but that has eluded her.

One morning these two women meet and from the first instance, it is explosive. The attraction is undeniable, the fears very real and the end without question will change them both forever.

In Name Only—JM Dragon—Sequel to The Fix-it Girl Can an agreement forged out of necessity actually work?

Denial—Jackie Kennedy Time spent in Somalia has Doctor Celeste Cameron accustomed to living and working in a war zone. Coming back home to America, Celeste is glad to see the end of the peril she has been in—or so she thinks.

Danger seems to follow Celeste and she finds it in the shape of Amy. What Celeste feels for Amy scares her more than anything she has faced in war zones.

Amy has the same feelings, but is in denial and vows to marry Josh, Celeste's twin brother, no matter what.

When fate brings them together again, will they give in to their mutual attraction or will they once again deny what they feel.

An Affair of Love—S. Anne Gardner From a dark past, a forbidden love, a secret comes. Among the confusion and the chaos of an unwanted reality, two women find something they neither want nor can deny.

Desert Heat—Dannie Marsden For Luce Diamond, an undercover policewoman, her life is in shambles. Her longtime lover left her and an automobile accident that resulted in a child's death haunts her.

Taming the Wolff—Del Robertson This is a high seas adventure with pirate captain Kris Wolff and Lady Alexis DeVale. ONLY ONE WOMAN...HAS THE POWER...TO TAME THE WOLFF...

Private Dancer—TJ Vertigo Reece Corbett grew up on the mean streets on New York City, abused, used and in trouble with the law. Faith Ashford grew up wealthy, with all the creature comforts that money provides. When they meet fireworks begin.

Miriam and Esther—Sherry Barker Miriam thought her life would play out in the bustling metropolis of Dallas, but after a life-changing accident, she moves to the small town of Cool Lake, Texas to get her head on straight and regain her senses.

McKee—A.C. Henley Private Investigator Quinlan McKee has returned to Los Angeles after a three-year absence, only to find herself embroiled in a world of child slavery and police corruption.

Bailey's Run—Ali Spooner Bailey Chambers mourns the loss of her lover, Nessa, in an unsolved carjacking. When Tommy, Bailey's brother becomes a victim of a gay bashing, Bailey assumes his case will be handled the same way as her lover's—lackadaisically.

Desi Dexter assigned to Tommy's case, feels Bailey's disdain toward her and her partner. Through tenacious police work, Desi, is able to uncover the reason for Bailey's attitude, and convinces her that she is sincere in solving the case.

Mutual attraction sparks, and before they can move forward with their fledging romance, Desi, and her partner Braxton, uncover the presence of a serial killer.

What will happen to Bailey, when, Desi, becomes engrossed in another case, can their relationship survive?

E-Books, Print, Free e-books
Visit our website for more publications available online.

www.affinityebooks.com

Affinity E-Book Press NZ LTD

Canterbury, New Zealand

Registered Company 2517228